William Joseph Roberts

Presents:

Heathens
&
Heroes

Three Ravens Publishing
Chickamauga, GA USA

William Joseph Roberts Presents: Heathens & Heroes
Is a collective work of contributing authors and Published by Three Ravens Publishing
threeravenspublishing@gmail.com
P O Box 851, Chickamauga, Ga 30707
https://www.threeravenspublishing.com

Credits:
Cover art by: J.F. Posthumus
Edited by: William Joseph Roberts
William Joseph Roberts Presents: Heathens & Heroes
by William Joseph Roberts /Three Ravens Publishing – 1st edition, 2024

Ebook ISBN: 978-1-962791-73-1
Trade Paperback ISBN: 978-1-962791-74-8

Table of Contents

WHY SWORD AND SORCERY?

By: Steven L. Shrewsbury

I heard tell that sword and sorcery was defined as: "…a sub-genre of fantasy characterized by sword wielding heroes engaged in exciting and violent adventures. Elements of romance, magic, and the supernatural are often present."

Well, isn't that special? I'm guilty of writing such tales by accident. They just come out that way, with no intent ahead of time.

Any introduction to sword & sorcery should include one's own birth into such a genre. Most folks my age would claim theirs came in the form of CONAN THE BARBARIAN comics written by Roy Thomas and drawn by John Buscema back when dinos ruled the earth. True enough, I did get to that route. Eventually.

Born with cataracts in days before laser or implant surgery, I struggled to see to read. My mother got me what were called" talking tapes" back in the day. Her first choices for me? THE KING JAMES VERSION OF THE BIBLE and TARZAN OF THE APES. I think that says a great deal about how I tell tales, but I digress. Listening to these tapes, I often built dinosaurs out of tinker toys as I dreamt of Goliath battling Tarzan.

After a few eye surgeries, I advanced in reading beyond everyone else in my country school. War comics, weird westerns and superheroes were cool, but something about Conan in the comics stuck with me. Intrigued by the barbarian character, I grabbed the paperbacks from my brother Mark after he returned from the military, beat up copies that collected the original Conan tales by Robert E. Howard. The rest was history. Transported away from the farm, this blind country boy escaped into realms beyond that I still never tire of visiting. In time I found more tales and books by Fritz Lieber, Lin Carter, Michael Moorcock, and Karl Edward Wagner.

But what is this genre I discovered and wish more people would enjoy? How does one know what it is apart from other genres in fantasy?

When I decide to write a story or novel, I won't classify it apart as fine as frog's hair. I don't say, "Well, golly, gonna write me up a new Sword & Sorcery novel." Nor do I say, "Well, this sucker is gonna be a high fantasy, but not too long, so it can't be an epic fantasy, but I better make it more diverse, so folks don't think it's a heroic fantasy or…"

Ugh. It's a story. The terms folks use for such things can be a pain and I oft blur such distinctions. A reader once told me he didn't like how horrific my books are and was turned off at such violence in a supposed fantasy book. Ok. Well, read more stuff, I told him. I hope he never finds George R. R. Martin. I'm just telling a story, not trying to compete with someone for a gross out thing. I'm just telling a tale, if any of those odd things happen in the book, it is a piece of the yarn. At no time did I consult a TSR manual nor play a video game to figure details out. The yarn all comes from reading history and at times listening to music. S'true. Dark metal & bluegrass ballads inspired the creation of Gorias La Gaul, Rogan the Kelt and Roan. There's a lot more Tony Iommi, Johnny Cash and Ralph Stanley in my characters & tales than Gary Gygax dreams.

Nonetheless, I once wrote an article about the differences between fantasy, and the classifications. I became kind of sorry I learned what the difference was, as don't sit down to make it in any special category. If a story is long and covers so much territory, have I veered into epic fantasy? Does that mean I have to write ten more books over a thousand pages one can use for doorstops? I don't think I could live long enough to do that, anyway.

It's a book, a story, a yarn that will take you away from the mundane stuff of everyday life. One doesn't need to look at social media, wonder which spoiled Hollywood celeb is sleeping with who or slapped who…or how many people are killing each other in Russia. All the arguments over silly political nonsense that distracts people from how much the government is screwing us can be quelled for a while by reading. How do I know?

All fiction should be a form of distraction and allow escapism from reality for a while within its pages. The times, a pre-flood world or up to the Middle Ages is full of crass individuals like today, but they are not snarky punks with no guts on the internet. They are flesh & blood jerks who want to see you die and our characters must fight them or fall victim to their desires.

What's refreshing about that? The desire to strive on, the will to survive and act while others cower…to explore the natural instinct to react to horrid things, no matter how grandiose. It isn't a programed behavior exercise where sudden violence is shocking, but perhaps the order of the day. It's a story of courage in the face of terrible odds and monsters, human and otherwise. Are the chimeras, demons, gorgons and mammoths the scary ones or does that moniker belong to the dire people of the tale? Perhaps one rivals the other.

This doesn't sound like a bright picture, does it? But it strips away the flesh of modern timidity or folk hiding behind keyboards and a lack of courage to show you REAL valor, from men and women, to fight on for retribution and the rest of their lives.

What am I after? To entertain, to tell you a story and to make you forget the world for a bit--Escapism, the purist form of storytelling and what all have sought after for thousands of years. Heroes, villains and monsters, devils, demons and all that…they will make you forget who is sleeping with who and why memes are considered near to scripture these days.

Take my hand and turn a page. Read a story that takes you away from all of that. Amid the lines one might learn a bit about legends and history, littered throughout the yarn. Ancient gods & demons, fabled cities, curses, basis for legends and creatures, all wrapped up to entertain, and folks up against such odds are good for you. IF done well, don't insult your intelligence. IF anything, they add to it.

Read and garner a desire to look for more works, not just my words, but tales from the past where these came. Breathe it in and ignore the absurdity of a damaged, contemporary world, one that has not learned from these tales of the past, from wars long ago...and times when one did what had to be done and may have been mistaken for a hero. This ideal alone, will bring more brightness to the world, as one will look onward and upward to greater things. Perhaps one will be reminded of a time when things were similar, yet crass, but there is light at the end of the tunnel, if one bashes the walls out a little, we can let the sunshine in, be it with sword or pen.

So, take a look at these tales within and escape for a little while. The way might seem a bit dark at first, but in time, it will lead on up to light.

Steven L. Shrewsbury

From the Country

The Red Wolf of Morragh

By: William Joseph Roberts

Draven's footfalls sloshed on the mossy path that led away from the Valley of the Mauga, his home. He trudged alongside his uncle's wagon as they left the Valley. The spring thaw was late this season, but the harsh winter had kept the raids to a minimum. No one enjoyed war, especially when the cold seeped deep into one's bones.

Laden with woodcrafts, high-quality furs, trinkets, and raw goods for sale at market, the small caravan slogged on. Draven was tasked to guard the load and to learn all that he could on this trip.

This was his first time venturing beyond the Valley. He'd met many others from other villages who'd come to trade with his people, but they were few and far between over his lifetime. They'd had visits from the short, squat blonde-haired clansmen of the Ashtabula from the north, whose proportions reminded him of the tales of dwarves and goblins of myth. Or the red-skinned beauties of the Bauneg from the north and east of the Valley. Draven had even met an Atlantean merchant once who had wandered in from the wilderness. He'd been turned around and lost his way after his caravan had been attacked and left for the carrion creatures of the forest.

"Why do we even need to leave the valley, uncle? Isn't it bad enough that we have to be on guard at all times against Euharleen and Xivitol slavers? Why do we want anyone else to know that we exist? Wouldn't it be easier to fortify and protect the village, relying on our own people for what we need?"

"That it would, nephew," Gera, Draven's elder uncle said with a grunted laugh.

"Then why do we not stay hidden?"

The old man smiled, then focused on the reins he held in his hands. He quietly thought for a long moment before he responded. "For wealth. Power. Adventure. Men do many things for many reasons that others do not understand. Take this venture for example. We seek our fortunes on what wares we have crafted over the long winter months. But also, we seek out the things we cannot produce, hunt, or forage for ourselves. Ingots of Atlantean steel, spices, dyes, and bolts of cloth that we may trade elsewhere or that our own people may use. But also on this venture, we will attend the court of Laird Morragh, high in his keep among Catair Cloiche, the city of stone. There with the other clans of the region, we will pledge our fidelity for the coming year. Should raids or war return to threaten the region, we respond as an army."

"I don't understand why, uncle. Why pledge to a Laird who does not lift a finger for us when the slavers come?"

"Because without the unification of the clans, the possibility of slavers and invasion would be that much greater."

Draven stared off into the snow-covered landscape, shaking his head.

"Why else would we do it, boy? Do you think that I prefer to travel for days on end, freezing my ass off on the seat of a wagon when I could be wrapped in the arms of a young wench, enjoying a warm fire and spiced cider?"

"I just don't understand why we have to rely on others when we are ourselves capable of much."

"That capability only goes so far, nephew. We negotiate deals and treaties for aid or to supply the like when needed. The gold and silver that we earn from trade go much farther in the world than just furs and the raw ore that we mine. Gold and silver rule the world, boy. And with that coin, we can buy much, or hire sellswords when needed for extra defense – though by the gods it was well before you were born that we needed that sort of assistance." Gera kissed his pinched thumb and forefinger before placing them against his forehead and muttering a prayer to himself.

"Then why am I here," Draven asked, almost demanding. "Why must I trudge along through the icy mud instead of tending to my duties in the valley?"

Gera reined in the wagon and turned in his seat. "You are here because I said you'll be here. You're here to help load, unload, and do anything else that I wish for you to do. You are here to provide protection to the caravan. And the gods help me, you are here to learn as much of the world as I can wedge into your stubborn mind."

Angry shouts of drivers came from the wagons behind theirs. Gera turned in his seat to face back down the path. His glare was enough to silence their complaints.

"Give me a half dozen Atlanteans or a score of Xivitol man-eaters over mindlessly trudging through the mud."

Draven drew the wide leaf-bladed Atlantean sword from the scabbard at his side. "I'd rather cut my path through the world than spend time jabbering like an old fool."

"If you think that the sword is the solution to every problem, then *you* are the *fool*, boy. I fear that I have done you a disservice, Draven. It is my fault that you have run with the hunters like a feral animal. By not teaching you these aspects of diplomacy and trade sooner, it has left your education off-balance."

"*You* wish for me to be a merchant. I'd rather seek glory by my own hand."

"I promised my sister that I would look after you should she cross through the veil to the other side."

"The man-eaters made sure she crossed over. How do we know she has crossed over? What if because of those bastard flesh eaters, her spirit still wanders this plane?"

"What I do know is that if you wish to continue warming yourself at my hearth, you'll do as I tell you or you can follow your feet and find your own way."

Draven glanced away, red anger flushed his cheeks. His jaw muscles bunched and chorded as he chewed on his anger.

"But I do not think you'll want to strike out on your own before We've arrived at the Oracle of Samoy," Gera continued.

"Why are we going there? Why not continue to the Laird's Keep?"

"It is over two days journey to reach Catair Cloiche from the Valley. The Oracle lies about halfway between the Valley and the keep, nestled in the crook of Morlee Cove."

"Seems a waste of time when we could continue through the night and arrive at Catair Cloiche that much sooner. Why stop? Why not continue and press on to our destination?" Draven snapped.

Gera threw back his head and laughed. "Because, *boy*… You will not find hospitality equal to that offered by the servants of the Oracle anywhere else in the world. Not even in the grand courts of Casstagou, the Fotabi Palace of Mimano, or the great mead hall of Atlantis itself, will you be treated as well as you will when in attendance of the Oracle of Samoy." He chuckled once again at Draven. "You will see, young one. Once we arrive and have paid our tribute, we may feast and partake of the Oracle's other generous offerings. It is something that you will not soon forget."

The night seemed to advance double after the caravan wound its way between narrow crags, entering the valley that was Morlee Cove. Torches were lit and placed in holders at the wagon's sides for the last hour of the day's journey.

Draven's jaw dropped when he spotted the dark forest temple, standing high on the hillside ahead of them. Torches illuminated paths leading up the hillside and several places both within and without the temple. A low drumming floated through the forest as if it were a lost and curious spirit.

Providing defense, an aged and moss-covered wooden palisade wall surrounded the temple. Three men guarded the gates to the compound. Each man was dressed in specialized armor. A mixture of heavy breastplates over shirts of scale mail that resembled the scales of pit vipers. Each man held a spear at the ready and were equipped with bronze-handled broadswords that hung in scabbards at their sides.

Having left the Valley well before daybreak during the small hours of the morning, they had pressed hard all day over frigid paths of semi-thawed mud to arrive at this moldy, moss-eaten *temple* when they did.

Draven would be glad to get off his feet and rest, but he would never admit that to his uncle. He hoped his uncle's boasting of the temple's hospitality was more than that. Sounds of laughter and moans of pleasure emanated from within the temple and found their way to Draven's ears from the structure above.

Gera pulled back on the reins, halting the oxen and stopping the wagon. He lowered the reins to his lap and held his hands out at shoulder height, palms out, fingers splayed to show they contained no weapons and that he approached with no ill intent.

One of the Guards stepped forward, taking control of the oxen by the bridle. Draven could make out that he was an older man in the flickering torchlight. Wisps of white stood out at his temples and in his short beard. "What brings you to the Oracle of Samoy?"

"We seek the Oracle's wisdom," Gera replied. "We bring gifts for the temple and items to trade after a long, frigid winter." The guard leaned out, looked down the line of wagons, and regarded Draven with an annoyed glance before turning back to Gera.

"You are of the Mauga?"

"We are."

"You've been here before, have you not?"

"I have, many times in the past, but not in nearly a decade myself."

The guard nodded. "Aye. Then that would be why you seem familiar. You may pass. Just be mindful and remember yourselves, but otherwise enjoy our hospitality.

Gera nodded and smiled, taking up the reins once again. "We will, friend."

"You may gather your wagons to the east side of the yard, near to the well. There is snow upon the ground in most places, but there, fresh grasses are poking through that your beasts may enjoy." He motioned to the other two guards, and they began opening the gates.

"Again, thank you. May Crom and Ebium bless you with success, friend." Gera said with a bowing nod toward the guard. He flicked the reins and spurred the beasts forward with a sharp *hey, yeah*. Guiding them through the entrance, he steered them to the eastern side of the complex, toward a small stand of trees near the palisade wall. Remnants of old campfires dotted the area.

"I've been here many times over the course of my life, but it has been quite a while. It's good to stretch my legs in the world once again," Gera said, as he pulled the oxen up to a stop and climbed down from the wagon. "Medicine men, merchants, hopeful farmers, and others have visited the Oracle for centuries. Some come seeking blessings, others for trade, and still others pray for hopeful predictions of the future. The Oracle is known to have been touched by the power of the gods and blessed with the sight of premonition."

"You speak as if the Oracle is ancient."

"Her spirit and powers are forever," Gera replied.

But how can anything be forever and immortal, Draven asked himself then shook it off as magical nonsense.

They rushed to set up camp, pitching their canvas shelters and tending to the animals.

"Retrieve two of the best furs and several blades from the wagon. Hurry, make yourself presentable then bring them along," Gera ordered, gathering himself after donning the fine silk vestment of a tradesman and merchant draped over a fine coat of velvet and fur. Reluctantly, Draven did as he was told and using fresh snow quickly washed the road dust from his face, pulling back his thick red locks he bound them with a leather thong in a top knot before falling into line along with others. He followed his uncle as he ascended along the steps cut into the hillside leading to the large wooden temple.

It was similar in construction to the two-story clan longhouse of the Mauga formed from large rough-hewn timbers that had seen better days and were long ago covered in moss. Slow-burning tapers marked the path up the hillside at odd-spaced intervals casting eerie shadows that danced in and out of existence about the hillside.

"It is said," Gera began, breaking the silence, "that the Oracle can call upon spirits, summon demons from the depths, and produce creatures of untold nightmares that would feast upon any who defiled the temple."

Draven stared at the dancing shadows as he continued along the path. Formless shapes bounced and weaved throughout the woods surrounding them like imps diving in and out of the darkness, mocking weary travelers on the final leg of their journey.

Several more guards stood before the entrance to the longhouse. Each were armed similarly to those men guarding the gate, small shields held at the ready in front of them as the group approached.

Gera produced several pendants from beneath his robes as he approached the first guard. "Thank you for all that you do in the Oracle's service. Thank you and your men for keeping her safe for the benefit of us all." Gera placed one of the pendants and a copper piece in the guard's hand which was quickly pocketed. Gera continued, repeating his words and actions with the other two men guarding the entrance. They each said their thanks, tucking away the small treasures as Gera led the party into the building.

Several men were gathered at low tables scattered around the main hall. Some played games of chance, tossing bone dice while others conversed in low grumbled tones. Low-burning tapers mounted to each of the room's main support beams hung suspended in cast iron sconces — casting a shadowy orange light about the chamber.

At the far end of the hall, sitting on a heavily padded lounge sat a young woman in nothing but a thin silken thong. Her face was as ashen as death itself but for the black marks that marred her smooth, delicate features. She did not look ancient to Draven. By the look of her, he'd guess that she was as young as him if not younger.

"Magic," Draven muttered under his breath and spat to the side. His uncle's hand came up an instant later and struck him hard across the face.

"Do not desecrate the holy place of the Oracle. Mind yourself or you'll not step foot from this temple alive."

A low rumble began deep within Draven's throat. He could return the strike, but the two older clansmen standing behind his uncle already had their hands on dagger hilts he knew were hidden within their robes.

Several drummers seated off to the side near the Oracle began a low rhythmic beat that resonated through the heavy beams of the structure. The Oracle slowly sat up straight, placing the palms of her hands together she raised them, stretching them above her head to the full extent of her reach before she rose slowly from her seat, swaying to and fro to what felt like the heartbeat of the temple.

Orators lounging on either side of the Oracle began a low murmured chant, joined quickly by those in attendance who feasted and gambled about the hall. The Oracle let out a shrieking wail, that at first sounded like a shrill of pain, but then devolved into something of unbridled pleasure. She laughed, almost cackling as she undulated to the beat. Her thrusts and moans sped up faster and faster to the drummer's rhythm. The chorus then deviated from the wailing screams of pleasure from the Oracle, adding discord to the cacophony with their own jeering shouts and cheers.

The Oracle went rigid from the intensity of release, letting out a long scream before falling back onto the padded cushions of the dais to a final staccato strike of the drums.

"Close your mouth, boy," Draven's uncle said, chuckling. Gera nudged his right-hand man who spotted Draven's red-faced glare and joined in the persecution.

"You look lost, boy. The oxen are outside if you prefer."

"Come," Gera said, motioning toward the front. "We must make our offering and pay our respects to the Oracle.

Angry, Draven held his tongue and fell into step behind his uncle. The men knelt before the dais, averting their eyes from the beautiful young woman lounging there among the plump cushions. Draven couldn't help but to take in every curve and swell of her nearly nude form. Noticing them she pushed herself upright, sitting cross-legged on one of the larger cushions before she noticed Draven's gaze. She smiled and let out a surprised giggle.

Gera grabbed Draven's arm and pulled at him. "On your knees and avert your eyes, boy. Do not disrespect the Oracle." This produced another amused cooing laugh from the young woman and an angry grumble from Gera.

"What brings you to my temple, travelers," the Oracle asked in a soft dulcet tone, similar to a mother soothing a young babe.

"Now that the passes are clear and spring flowers push their way up through the winter snows, we travel from the Valley of the Mauga to the folkmoot held at Catair Cloiche. We bring you these hard-won gifts and ask for your favor in our travels and endeavors. We've toiled away over the dark winter."

Carefully, Gera took the bundle from Draven's arms and began to lay out the gifts before him on the edge of the dais. "We bring you newly made blades of excellent steel that I'm sure your guards will welcome, excellent furs in which to wrap yourself, and beautifully crafted tools of silver that your kitchens are sure to appreciate."

Lazily she waved her hand and nodded her acceptance of the items before laying back on the cushions and propping herself up on one elbow. "Your offering is welcome. Thank you, and blessing to the Mauga."

"What say the gods of our travels and future dealings?" Gera nervously asked as if he were now overstepping his bounds. "Do we prosper, or is there failure in our future?"

One of the Oracle's assistants rushed over with a small bronze bowl encrusted with precious stones around its circumference and a small smoking brazier. The assistant helped her to sit up and drink from the bowl then she inhaled deeply of the perfumed smoke and leaned back on the cushions. She stretched, then rolled over onto her stomach and propped herself up on both elbows.

The drums began once again. Her head swayed to the slow beat, humming a tune to herself before letting out what felt like a banshee's wail. She rolled and writhed to the slow cadence. Rolling her hips from side to side, she caressed herself from neck to thighs, moaning in time to the hypnotic beat before rising up on her knees, straddling one of the larger velvet cushions.

Boom, bada boom, bada boom, bada boom, the drums continued — the speed of the measure increasing as she rocked and writhed, faster and faster, her panted breaths mixed with whispered prayers and incantations that Draven could not understand.

"By the blessed Corimaen," she moaned and shook, ripples of pleasure pulsing through her lean muscles. Then letting out a wailing scream, she arched her back and fell back upon the plump cushions of the dais. Small sounds of contented pleasure escaped her full lips as she continued to gently caress herself.

Rolling over, she propped her chin in the palms of her hands and stared at Gera with a burning gaze. He averted his eyes, staring at the floor in front of himself. He dared not look her way. Draven did not share his uncle's apprehension and smiled at the Oracle. She returned his longing gaze and chuckled before turning her attention back to Gera.

"Crom and Mitra favor you on this journey, son of the Mauga. The gods tell of a boon ahead for you and yours once you reach the fortress of Morragh."

The Oracle let out a sharp hiss and snatched at the empty air before her. "But do not delay in your travels, merchant. Be very wary and make your visit brief. If you linger too long, you will be the spark that invokes death incarnate…a ferocious and fiery devil that will destroy all in its path. The people will whisper its name in silent curses and pleading prayers for generations to come. *The Red Wolf of Morragh…*."

She sucked in a deep breath and cackled maniacally.

"Your boon will be lost, and misfortune will fall upon you and yours, son of the Mauga."

Her baleful gaze snapped to Draven, and once again she let out an angry, cat-like hiss. She laughed, relaxed, and laid back as one of her attendants rushed over to quietly collect the gifts.

"Enjoy our hospitality," the Oracle said, exhaustion filling her words. She lazily waved them away. "But remember my warning if you value your lives. The Red Wolf of Morragh is not a demon to be invoked lightly. You know in your hearts that my words are truth."

"Thank you, great Oracle," Gera obsequiously replied. He backed away as he rose to his feet. "We shall heed your warning." Grabbing Draven by the arm, he tugged. "Come boy."

Gera led them to the side where they took their place at one of the many low tables along the side of the chamber. A young serving wench dressed in as little as the Oracle herself brought around bowls of hearty stew and pitchers of chilled cider. Draven eyed the comely lass. She smiled down at his wanton gaze.

"Is there more that you desire, young master," she asked, her voice meek and mouse-like. Setting down the last bowl, she rested her hands on Draven's shoulders and began to work the tense knots left from the day's travel from his muscles.

Gera's right-hand man chuckled, then dug into his bowl of stew. "We did warn him, did we not, Gera?"

"That we did," Gera replied, smiling. He leaned over the table, closer to Draven. "Go, enjoy the humble offerings of the Oracle, but be mindful to not disrespect her or her temple."

Draven stood, then took her hand and the pitcher of cider, letting her lead him away, deeper into the temple.

The next morning, they set out at daybreak, pushing the animals hard, attempting to make the gates of Catair Cloiche before the darkness of night could fall. And just as the setting sun rested on the edge of the rolling hills to the west, they began their ascent along the narrow mountain path that led to the fortress of Morragh.

Winding along the hillside as darkness fell, the large hand-hewn stones of Catair Cloiche and the Keep of Morragh came into view. Built onto the side of a sheer facing cliff, the only way in or out of the city was the path they currently traveled upon.

Draven gasped at the enormity of the structure that seemingly clung unfettered to the side of the granite cliffs. The rocky face easily stretched a hundred feet above the structures if not more.

The gate guards hurried about their duties as the sun crept lower behind the hills.

"Come forward," one of the gate guards said, waving them forward after another wagon laden with sacks passed through the gates. Gera snapped his reins and drove his wagon forward. "What's your business?"

"We're traders and huntsmen from the Valley of the Mauga," Gera answered. "We're here for the folkmoot to trade our wares and to pledge our fealty to Lord Morragh for another season."

The lead guard was a massive beast of a man who easily stood two heads taller than Draven and as nearly as broad as an ox. The guard scowled and huffed at Gera.

"The stable area is to the right as you approach the keep. Park your wagons near there. Lord Morragh has been gracious enough to supply a feast for the folkmoot. He will receive tributes later this evening."

Gera retrieved a coin from his belt purse and palmed it off to the guard who accepted and pocketed the small token as quickly as it was handed off. "May the gods and Lord Morragh look favorably upon you, guardsman" he said, then urged the oxen forward.

The guards rushed the small trade caravan through the gates, securing them behind Draven's party for the evening.

Gera led the way to the stables set around the outside of the keep. Draven's uncle stepped down from his wagon and stretched before turning to his small group. "Remember that Lord Morragh is testy at best. We're here to trade, nothing else. Start no troubles and we'll be back on the road by midday tomorrow." He spun, looking about his people. "Fuda, you'll stand watch over the goods. Colto can relieve you in a few hours." With that, they each hurriedly secured their animals and left together for the feast.

As they approached, Draven could easily hear music and laughter that resonated from within the grand stone hall of the fortress. Crossing the threshold of the fortress, the entrance led to a low passage lined with murder holes to either side.

Draven emerged from the passage behind the others into the keep's grand hall and took in all that Lord Morragh had to offer. In a far corner off to the right, musicians plucked at strings and tapped at the drums that he'd heard from outside. Other patrons relaxed on cushions and diced or ate at low tables all around the chamber. At the far end of the chamber was a raised platform, and on it sat a cold grey stone throne draped in what looked to Draven like expensive cloth and furs.

A feast of roasted meats, broiled vegetables, and fresh baked confections were spread out on a long table in the middle of the chamber, available for all to pick and choose from at their discretion.

Draven hoped that the two exotic, raven-haired beauties dancing about the chamber would be on the menu for the night. They shifted and swayed to the light-paced tune, mirroring each other move for move, dropping bits of silk clothing, revealing more and more flesh with each step. Their hips swayed and bounced to the rhythm of a high-pitched flute that joined in the revelry, accented by the rattle of bells attached to thin chains that were wrapped about their equally thin waists.

Gera turned to find Draven and pulled him in close, then nodded at the exotic dancers with a smile.

"Go, boy. Enjoy yourself. Do not cause us any trouble. We will be speaking with several other merchants," he said, pointing off to the right where a number of older men in robes and several warriors sat around one of the low tables. He slapped Draven on the back and continued with the others to the table of merchants.

Draven scanned the room, finding space among a group of younger warriors like himself lounging on plush cushions around one of the low tables near the entrance, tossing dice, and carousing with the serving girls.

"Is there room at your table for one more?" he asked as he approached.

"There is," a wispy thin blond-haired youth replied with a dead serious stare. "If you have the coin to join us."

Draven smiled and shook the coin purse hanging from his belt. The all-too-familiar tinkle of silver and gold drew the attention of everyone surrounding the table. The blond-haired youth's stone-like expression melted away as he returned Draven's smile. "That will do nicely," he said, motioning to an empty seat opposite from himself. "Please, join us."

Sitting, Draven took up one of the wooden cups and reached for the pitcher of chilled wine. The blond-haired youth placed his hand on top of the pitcher. "Not before We've tossed a round, my friend."

Another young man of dark hair and olive-toned skin sitting to Draven's right placed a cup in front of him that rattled with the sound of bones.

"Toss the dice and let's see if you have the right to drink with us," the blond-haired man said, then smiled wide like the viper that Draven suspected the man was. Draven glanced down at the cup then back up at the man.

"And what did you say your name was," he asked the blond-haired youth, heavy sarcasm in his tone. The blond-haired man smiled even wider. The look of a predator glinted in his eyes.

"Sven."

Draven nodded. "It's a pleasure to meet you, Sven. I am Draven of the Mauga." Draven pulled his hand away from the pitcher of wine and took up the dicing cup. Rattling its contents, he looked about the table, taking in each man seated nearby. "What's the wager?"

"Coppers, silver, gold if you like. We're not particular as long as we're winning." Sven started to chuckle and the others around the table joined in his laughter. Draven retrieved a small coin from his coin purse and glanced at it. It was a small silver Atlantean fanning. He dropped it on the table in front of himself.

"Will that suffice to start?"

Sven smiled again and nodded. "That will do. Please Draven of the Mauga," he said, motioning for Draven to get on with it. "Toss the dice. Let us see who the gods favor this night."

Dicing was one of the simpler games Draven had learned from his father before he'd fallen ill and left this world to stand beside Ebium in his great hall among the ranks of the fallen. His father would take Draven with him when he was young to the different mead halls of the Mauga. They traveled to trade, converse, and learn any useful news there was to be learned from across the valley and their widespread community. Merchants and farmers alike talked and traded information freely over a mug of anything that had a bite to it, but Draven rarely had the ear for prattling and positioning. He preferred to hear tales of great warriors, or tips of physical skills and prowess that he could attempt to emulate instead of useless banter.

Draven shook the cup and poured out the dice, rolling a pair of sixes. Taking up the dice again, he followed up with a total of ten.

"You do know how to play this game, don't you," Sven asked.

"If you are playing against the odds of matching sums as most rolling old bones do, then yes."

Sven added his own coin to the pile, then took up the cup and dice, rolling a total of three.

"Not an easy number to roll, even with the gods on your side."

"That, we can both agree on, friend." Sven chuckled under his breath and rolled, rolling a total of three once again. He picked up the coins, adding them to the small pile on the table in front of him. "Bad luck, friend."

"Perhaps. Perhaps not." Draven poured himself a mug full of wine and took a long drink.

Sven placed another silver on the table and rolled the dice, totaling eight. "I do not remember seeing you in this hall before, *friend*. Is this your first time in the keep of Morragh?" He took up the dice once more, rolling eleven.

"Looks as if my luck has rubbed off on you, *friend*," Draven replied, then took another long draw of wine. Taking the dice, he dropped another silver on the table and rolled again, producing a five. "This is my first visit to the keep."

"It's impressive, wouldn't you say?"

Draven nodded. "It is. The sheer amount of time and the number of workers involved in its construction is hard to imagine." He rolled once more, drawing a pair of ones.

"Bad luck…" Sven hissed. He added another coin to the pile and took the dice back. "I saw you enter with several others. You're clansmen?"

"My uncle and others from the Valley."

"Were the snows as bad as we'd heard?"

"That they were. It never seemed to stop snowing throughout the winter. We were blessed that last season's harvest was as bountiful as it was, or we might have starved before the spring thaw began in the Valley."

"Remind me. What valley was that again?"

"The Valley of the Mauga."

"That's three to four days of travel to the north, isn't it?"

"To some, maybe. It was two hard days travel by oxen-drawn carts, but they were driven hard and steady both days." Draven drained his mug and then poured himself another.

Sven leaned slightly to the side, looking around Draven and chin nodded in that direction. "Would those be your clansmen?"

Draven turned to spot his uncle and the others still at the table in the far corner where they'd seated themselves earlier.

"They are," Draven confirmed.

"I hope they are well-mannered."

"And why is that?"

"The orange-headed man at the table with them is known as Waght. He is prone to headedness, especially when drink is involved, and is known to be quick to anger. Laird Morragh does not take kindly to disruptions in his hall."

"And what if they do anger this, Waght?"

"Laird Morragh's punishments are known to be fairly severe, so I hope that your kinsmen can keep their tongues. Especially since Waght is a personal friend of the Laird."

Draven shrugged and topped off his cup. "Makes no difference to me. If they do, it'll be of their own doing. I wasn't keen on this trip to begin with."

Sven perked up at the potentially new and interesting conversation. "Do tell, Draven of the Mauga. Why would you not want to grace us with your presence?"

"Because my place is defending my people, not gallivanting around to trade for trinkets. My time would be best served hunting down those who would steal or harm any of the clan."

"I see. But aren't you protecting your clansmen by being along with them?"

Draven nodded slowly and lifted his mug once again. "I suppose you are correct. It does hold some truth, but it is not the same as protecting the Valley."

"It might not hold the same weight as patrolling your homeland, but you are still protecting some of your people. What if they were to perish on your watch?"

Draven shrugged. "Then I do not know. Perhaps I would be welcomed back, but that I highly doubt. Failure is severely looked down upon, but by venturing out of the Valley on their own, they willingly endanger themselves."

"And if that were the case?"

Draven drank and thought quietly for a moment. "Then even deeper into the world I would be forced to go."

"How about another roll of the dice, friend Draven? This game is easy. The highest roll wins the round." Sven shook the cup and rolled a pair of fives. "Ha, luck is with me. Beat that with a single roll."

Draven added a silver to the pile and rolled the dice.

"Ha!" Sven chortled. "Better luck next time, Northman." He collected the winnings on the table and placed a single piece of copper on the table. "Just in case your purse is feeling a bit light this night, *friend*."

"There is nothing light about my purse," Draven said, almost growling back at the other man. He downed the remainder of his cup, refilling both his and Sven's once more before he placed his bet and took up the cup.

Sven flashed a toothy, predatory grin. "Shall we?"

Dice rolled and drinks flowed into the small hours of the night when the musicians had all but wandered away and most of the laughter had died down to whispers. Snores from overindulged patrons sleeping off wine fumes resounded from dark corners of the hall.

An angry roar erupted from the far end of the hall followed by the hard thump of a table being turned over. "You son of a godless whore! No one cheats me!"

Draven turned to find Alrais, Gera's right-hand man defending himself from the red-haired man known as Waght. The low table they had been sitting at had been tossed to the side as if it were a child's toy.

Draven turned to stand but found several sets of hands clasped atop his shoulders, pushing him back into his seat.

"Not so fast there, my Maugan friend. Let's see what will transpire without interruption," Sven said, the hiss returning to his voice. He leaned back, laughing into his cup as he began to sip his wine. Draven turned as much as his captors would let him and looked back over his shoulder.

Alrais drew a dagger from his belt and thrust it deep into Waght's belly. Slicing sideways across the girth of the red-headed man's gut, the wound split, spilling blood and entrails. Even from this distance, Draven could smell the stench of bile and filth falling out of the man.

Four others around the table, including Gera, scrambled to their feet, drawing weapons themselves.

The large burley gate guard appeared from the darkness, sword in hand. He bellowed, "Stand down! Stay your weapons!"

More men rushed into the hall, surrounding Alrais, Waght, and the others with swords drawn.

"Call for the Laird," the large guard said, pointing at one of the other armed men.

Alrais stepped toward the guard who countered by placing the tip of his blade to Alrais's nose. "You'll stand where you are, stranger."

"This fat pig attacked me."

"It doesn't look that way to me," the guard replied. "From where I stand, he's gutted and dying and you're holding a bloody blade. This *fat pig* is Waght the Red, the right hand of the mountain, a personal friend of the Laird. Morragh will not be pleased with you."

The guard's eyes darted about to his men. "Take their weapons and place them in chains."

Two of the guards hurried from the room. They returned moments later with black iron shackles, clasping them about the men's wrists after removing their weapons.

Draven had been in enough brawls to know he couldn't do anything to help if he were shackled like the rest of the Maugan men. No matter how hot the fire burned within him he had to wait as if he were the coiled serpent waiting to strike. To leap into the fray now would leave him outnumbered twenty to one. Only an insane or desperate man would attempt to fight their way out of the hall at this moment.

Turning back in his seat to face Sven, Draven took up his cup once more and sipped slowly.

"That's it, Northman," Sven said, chortling to himself. "It's good that you realize your place."

Sven was beginning to grate on Draven's patience. Draven waited calmly and quietly, even though he seethed on the inside. He wanted nothing more than to remove himself and his kinsmen from this place. He thought through his options as he slowly sipped at his wine, observing each man for a possible weakness. Draven had been in more brawls and tavern fights than he could count along with border skirmishes with flesh eaters and slavers. He knew how to fight. He knew how to hold his own. With luck and speed, if the gods were on his side, he might have enough of an edge to cut his way to his clansmen and free them. He waited, slowing his breathing as he could, trying to focus against the wine fumes starting to creep in at the edges of his senses.

With the speed of a deadly asp, Draven grabbed the hand resting on his left shoulder and snapped several fingers, bending them backward at an unnatural angle. Cold steel pressed into the flesh at the base of Draven's skull as quickly as he had broken the other man's fingers.

"You so much as move," a voice from behind him said in a quiet yet firm tone, "and I'll skewer you like a pig on a spit."

Bleary-eyed, Laird Morragh reappeared and took up his seat at the head of the hall. The chained offenders were led before him. Sven rose from his seat and poured himself another mug of wine. "Shall we see what Father wishes to do with these nuisance peddlers?"

"Father?" Draven asked. Two of Sven's men nudged him to stand, each of them keeping a large hand securely on Draven's shoulders.

"Aye, Northman. Father." Sven flashed an amused smile. "Does it surprise you that the old Laird had a bastard that survived, or that you were dicing with the second most powerful man in Catair Cloiche?" He continued forward toward the throne. Those sober enough to walk and witness the judgment followed behind him.

Rage began to boil up within Draven and he watched the young lordling strut away. But it was guaranteed suicide to attempt to fight his way out. There were too many of them loyal to the Laird versus Draven and his clansmen. And half of them, even though they could hold their own in most fights, were no match for professional soldiers.

They led Draven forward, stopping him just behind his kinsmen.

"You come into my home," Laird Morragh roared to start. Spittle flew from his lips as he continued. "You bastards drink my wine, eat my food, and repay my kindness by slaughtering my right-hand man? What outrageousness! What Insolence! Do you seek my position as well? Was that your plan from the beginning? Arrive in my home, then when the time was right you'd slip in and slit my throat when I slept?"

The old laird shook his head then glanced about, looking for someone. Spotting his servant, he waved them forward. They hurried to Morragh's side and handed off a small, ornate box that he opened then pinched some sort of powder within. Placing it to one nostril he snorted, repeating the process for the other nostril. Laird Morragh coughed furiously, trying to catch his breath. He sniffed and snorted, rubbing at his face as if the brown powder burned.

Regaining himself, he handed the box off and continued. "You dare to come into my home to take my position from me?"

"No laird! Nothing of the sort," Gera said, pleading. "My Kinsmen and I are here to pledge our fealty to you and to trade our wares. Nothing more."

Morragh let out a wailing scream then ripped a sword from the grip of the nearest soldier, plunging it deep into Gera's chest. "Your insolence will be repaid with death!"

The laird's guards sprung to action, slaughtering the bound men in moments.

Draven roared, fighting against those restraining him, he pushed forward. Half a dozen other hands gripped him tighter and drew him back, forcing the Northman to his knees they bound him with a set of black iron manacles like the ones used on his kinsmen.

"What is this?" Morragh shouted, turning toward the commotion.

"The last of the Maugan's that traveled here to take your throne, father," Sven answered, stepping forward to stand beside Laird Morragh.

"Then he should die with the others."

"You'll be the one to die!" Draven roared.

Sven glared down at Draven. "And you'll silence your tongue, Northman."

"No, Father. He had nothing to do with what happened tonight. He was with me and my men. I will swear to it as truth. I ask that you spare his life."

Laird Morragh stepped back and glanced at his son. Unsure confusion that turned to curiosity flitted about his features. "And why should I spare him? What favor does this stranger owe you that you'd ask this of me?"

"None at all, father. You'll spare him because I asked of it. I wish to give him to the ogre. He's been bored as of late and needs a plaything."

Lord Morragh's face twisted in disgust at the thought. After a moment, he answered. "Very well. If you must, but he does not leave this keep. He is under your watch and care. If not under your direct control, my men will kill him on sight."

Sven nodded, then bowed and backed away from his father. With a snap of his fingers, Sven headed for a side passage. "Come, friends. Let us pay the ogre a visit."

Draven struggled, testing their grip on him, but several points of sharp-tipped steel dug into his flesh. They led him along into the bowels of the keep. Perhaps their numbers would dwindle at some point, or an opportunity for escape would present itself.

"I would almost place a wager that you may just enjoy yourself, Northman." Sven turned, walking backward as they continued down the corridor, leading the party. "I know from experience that the ogre will be thrilled to meet you. He's a very strange lot. We found him wandering in the nearby forests some time ago. He wasn't much more than a pup shortly removed from its mother's teat. I was young as well when he was brought to us, so I have had plenty of opportunities to study him and his reactions over the years."

Sven turned back around, taking up a burning torch from a wall sconce, and continued down a set of stonework stairs. Several of his men took up lights as well as they continued. "I keep him happy by bringing him things to play with. It's so interesting to watch his mind at work. Sometimes I see compassion in his eyes, other times lust or sadness, but mostly they are filled with rage like yours are right now." Sven looked back over his shoulder and flashed a sadistically knowing smile. "Rage meeting rage is one experiment I have not witnessed, so I hope you will be willing to oblige me and my curiosity. In the end, the result is always the same. The ogre does have to eat, after all. I would have to guess that you would approve of his favorite method of dispatching his prey. I wouldn't expect someone like you to understand much more than brute force."

The lordling let out a short self-satisfied sounding chortle. "It has been interesting to watch him learn to enjoy himself. Take his time by slowly removing appendages, stripping the meat from each finger. Eventually, he'll have his way with you. Living or dead hasn't seemed to matter much to him. He's a creature of few emotions. He seems to live in the moment, enjoying life to its fullest."

Reaching the next landing, they continued down another dark corridor ending in a wide spiral staircase leading further into the mountain. Draven could hear the grunts and excitement of something at the bottom.

"I believe the ogre has noticed our approach." The excitement in Sven's voice was unmistakable. "This should be a treat for all of us." He let out a deep, chuckling belly laugh as he reached the bottom of the stairs and a large wooden door where he lifted several latches, sliding them to the side, he unbarred the door and pushed. The door swung slowly, its iron-bound hinges creaking and popping from rusty age.

Chains rattled from the darkness beyond the doorway, followed by the sniffing blows of a dog or possibly a bear, Draven thought. The stink of rot and offal that emanated from the open door was enough to turn his stomach.

"What sort of man keeps a beast confined to the dark confines of a prison?" Draven slowed his descent, pushing back against the men leading him. His reluctance to move forward was answered by steel. The tips of two daggers stuck into the back of Draven's neck, one near the base of his skull, the other he could feel was aimed at the main vein of his neck. A simple thrust of either blade would be enough to end his life.

"Not so fast, Northman," one of the guards said. Decay and pickled fish that tainted the man's breath wafted over Draven's shoulder.

Sven turned and let out a disappointed sigh. "This goes so much easier when the Ogre's playmates give themselves over to the realization that this is the end. There is no turning back. You are witnessing your last moments, Maugan. Pray to your gods if you must but do it quietly and try to enjoy each moment before they run out."

"You're a madman."

Sven shrugged and continued through the doorway. "Perhaps," he said and entered, thrusting the torch ahead of him, and turned to the left just as he crossed the threshold of the doorway.

A small stone walkway possibly wide enough for two men standing abreast, illuminated by Sven's torchlight appeared just inside the room. Sven's men forced Draven through the opening and guided him to the left.

Sven lit torches mounted in holders along the wall as he continued around the circular walkway surrounding a wide pit. The movement of something large hidden down within the darkness of the pit caught Draven's eye as it shifted its position. Draven could hear the shuffle of movement from below and the clank of chains on stone. Once Sven had lit nearly every torch around the chamber, Draven could make out the shadowy figure of something man-shaped, crouched on its haunches at the bottom of the pit. If it were a man, he would have to be twice as large as Draven if not more.

"Ogre," Sven said in a sing-song tone that echoed within the chamber. "I've brought you a new plaything."

"Plaaaaay," the thing said as it rose.

"By Crom and Ebium," Draven gasped. He stared as the creature stretched to its full, hunched height. Gangly elongated limbs unfolded as it stood, the torchlight revealing a thick covering of coarse black hair on its body and a grotesquely malformed, drawn-out face that looked vaguely man-like. Sharp, spine-like fangs protruded outward over both upper and lower lips.

It began to speak in a tone so deep that it resonated, reverberating about the room so loudly that Draven couldn't make out the words.

"Yes, Ogre," Sven said calmly, almost like a patient father. "I have brought you a new plaything."

The beast-man screeched. Bouncing with joy it clapped, rattling the heavy chains attached to its wrists. The childlike laughter that followed sent a chill deep into Draven's soul.

"Do you see the joy you have brought this poor, pitiful creature," Sven said, waving a hand towards the beast. "Know that your death will not be for nothing. It will brighten this one's life for some time to come. At least until there is nothing left for it to play with."

Sven's men shoved Draven forward. Skidding to a stop at the edge of the pit, Draven turned, squaring off with the two men. "Only a damned fool would willingly give up and lay down his life for nothing. Especially for a corrupt lordling's pleasure."

Sven laughed. "Be my guest, you are unarmed and outnumbered," he chided, then drew his own sword as if to accent his words. "You have no chance of leaving this place. Ever. But since you are a gambling man as am I, let's make this interesting. Options of your release may be discussed should you survive your time with the ogre."

Draven looked down at the gaping maw of the creature. The fetid stench of the creature's breath as it panted with excitement seemed to fill the room.

"I'd rather take my chances against your hired hands than a lordling's bastard," Draven growled, motioning toward the thing in the pit.

"As you wish," Sven replied. His men advanced, drawing their own short, leaf-bladed swords. Draven rushed forward, diving under the downward swing of the first man, he shouldered the soldier just enough to nudge him into the pit. Flailing to catch his balance, the man fell. The soldier's panicked scream nearly drowned out the bestial roar of the creature below.

Draven continued his rush. He rose, both fists clasped together into a hammer hand that he swung upward and to the right as he rose, smashing in the next man's face. He grabbed the soldier by the hair of the head with one calloused hand, and the grip of the soldier's sword in the other. With the soldier still dazed, Draven forced the man to turn and shoved his face forward, smashing him into the stone wall. Shouldering the dazed soldier to the side he freed the sword from his hand but failed to completely grasp the grip of the blade before three more men slammed into him, tackling him to the ground.

The wind left Draven's lungs in one harsh woosh as the weight of the three men crashed down on top of him. He fought, smashing an elbow into one man's side hard enough that he heard the unmistakable pop of bone giving way under the force of the strike.

They struggled, lifting Draven to his feet by the braids of his fiery red hair, and turned him to face Sven, who looked upon Draven with a smug, almost contented smile. Motion and a sickly slurping sound drew Draven's eyes back to the pit. His stomach lurched at the scene his eyes fell upon. The beast held the disembodied head of the unfortunate soldier who had fallen into the pit. It poked, prodded and sucked at the eye socket, squeezing the sides of the skull as it did.

"I must not have made myself clear, Northman. You will *not* be leaving this place so quickly."

Several sets of hands forced Draven forward with a sudden shove, off-balancing him and sending him over the edge. He landed with a small splash among the scattered bones that littered the soft muddy bottom of the pit, covering him in filth.

The creature let out an ear-piercing chortle and lunged forward. Draven backpedaled, getting his feet under him as quickly as he could. The beast came to a sudden stop, held in place by the heavy anchor chains that stretched from its wrists and secured to a ring in the floor at the center of the pit. The beast had just enough chain that it could touch the walls of the pit with its feet, but nothing else.

Draven pressed his back against the wall of the pit and stood straight. The creature jerked at the chains, letting out an inhuman scream. The coppery tinge of blood was heavy on the creature's breath. The sides of the depression were at least twice the height as Draven was tall and climbing the smooth walls of the pit would be all but impossible as long as the creature was still a threat.

It kicked, striking for Draven's head with a long, powerful leg. Draven dove, rolling to his right and away from the beast. It leapt, getting ahead of Draven's escape, and again struck out with a powerful kick that just clipped his arm. The strike might leave a bruise later if he managed to survive but was otherwise minor.

Draven struck out, hammering a fist to the creature's inner thigh. It howled in pain, hopping backward and away from the young warrior.

Quickly glancing about the dark depression Draven spotted the unfortunate warrior's remains lying on the other side of the pit. Sprinting, he covered the distance to the corpse in moments.

The beast roared and charged in Draven's direction. Finding the fallen soldier's leaf-blade sword, Draven sprinted away from the creature heading once again for the wall.

The chains snapped taut, stopping the creature. It let out a roar. Enraged, it furiously fought against its bonds to reach Draven. Sidestepping the creature's kick, Draven sliced upward, connecting with a solid strike. The blade bit deep into the creature's wrist, but only about a quarter of the way through the joint. Draven jerked the blade, pulling it free. Howling, it backed away, clutching the wound with the opposite hand.

Not wanting to lose the advantage, Draven charged forward and leapt high into the air. He pushed his exhausted leg muscles to their limits and soared onto the creature's back. Gripping the beast by the coarse black hair covering its back, the experience reminded Draven of attempts to tame and ride wild boar when he was younger.

The creature screamed. Panting with panic it spun, attempting to reach the nuisance that had landed on its back, and began bucking like a wild, untamed stallion. Draven dug the heels of his booted feet into the creature's sides.

Attempting to guide the beast, Draven leaned, pulling the creature left. This guided the creature closer to the wall of the pit. Nearing the edge, Draven plunged the blade into the beast's back. It leapt and howled, doubling its effort to remove its rider.

Again, Draven plunged the leaf-bladed sword deep into the thing's flesh, hoping its heart would be in the same place as a man's. Black blood and bile initially gushed from the wound which quickly turned to a trickle.

Weakening, the ogre began to totter. Draven could feel the strength leaving the creature's powerfully muscled frame.

Draven climbed, pushing his exhausted limbs even harder so he could scale the creature. He gripped the beast by the hair of its head and pulled himself to a crouched position on its shoulders then hurdled himself across the gap to the wall of the pit.

Impacting the corner edge of the pit, the breath was knocked from Draven's lungs. He scrambled, fighting to get a grip on the worn stone before he slipped back into the pit with the beast. Pulling himself along on his elbows Draven inched himself onto the walkway. Rolling over onto his back, he took a moment and stared into the flickering flames of the burning taper mounted to the wall above him.

He focused on the sound of the creature's whimpering ragged breathing as it clung to the last moments of its life.

"By the gods…," Draven gasped quietly to himself.

"Such a pity," Sven said. "I raised that poor creature from the time it was an infant. It was possibly even the last of its kind, and you killed it."

Draven had all but forgotten the young lordling amid his struggle to survive. Glancing in the direction of the voice, Draven found Sven still standing where he had been when he'd been pushed into the pit but now, the noble was alone. Quickly taking in the rest of the room, he did not see any of Sven's men.

Rolling slowly to his knees, Draven stretched already sore muscles and adjusted his grip on the ichor-coated sword. "Do your men not have the stomach for blood, or the balls for battle?"

Sven let out a dissatisfied grunt then slowly took a step, making his way around the walkway toward Draven. "Apparently neither. One of them mumbled something about fighting as fiercely as one of the red wolves of the forest before they scurried away with their tails tucked."

Those words suddenly struck at something in the back of Draven's mind. The Oracle. She had mentioned something similar. A warning. Draven thought back to her words.

The Red Wolf of Morragh is not a demon to be invoked lightly. You know in your hearts that my words are truth.

Could be the Oracle was right, or could be a complete coincidence. Neither mattered in the end if it was something he could use to deter and distract his enemy. Draven shook off the thought and focused back on Sven.

"But they've left you to fend for yourself," Draven replied. His words brought a perturbed grimace to the lordling's face.

"No matter. You'll take little effort for me to deal with. While those guards will be severely punished for their insolence and their *replacements* will be more aptly trained." He lazily stepped forward toward Draven and brought his sword up to a defensive posture, almost as if it were more of a hassle than anything else.

"I thought you were a gambling man, *Lordling*," Draven asked. "I defeated your beast, and your men ran off with their tails tucked between their legs." Draven took a step forward, bracing himself in a simple attack stance, the sword poised for a powerful downward strike. "Are you certain you wish to take your chances against me? The odds are not in your favor."

"The odds are always in my favor," Sven roared, his rage overtaking him. He charged forward, thrusting with his sword. Draven easily deflected the attack, swatting the sword away with a powerful strike of his own. Draven did not yield. Instead, he pressed the attack, using the momentum of the strike to redirect the sword he pressed forward and aimed the blade for the Lordling's throat. Sven brought his sword up just in time, blocking the movement.

"Are you certain your luck will hold, *my lord*," Draven taunted. "Or would you like to tuck your tail and follow your men's example?"

Enraged, Sven responded with a furious cry and a flurry of wild strikes. Draven had hoped that tormenting the young lordling's ego would unsettle him, and his hunch had paid off.

"By the gods, you swing like a mad *woman*." Draven parried each ill-placed strike, hoping to the gods that Sven did not get lucky and that he could end this quickly. Sven continued, pushing forward to the point he landed a kick to the side of Draven's leg.

Shifting his weight, Draven stepped back, blocking another series of blows before he pressed forward. Ducking low, he struck with an upward thrust that easily penetrated the lordling's loose robes with the sharp tapered tip of the leaf-bladed sword. Bone and flesh relinquished to the force of the attack. Sven coughed, dropping his sword he spewed a bloody red mist over Draven. Rivulets of blood trailed down from the edges of his downturned mouth.

"My father…will avenge me," Sven hoarsely growled, choking on his own words.

Draven stood, pushing against the blade as he stepped forward. Sven quickly clasped Draven by the wrists. His strength failed him, his grip was like that of a child. Draven continued, backing the lordling against the stone wall of the chamber.

"*Your* father... will suffer for *his* insolence toward my uncle and my people. *Your* father will not know that I stalk his halls, until the moment that I strike. *His* men will not see me coming, before their lives have been forfeit for his failure. *Your* father... will perish by my hand, as slow and as sure as the sunrise," he whispered into the lordling's ear slowly, drawing out each and every word.

Draven twisted the blade slightly, causing Sven's entire body to convulse. Sven gasped, blood choking his words. "You will die before you reach the great hall."

Draven's stare bored into the young lord. "That may be, but it will not stop me." Sven laughed, coughing, holding Draven's wrists tight.

"Then you are a fool, Northman."

"No, little lordling." Draven smiled wide. The fires of revenge burned as an inferno in his eyes. "The Oracle of Samoy saw what was to come... By her words, our boon would be lost to misfortune.

Should we linger, we would unleash a ferocious and fiery devil that would destroy all in its path. She spoke the name of the demon. *The Red Wolf of Morragh.*"

Sven's eyes went wide at the realization of Draven's words, and the blade that now fully penetrated his body.

"As the Oracle predicted. *I...am...here.*"

"I *am* the Red Wolf of Morragh."

Melkart And The Sage

By Mark Mellon

The noonday sun was hot, and shade was scarce. The man urged the heavily laden mule onward. His dog paced alongside him. The path through the hills was arduous and stony, but the mule was well shod, and he wore high Assyrian boots with hobnailed soles. A goitered gazelle peered down from a hilltop. The only sound was the crunch of loose rocks.

"Look what we found!"

"Travelers, ripe for plucking."

Voices came from just ahead, around a bend in the trail, more like jackals with fresh caught, helpless prey than men. He tethered the mule to a rock outcropping. With a bow, a quiver, and a sword, he advanced cautiously with the dog.

"Let's strip and kill them."

Brigands capered gleefully around their captives, an old man and his young companion. Dressed in filthy rags, the hill thieves brandished swords in their faces and screamed threats. The travelers were unnaturally calm despite the danger.

"We're paupers," the old man said. "We have no money or valuables."

"Then you'll be our slaves, hew wood and draw water for us."

The man took an arrow, nocked it, pulled back the bowstring, and fired. The long shaft landed in a brigand's stomach. He fell screaming to the ground.

"AAAAAUUUUUUUGGGGHHH!"

"An attacker. We outnumber him. Slay him."

The remaining brigands charged, but fast as fleet footed Akhilleous, the man and dog were already among them. The dog savagely bit one man's bare calf. The bandit cursed and raised an arm to strike the dog, but the man hacked it off at the elbow with his sword. He cracked another's skull with the flat of the blade.

He waved his blood stained sword at the two remaining bandits. The dog snarled at them.

"Run while you can."

Averse to the odds now, they followed his advice and took to their heels, dead and wounded comrades left without a thought. The big man went to the arrow shot brigand, put his foot to the man's chest, and yanked out the arrow.

"You miserable bastard," the brigand hissed in Aramaic.

"Good shafts are hard to come by."

He took his sword and pulled the man's head back by his hair.

"Hold," a quiet voice said.

Calm as ever, the old man gently smiled. "He poses no threat now. T'is wrong to slay him."

The man cut his throat anyway. He also killed the unconscious brigand. The one whose arm he severed had already bled to death. He wiped his sword on a dead man's tunic.

"They were naught but brigands. They'd only set to thieving and killing again for t'is all they know. I must fetch my mule."

"As you will, my friend. Damis and I will see about burying them."

"Bury them? They were going to enslave you."

The old man ignored him. "Pull the bodies together and we'll heap stones on them."

They set about their grisly task. The man retrieved his mule. When he returned, they were heaping small stones onto the dead men.

"You'll never finish that way. Against my better judgment, I'll help you."

He tied up the mule and piled large, heavy stones onto the bodies with amazing speed and strength. Soon a proper cairn was built, the bodies secure against marauding animals. The big man wiped away the sweat that streamed down his brow.

"Let's be off."

"After we pray for their souls."

"Do you plan to spend the day here, father?"

"You needn't wait. We're grateful you helped us, even if it wasn't necessary."

"Nay. The gods would frown on me. T'is like leaving infants in the wilderness. Say your prayer and let's leave while there's still light."

"Pray hold hands with us."

He forced a smile and complied. The old man chanted prayers in Greek and Aramaic. The ancient's face glowed with a numinous aura, sunlight dancing in his snowy white locks. A strange sensation swept over Melkart, akin to awe, as if he were in a temple before the gods. The ceremony done, the three men left.

"I am Melkart of Tyre, a merchant."

"Peace unto you in this world, Melkart. I am Apollonius of Tyana. This is my disciple Damis, a son of Nineveh."

The lithe, dark young man smiled shyly at Melkart. They traveled the afternoon, but progress was slow on switchback trails over rugged, high hills. Near twilight, Apollonius called a halt.

"We should camp elsewhere, father. Someplace with water."

"Pray keep still, my son."

A bevy of doves cooed from a stand of pine trees. Apollonius listened intently, as if he heard human conversation. "The valley ahead has a creek with good water. We'll camp there."

Puzzled, Melkart nonetheless followed Apollonius. He led them up a hill in the gathering darkness.

"Master understands the birds' tongues," Damis whispered.

They crested the hill and heard rushing water murmur below, confirmation of Apollonius's prophecy. By the creek, Melkart unloaded his mule, loose hobbled him, and cut fodder for the mule with his sword. He gathered dry wood and started a fire with flint and iron while Damis and Apollonius ritually cleansed themselves of the taint of murder in the creek.

They sat around the fire. Kaleb put a front paw on Melkart's leg and whimpered. Melkart scratched his head.

"Aye, boy. Catch your fill."

The dog eagerly ran off.

"He hasn't eaten since this morn. Nor have I. I'll take my bow and see if I can bag some game, perhaps a roe deer."

Apollonius made a horrified face. "There's no need for that, Melkart my son. We have sufficient rations to feed you as well."

Melkart smiled broadly. "That's kind to share your food with me. I don't have to take any trouble for my supper then."

"Damis, give Melkart a double portion since he's so big."

Damis reached into the linen sack he carried. He handed Melkart two onions and two small loaves of twice baked bread. Damis and Apollonius contented themselves with a loaf and an onion apiece. Melkart forced another smile.

"My thanks. Now that you've shared your food, I'm your guest friend."

"And we yours, Melkart. Let us pray to the God in gratitude for our meal."

They held hands and prayed again. Melkart ate the meager meal, washed down with creek water. Kaleb returned, tail wagging, snout red with blood. He ran up to Melkart, but he shooed him away.

"Go wash in the creek first. Then you can curl up with me."

Kaleb obediently trotted off. The air grew chilled. Damis and Apollonius drew close to the fire, thin mantles pulled tight around their shoulders. Melkart donned a lion skin cloak.

"You said you're a merchant, Melkart. Do you journey to Antiok?"

"Aye, Apollonius. My mule bears a talent of amber stones, tears of Apollo, brought from the land of the Scythians. I acquired them in Commagene. After I sell the amber in the agora, I'll buy passage on a ship to Tyre and start a new venture there with my profits."

"Perhaps a journey to Gades and on to Albion where the blue skinned men mine tin?" Melkart's eyes went wide. "Have you been to Gades, father?"

"Aye, he has," Damis said. "And to Aegyptus as well and Kush. My master has even traveled beyond the Indus, to Taxila and beyond. I know because I accompanied him."

"Pride is unbecoming, Damis."

"Yes, master."

"You've traveled further than a Tyrian. Tell me, father, where do you go now?"

Kaleb returned, muzzle and paws wet. Melkart dried him off and spread out a rough wool cloth where the dog curled up and slept.

"We too travel to Antiok."

"You're welcome to my protection until we reach the city. You know, father, King Seleukos forbids philosophers from entering his capital on pain of death. He considers someone like you nothing but a troublemaker. Why do you go then?"

"The God told me to go. Antiok's cultic practices must be reformed. The priests must give up blood sacrifice. Taking life needlessly is an abomination in the God's eyes. They should only offer pleasing sacrifices."

"Myrrh and frankincense like the Magi of Persia," Damis said.

"You may be right, father," Melkart answered, "but you won't be well received by the king or his priests. Seleukos is wealthy with hundreds of hoplites at his command. I can't protect you once we enter the city, Apollonius."

"Whatever happens is the God's will," Apollonius said, maddeningly calm as always. "Let us sleep. Another day's travel and we'll reach the city."

Damis and Apollonius embraced each other for warmth and slept. Melkart rolled himself up in his lion skin and lay by the fire, Kaleb by his side. His stomach rumbled throughout the night. On the morrow, the two ascetics broke their fast with water and set off. Melkart filled his waterskins and followed them. Their frail appearance and meager diet, both men proved much tougher than they looked. They easily kept pace with Melkart's long legged strides. Near midday, Apollonius paused to cock his head as a buzzard passed overhead and squawked.

"The plain lies ahead. We should reach the city well before dusk."

They left the hills and descended into the broad alluvial plain. A gray ribbon gleamed to the west, the broad, fast flowing Orontes. Southward, white walls and towers wavered on the horizon, a glimpse of Antiok Upon The Orontes, the greatest city in Anadolu.

Melkart was so hungry, his broad shoulders were about to sag. They plodded down a dirt path, headed toward the paved road that paralleled the river and led to Antiok. Small farms and substantial villas dotted the fertile plain. Hinds chased their restless flocks while women threshed wheat. A wretched hut was near the path. Cries and wails erupted from inside.

"He died. My husband died, left me with the children and no money! What am I to do?"

"Hold, Melkart."

Apollonius entered the hut. Melkart handed the mule's tether to Damis and followed him. A man lay on a low rope bed, face waxen, plainly dead. A woman wept beside him, surrounded by three small children. She looked up, her face a contorted mask of grief.

"Are you brigands come to kill us? T'would be a mercy."

Apollonius smiled. "Peace, woman. We mean no harm, just the opposite. Step away from your husband."

She silently complied, drawing the children with her. Apollonius stretched his hands over the corpse.

"O God, look upon this humble sinner. Expel the evil inside him and bring him back to provide for his family."

Colorless features suddenly flushed wine red. The man bolted from the bed. He heaved an enormous wad of black bile from his mouth, violently coughed, and gasped for air. His wife and children shouted with surprise. Tears of joy streamed down their faces as they crowded around him.

"Wife, what has come over you?"

Apollonius gestured for Melkart to leave.

"How did you do that, father?"

"I didn't do anything, Melkart. The God did it."

A short way down the path, the woman ran after them, a loaf of bread in one hand. "Here, please, it's fresh baked."

Apollonius raised his hands, about to decline, but quick as ever, Melkart had already accepted the loaf with a grateful smile. He broke off half, handed it to Damis, and bit deeply into the bread. Damis split his half and gave one part to Apollonius who reluctantly accepted it.

"That family was poor, Melkart. You shouldn't have taken the loaf."

"I'm hungry, father. Now you brought her husband back, he can kill a chicken and they can feast."

They reached the main road and joined a long line of wagons and travelers on foot, bearers loaded down with packs, headed like themselves to Antiok, a key juncture in the trade routes for valuables goods like fine silks from beyond the Indus, spices from Sheba, and reddish gold from far Ophir. The city came into view. Girdled by a high curtain wall, Antiok encompassed four separate quarters, one a large island in the river, walled and connected by two causeways to the city proper.

The line slowed to a halt as they neared the city. Hoplites stationed at the North Gate carefully inspected everyone before allowing them into the city. Merchants paid stiff fees for the privilege of trading. Beggars were driven away with spear shafts.

Melkart whispered. "I'll see if I can get you inside, but they may turn you away."

"T'is in the God's hands."

Their turn finally came. A hoplite barred their way, hands on hips, short sword at his side. Pale blue eyes stared at them through helmet holes, bored and full of malice.

"What have we here?" he said in Greek.

"A merchant of Tyre with a talent of amber to trade in the agora," Melkart replied in the same tongue.

"Show me."

He partially unloaded the mule with help from Apollonius and Damis. The hoplite carefully searched the mule and inspected the amber.

"You don't seem to be lying, a rare thing for a Tyrian. One silver shekel to enter."

Melkart took a shekel from a leather pouch that hung by a thong from his neck. The hoplite carefully inspected it.

"Don't forget to take your marker so you can prove you paid. Now get moving."

Melkart reloaded the mule and led the animal forward. Apollonius and Damis tried to follow, but the hoplite barred their way with his drawn sword.

"And where do you two wretches think you're going?"

"They're with me," Melkart said. "I hired them to make camp and to care for my mule while I rested."

The hoplite scowled. "You don't feed them much, do you? Go on."

A slave handed Melkart a potsherd marked with cuttlefish ink, his token of payment. They passed through the high gate onto a broad, colonnaded street, adorned with marble and bronze statues, triumphal arches, and inscribed altars. Laid out in a grid pattern, Antiok was graced with the public buildings a Greek city required, a palaestra where young men exercised, a library where their elders studied and orated, and a theatre where plays and wild Bacchic rites were held. Interspersed among the buildings were large public gardens, fragrant with oleander. Despite the Greek layout, all the world's tribes mingled in the streets, numerous Habirus prominent among them, distinctive with their long beards and knitted skull caps, full citizens of Antiok.

"I'm going to the agora. You're welcome to come."

"You've already done enough, my son. The God sent you to help us reach Antiok. We'll go our own way now."

"Our friends here will help us," Damis said.

"As you will. May Ba'al Hammon, Ishtar, and Marduk preserve and protect you both."

"May the God keep you also, Melkart."

Melkart went to the agora. Although twilight approached, merchants still did business by the lights of blazing iron flambeaux outside their tents, up all night like virtually everyone else in Antiok, famous throughout the Great Green Sea as a city that never knew sleep, dedicated to pleasure and revelry. Melkart led his mule to the jewelers' street with booths full of fine necklaces, bracelets, and crowns made from silver, gold, electrum, and the rarest, finest jewels.

While Kaleb guarded the mule, he went from tent to tent, showing each merchant a few choice stones, until he found a bidder who offered a price to his satisfaction, two silver talents, enough to fit out a merchant ship in Tyre for a long voyage. Melkart sold his mule to a livestock dealer, haggling again until paid to his satisfaction. Freed of his cargo and the mule, pouch weighed down by silver, and ravenously hungry, Melkart stopped at the first likely inn.

Guests sat outside in the back among shady trellises, the vines festooned with purple grapes. A fountain burbled soothingly. Slaves grilled lamb, chicken, and goat meat in the open air. Mouth watering uncontrollably, Melkart sat at a table. Kaleb rested beside him. A boy in a short tunic handed him a linen napkin with a wide smile.

"What will you have, master?"

"Bring me that boar haunch, three loaves of bread, olives, whatever green vegetables you have, and a small amphora of red wine mixed two to one. Oh, and bring the dog some beef and a bowl of water. Hurry, boy, hurry!"

The boar meat was set before him, glistening in reddish pomegranate sauce. Clay plates heaped with food were placed beside the haunch. The boy filled his krater full of watered wine. Melkart tied the napkin around his neck, took his dagger and a long spoon, and set to his food. Kaleb devoured meat beneath him.

"Be careful you don't eat the table, big man."

A young woman sat opposite Melkart, clad in a thin silk gown, lithe and beautiful, with dark hair and eyes like his own. She wore golden bracelets and a necklace adorned with a large emerald. She held out a krater.

"Might I have some wine?"

Melkart waved to the boy who filled her krater. "Don't let me stop you from eating. You haven't completely gnawed the bones."

He untied his napkin, held out his hands for the boy to pour rose scented water over them, then dried his hands with the napkin after he wiped his beard and mouth clean. "I'm full now, thanks to the gods, after near two days with no real food."

"Were you set upon by bandits?"

"Nay. I came upon two travelers being attacked by brigands and drove them off."

"That was brave of you."

Melkart shrugged. "I paid in full for my good deed. They're mystics, philosophers, full of odd ideas, especially the old one, Apollonius. He wouldn't let me hunt game, said that killing was wrong. All they gave me was hard bread and onions."

"A big man like you needs more to eat than that." She reached over and ran an appreciative hand over a massive arm.

"My name's Daphne."

"I'm Melkart, a merchant of Tyre."

A Greek struck up a merry tune on a lyre. Men and women sang a hymn of praise to wine and Bacchus. They danced to the music. Daphne signaled to the boy to refill their kraters. They drank deeply of the sweet wine.

"This must suit you better than the company of mystics. You don't seem the kind to wear a hair shirt and fast."

Melkart laughed. "I'm not. I like my food and wine and good company too. Still, I grew fond of them, especially the old one, Apollonius. He's plainly in the gods' hands. With my own eyes, I saw him raise a man from the dead."

"You must tell me about it. I have a room upstairs with chilled wine and a soft bed. We'd be much more comfortable there."

Daphne looked directly at Melkart. He smiled in turn.

"Why not?"

Soft, early morning light filtered past the wooden shutters. Outside, street vendors cried out their wares, fresh baked loaves of bread, sweet melons, eels just caught in the river. Melkart and Daphne lay entwined on the round bed, asleep. She awoke first, put on a silken robe, and sat on a three legged stool while she combed her hair with a fine toothed ivory comb.

"You look wonderful."

"Thank you. Would you like your hair and beard trimmed? I have scissors and a sharp razor."

"Nay. I think I'll just lie awhile. T'is months since I rested on a real bed instead of hard ground."

"Do as you please. T'is usually quiet in the morn--"

A sudden uproar from outside drowned them out, thousands of screaming, shouting voices full of rage, a mob's savage outcry. Melkart rose, dressed, and donned his belt with his sword and dagger. He opened a shutter.

"They're gathered around the theatre on Mount Silpius. What stirred them up so, I wonder."

"I'll send a boy to run for news."

There was a knock at the door. A young, blonde, Greek woman ran in, eyes wide, hands aflutter.

"They've taken them captive. Two of them."

"A moment, Hestia. Slow down and start from the beginning."

Hestia took a deep breath to steady herself. "Two blasphemers, an old man and a young one, interrupted the priests of Hekate during their sacrifice of a black goat. The news is all over the agora. There's going to be a trial in the basilica. The king himself will preside over their case. Everyone's going."

Daphne grimaced. "To see men put to death. I'd rather stay here. Where are you going?"

Melkart donned his lion skin cloak. He headed toward the door. "T'is Apollonius and Dismas. They said they'd try to reform the priests. Like the naive fools they are, they stirred up a hornets' nest. I must help them."

Daphne took Melkart by the arms. "Why? You can't save them. Stay with me."

"I wished I could, but they're my guest friends. We broke bread together. They're helpless. At least I can speak up for them."

"If you're determined to go, leave your weapons behind. The hoplites won't let you in the basilica with them."

Melkart removed his dagger and sword and set them on a table along with a silver shekel.

"That's by way of thanks."

"You'll come back, won't you?"

"If I can."

He kissed her gently and left, Kaleb at his heels.

The basilica was a large, rectangular building in Antiok's center with a peaked roof supported by columns of red, white, and mottled marble and seven iron gates chased with gold, each gate topped by a sacred talisman to ward off evil. Trials were held inside the walled courtyard where a large bronze clepsydra, a water clock, timed arguments' length. Antiokenes gathered outside, anxious to see the heretics condemned to death.

"Wait here," he said to Kaleb.

Melkart pushed past the crowd, into the courtyard. Apollonius and Dismas stood inside a ring of hoplites, weighed down by iron fetters. The seats were taken by rich merchants with soft pillows to cushion the hard stone, fetched by their slaves. They wore gold and silver diadems, spotless white linen himations and imperial red mantles, and their scant hair was styled into ringlets. A tin salpynx sounded a discordant note. A steward rapped his ivory staff of office on the polished marble floor.

"Hail to King Seleukos, lord of the greatest empire known to man, stretching from the Great Green Sea to the River Indus, come here to sit in judgment. All bow before him!"

Men rose from their seats and bent their heads low. Melkart bowed as did every commoner and slave in the courtyard. A young man sauntered in, dressed in a linen tunic and a petasos, a broad-brimmed straw hat to keep off the sun. His only badge of rank was an iron headed mace in one hand.

Seleukos slumped onto his throne and waved his mace. "All right. My court's in session. Are these the ones that stirred up the riot?"

"Aye, My King," the steward replied.

"What are your names?"

"I am Apollonius of Tyana. This is my disciple, Damis."

"Disciple? That must mean you're a philosopher, a magician. Do you admit it?"

Apollonius lifted his shackles in an eloquent shrug. "How can I deny the God's truth?"

"Well, there, you see. He's guilty by his own admission. I don't even need to hear from my procurator, I can simply pronounce sentence and end the whole business forthwith. I've specifically forbidden philosophers or any other so called wise men from entering the city. Now you can pay the penalty."

"You have no right to judge us. Only the God has that authority. I only perform the God's will. I need offer up no more defense than that."

Seleukos scowled and shook his mace at Apollonius. "So, you want to argue, eh? Another thing about philosophers that I hate. I was going to be merciful and have your throats slit, but now I'll have you flogged to death instead!"

"Hold, O King," a loud, deep voice shouted.

"Who speaks out of turn in my court?" Seleukos cried.

"I do, O King."

Melkart strode forth from the crowd, an impressive figure in his lion skin cloak and imperial red tunic. He bowed low before the king.

"Great King, I am Melkart of Tyre, a humble merchant. These are good, worthy men. I traveled with them to Antiok. With my own eyes I saw Apollonius raise a man from the dead and restore him to his family. Surely a man who can perform such a miracle must enjoy the gods' favor. I beg you to spare them. Let them leave the city instead under my charge."

Seleukos smiled thinly and leaned forward as if about to impart a confidence. "You're new, commoner. You have no idea what things are like here. Philosophers and magicians plague the city like locusts. There was Diagonos who lived in an old amphora and wandered the agora in broad daylight with a lantern looking for an honest man. And Sokratis with his constant, annoying questions and total disrespect. At least I had the pleasure of seeing him off with a dose of hemlock. And what of that madman Peregrinus Proteus? He burned himself alive in the agora to prove his principles. It took days for my slaves to clean up the mess."

"Very unfortunate, O King. I know my friends have offended against your laws and sacred rites, but still, I ask you to be merciful."

"Aye, Melkart, and you've only annoyed me further. If your friends' plight moves you so much, you can share their miserable fate. That can be your consolation. Guards, arrest him and put him in irons!"

Hoplites surrounded Melkart, spearheads pointed at him. Outnumbered ten to one and unarmed, Melkart could only surrender. Heavy irons were placed on his wrists, and he was forced to stand with Apollonius and Dismas.

"Do not despair, my son. The God will protect us."

"Hold your tongue, old man. I'm about to pronounce sentence."

Seleukos removed his petasos and donned a golden radiate crown, thin spikes agleam in the sun. He sat up straight and held his mace high.

"All three of you are guilty of sacrilege and disrespect to my royal person. I sentence you to death by flogging with the sentence to be carried out here and now for my pleasure. What do you have to say to that, magician?"

Apollonius raised his thin arms high. The heavy chains dangled from his wrists. The same numinous aura danced in his hair again. His body softly radiated light.

"You cannot judge what you cannot understand. Behold the God's power!"

He gestured with his hands. The fetters fell from his wrists, crashed to the floor along with Melkart and Dismas's chains. Seleukos recoiled in shock.

"Seize them. Restrain them."

"And you cannot seize what you cannot hold," Apollonius said.

He clasped his hands in prayer. Burly hoplites advanced, hands outstretched to grab him. Yet to their amazement, the ancient faded away.

Like a sheet of papyrus thrown upon a fire, he spindled and curled before them until only his outline remained, traced by wavering lines of smoke.

Apollonius disappeared.

Pandemonium broke out. Unmanned by Apollonius's magic, hoplites threw down their arms and fled along with rich men, commoners, and slaves, headed for the seven gates. Melkart took advantage of the chaos. He snatched up Dismas and carried him away from the basilica.

"We must leave Antiok."

Kaleb still patiently waited where Melkart had left him. He whistled for the dog to follow. As he hoped, as rumors spread of the bizarre miracle at the basilica, in the wild confusion and panic throughout the city, the South Gate was left unattended. Melkart hustled Dismas away from the city. He struck a quick pace toward the Great Green Sea.

"We were lucky to escape by the skin of our teeth, boy. Your master certainly is full of surprises. When will we see him again?"

"We won't," Dismas replied. "Apollonius has moved on to a higher plane. He's one with the God now."

Melkart halted. "So, he's left you alone in the world."

"Nay, Melkart. He'll always be with me just as the God is always with me. This is just his sign I should take up my own mission to the world."

"You're welcome to travel with me to Tyre and beyond. See Gades like Apollonius."

Dismas shook his head. "I shall travel to Babylon to study the Chaldean wisdom."

"Very well. Take a few shekels for the trip."

"They'd only be stolen from me. The God will provide, just as he sent you to help me escape Antiok. May he bless and keep you. I'm sorry you lost your weapons."

"No matter. I still have Kaleb, my lion skin, and the silver I need to finance a new voyage. Farewell, sweet Dismas. May the gods protect you."

They embraced and kissed like brothers. Dismas parted from his companion. Melkart watched him trudge away, head bent as he set down one determined foot after another, a holy fool traveling the world alone with no more than the clothes on his back. He turned to face Melkart, raised his hands over his head in a final blessing, and was gone, never to be seen again. Melkart headed with Kaleb toward the Great Green Sea, there to take ship for Tyre where once more he could seek another adventure in a strange land, like the restless, eternal wanderer he was.

The Escape Plan

By Z. M. Renick

They had to wait until the Shining Prince and his escort passed by. Reirig watched the procession with annoyance but also a certain amount of curiosity. This was his first time in the capital since the ascension of the new ruler, and he wanted to see something of this legendary man, this descendent of the divine, this favorite of the god and the only one worthy to worship him directly.

He was disappointed. This new Shining Prince was even more pathetic than the last one had been. He was short and skinny, with a shaved head that served to show off his misshapen skull. He was dressed in fine linen, and was wearing bracelets and necklaces of gold that shimmered in the desert sun, but all the finery in the world couldn't disguise the prince's hesitating movements, his stick-like arms, and the fact that even the weakest warrior of the Sumerai tribe could break him in two without effort.

Beside him, Reirig's young companion Hisum clearly had the same opinion. "How could a man like that convince others to worship him?"

Instead of answering, Reirig gestured to the soldiers that surrounded the prince. There were at least half a hundred of them, and they were not weak. Reirig thought that he could take most of them in a one-on-one battle, but there were a couple that he knew could defeat him. And, of course, he would stand no chance against all fifty of them at once. This was only a small part of the prince's forces. His army had enough power to force the people into worship.

As to why the army followed him…. Gold, Reinig supposed. That was why most people accepted the leadership of those weaker than themselves. People would do anything for wealth—and if he were being honest with himself, Reirig had to admit that the same was true of himself and Hisum. They were here to trade and find work, acquire luxuries that could be taken back to their tribe. That was why they were in this part of town, across the street from one of the few taverns that would admit foreigners. There was a client waiting for them there, one who had promised them more wealth than they could imagine.

At last, the procession finished, and Reirig and Hisum made their way to the tavern. Even in the early afternoon, it was hot, and men craved wine and ale to cool their throats. But despite the crowds, they had no trouble finding the man they had come to meet. He was tall and broad-shouldered, and though his brown tunic was of the same style as the other men in the tavern, it was considerably cleaner. His face was wrinkled, and he seemed to view the entire building and everyone in it with distaste. It was obvious that he didn't belong. Reirig and Hisum went to his table and sat down.

"Good day to you, friend," Reirig said. "What are you drinking?"

"Nothing here," the man said. "Not unless I wanted my guts to turn to mush. Are you the men from the Sumerai?"

Reirig could sense Hisum growing tense. He said, "We are, but there's no reason to disregard the pleasantries or be rude to the people of this excellent establishment."

The man grimaced at Reirig's description of the tavern but said, "If you wish to drink, I shall not stop you. In fact...." He raised his voice. "Girl! Bring wine for these men. The best you have. If you bring them water with a taste of vinegar, you'll end up thrashed."

The woman that their client indicated was hardly a girl—she had to be at least twice Reirig's age, and he was no longer in his youth—but she nodded and hurried to obey.

The man returned his attention to Reirig and Hisum. "I am in need of an escort across the eastern desert to the Port of Makara. I'm told that you are as familiar with the desert as anyone and can assure my safety."

"We can," Reirig said slowly, giving a slight emphasis to that last word.

The stranger caught his inflection. "But you haven't decide whether or not you will. I suppose that depends on how much gold you would get out of it."

"Among other things. We like to know what we're getting into before we make any promises. So, if you'll tell us *why* you're so desperate to get to Makara..."

"My business in Makara is my own. But if you'll get me there, you can have this." The stranger reached into his pocket and pulled out a gemstone the color of blood. It was the size of his palm.

Reirig could feel his greed arising at the sight of the gem. He forced it down and said, "I don't think we're the right people for this job. Good luck finding someone else." He rose to leave.

"Wait!" The stranger seemed incredulous. "I offer you my greatest treasure, something that I'm sure could buy your pathetic village five or six times over, and you reject me?"

"Precisely. That is a valuable gemstone—much too valuable to trade for an escort across the desert. If you're offering that much, you're in serious trouble, and I'm not going to risk my neck without knowing exactly what sort of trouble it is." Reirig gave a contemptuous snort. "Either that, or it's fake, and you're trying to cheat us."

"It's not fake. This gem is worth more than you can possibly imagine." The stranger was practically shouting. He took a deep breath, then lowered his voice. "Very well. If you must have my story, I will give it to you. But then we must leave."

The man went silent as the old woman he had sent to get their drinks returned and set goblets before both Reirig and Hisum. The man contemptuously tossed her a gold piece. She seemed surprised by the gesture, and flailed about a bit, trying to catch the coin, before dropping it on the floor. She knelt to pick it up, and as she did so, she brushed her hair to the side, leaving the back of her neck exposed. At the base of her skull was a small, red, diamond-shaped mark. To almost everyone in the Land by the River, it would appear to be a birthmark or perhaps a scar. Only those of the desert tribes knew better: this was the mark of one who had been dedicated to the god Sumer, the Lord of the Desert. This woman had been born to the tribes.

The woman stood up and let her hair fall back across her neck. She bowed to the man who had paid her and said, "Thank you, Lord, for you generosity." She scurried away.

Reirig looked to Hisum, who gave him a short nod. So, Hisum had seen the mark too. But now was not the time to discuss it, not with this Riverland stranger sitting in front of them, still impatiently waiting for them to agree to be his escorts.

Reirig sat back down, picked up his goblet, and took an exaggerated swig. "It's good wine, and you paid for it. I guess that gives you the right to talk while we drink. You have until we finish to convince us to help you."

"And how can I do that?"

"Let's start with a name."

"You may call me Ferochi."

"Well, then, Ferochi, why don't you tell us why you're so desperate to get to Makara?"

Ferochi was silent for a moment as if composing his thoughts. Then he said, "I am the High Priest of Ar, king of the great gods of Tepergy, forever shall he reign over the world."

Reirig was momentarily confused until he remembered that "Tepergy" was the name that the Riverlanders in this area gave to their kingdom. To the tribes, none of it mattered. Call the lands Tepergy or Lonbaiden or Sarrissa or one of a dozen other names. They were all the Lands by the River, and whatever differences existed between them were trivial as compared to the differences between them and the tribes.

Ferochi continued. "Ar, with his wife Rotha and his son Tetsab, created Tepergy and gave to its kings the right to rule the world. But one of those kings betrayed the very god who gave him power and breathed life into him. This abomination, whose name I will never speak, created his own god and devoted his worship to this monster of his own creation. Worse yet, he forbade the people to give their worship to Ar and Rotha and Tetsab, insisting that they could pray only to him, that he might intercede with his make-believe god for them."

"Yes, yes. We didn't come here for a history lesson," Reirig said impatiently.

Hisum held up his hand and spoke for the first time since they had come into the tavern. "Wait, Reirig. We asked for this man's story. We should let him tell it the way he sees fit."

Ferochi smiled. Reirig scowled and looked into his glass. "I'm about a quarter of the way through my wine. You have three-quarters left until I finish and leave."

"For three generations, we have fought against the Abomination and his false god. And make no mistake, we will win. Ar will destroy all of the blasphemers and restore his worship to this land. Only … the Abomination's grandson now sits on the throne, and many of my order have come to realize that Ar's victory may not come about in our lifetimes or our children's lifetimes. We are marked for death here, and if we die without training the next generation of priests, who will restore right worship when the ways of Ar return? We must live in exile rather than throw away our lives trying for victory before Ar is ready to grant it."

"You mean that you've become cowards, ready to abandon your god and your temples if it means saving your own skins," Reirig jeered. "It seems to me that, if you really believed Ar's ways would inevitably come back, then you'd trust him to teach his new priests whatever they needed to know."

Hisum sighed. "Reirig, is this really necessary?"

Ferochi grimaced but did not deny Reirig's charge. He held up the gem again. "This is one of the last of the relics of the Great Temple of Ar that once stood in the center of this city. It's … all I have. That coin I tossed to the hussy who runs this tavern was the last one in my purse. Giving this jewel to you, who know nothing of its true value, is loathsome to me. But better that it fall into the hands of heathens then end up in the treasury of the Abomination. And the true wealth of Ar is not kept in gold or gems but in hearts."

"Okay, we'll do it!" said Hisum. "We'll take you to Makara. Keep you safe from this so-called Shining Prince who worships only himself."

Reirig glared at his companion. Hisum was brave and honorable but still young. Reirig was the one who was supposed to be making the decisions about what jobs they would and wouldn't do. Hisum shouldn't be making promises for the pair. Still, the decision Hisum had announced was the same as the one that Reirig was about to make. He gave a quick nod and said, "Meet us by the east gate at the hour when the sun first touches the walls. Take as much food as you can, and as many waterskins as you can carry; it's ten day's journey to Makara, and though we will be able to find some water on the way, the desert is unforgiving to those who let thirst weaken them. Beyond that, travel light. Hisum and I are your guards, not your porters. We will not lug packs full of religious relics to Makara."

"Then I will see you when the sun touches the walls. I need take no more of your time. Enjoy your wine." Abruptly, Ferochi stood up and left.

Reirig watched him go, then turned to Hisum. "When will you learn not to speak out of turn?"

"But the choice was obvious! So much wealth for such a simple job! And, besides, it's the right thing to do. Ferochi is being hunted because he will not worship that weakling of a prince."

Reirig shrugged. "And? We are children of Sumer, remember. The gods of the Lands by the River are nothing to us. It's not our business if the Riverlanders worship this Ar, or the prince, or a herd of goats!"

"But I can't imagine—"

Reirig held up his hand to silence his partner. The old woman who had delivered their wine had just reappeared on the edge of his vision. Reirig addressed her. "Come here, Sister. You have nothing to fear from us."

She shook her head but stepped closer. "I am no sister of yours. You two are Sumerai, are you not? I was of the Sumerleah tribe, back when I was a girl."

"Still, you are a daughter of Sumer, as we are his sons."

"I don't know if I can claim even that." The woman came even closer and sat down in the chair Ferochi had left. She lowered her voice so that both men had to lean close to hear her. "I was given to him when I was small, but I was a maiden still when I last did the rites. I doubt he still accepts me as his."

Reirig could guess this woman's story. Every year, some of the children of the tribes ran off to the Lands by the River, thinking of a richer and easier life there. Most ended up as drudges or prostitutes in the alleys of cities like this one; a few repented of their weakness and came home to the tribes. This woman had clearly been doing better than average if she had risen high enough to own even a small tavern.

Reirig said, "But you showed us your mark—it was obvious you did it deliberately. You wanted us to know who you were. Why?"

The woman hesitated. "Because, even though I've given up his worship, I *was* dedicated to Sumer and … I suppose you two are still my brothers. I couldn't let you go without some kind of warning. That man you were talking to—he's the High Priest of Ar, the old god of this land."

"He told us," Hisum said. "He wants to leave so that he won't die or be forced to worship the Shining Prince."

The woman frowned. "Is that what he said?"

"After a fashion," Reirig responded. "Hisum is making it sound more noble than it actually is. A weak and cowardly man is abandoning his post, and he wants us to help him run to Makara."

"No! That's not it!"

Reirig was surprised by the vehemence in the woman's voice. He said, "Explain, please."

"I came to the city when I was very young, a long time ago. Long enough, that I remember the time before the first Shining Prince took that title and cast down the priests of Ar. I remember when those same priests used to rule this city. I remember their cruelty. I remember the blood sacrifices. I remember the trials, where men accused of crimes were thrown to crocodiles, with the priests declaring that their gods would protect any innocents. I remember seeing—" Abruptly, the woman stopped, as if the memory was too much for her.

After taking a few deep breaths, she continued. "The priests of Ar were the closest thing to evil that I have ever seen. I heard the two of you talking when the Shining Prince passed by. You wondered why anyone would worship him. And the answer is this: the Shining Prince is weak and greedy, but he's not cruel. He takes wealth from the kingdom, but for him to do that, there must be wealth to take. He does not kill needlessly or leave the people so weak they can barely work the fields. His god is no more than a figment of his imagination—I don't think even he really believes in it—but Ar and the rest of the old gods.... When we were children, we were told stories about how Sumer battles the demon of the land. I think that Ar is one of those demons.

"No weak or cowardly man could rise to become High Priest of Ar; if Ferochi lead you to believe that he was those things, he was lying. I don't know what he really wants from you, but whatever it is, it's to further the goals of his god—and that means nothing good.

"You're supposed to meet him in the morning? Then leave, right now. You can be back in your village, safe from his schemes, before he even realizes that you've gone."

Hisum said, "No. We've given our word. And besides, I won't help the Shining Prince destroy his enemies. It's loathsome in the sight of Sumer to force one mortal to worship another."

"Everything Ar does is even more loathsome in the sight of Sumer. The Shining Prince is no friend of Sumer or his people, but an enemy of Ar is at least an ally."

Reirig sighed. "My friend is a bit too honorable. But he is right on this. We've promised the priest our aid, and we can't go back on our word."

"Then Sumer protect you." The woman crossed her hands, hooking her thumbs together, and placed them across her heart. Slowly, she moved them in a circle, towards her left shoulder, over her head, down to her right shoulder, then back over her heart. It was an ancient gesture among the tribes, asking Sumer's blessing on those about to go into danger. When she was finished, she seemed almost embarrassed. "It's been years since I've done that. Perhaps the novelty of seeing it from me will convince Sumer to stay with you and bring you safely home."

Reirig made sure that he and Hisum were at the east gate an hour before the appointed time. They had to keep their word to the priest, but Reirig was not about to disregard the old woman's warning. As soon as they reached the gate, he and Hisum split up and looked for any signs of an ambush. If Ferochi had something evil planned for them, they would spot it before the trap was ready to be sprung, and make the priest understand that the men of the Sumerai were no one's fools.

But the courtyard inside the east gate was almost deserted at this hour. Reirig examined every guard, every early morning traveler, every merchant just about to set up his wares, but he couldn't find anyone who seemed out of place or was preparing for trouble. Reirig walked the courtyard six times, trying to find booby traps or hidden weapons or anything that suggested Ferochi was about to betray them, but he saw nothing.

The first rays of light had just brushed the top of the outer wall when Ferochi appeared at their side. He was wearing a small pack on top of the same brown robe he'd worn the day before. He had six waterskins, three over each arm. He had nothing else.

"Not much luggage for a man leaving his whole life behind," Reirig said when Ferochi came up to them.

"You said to travel light. Besides … I told you, I have almost nothing left. Nothing except this." He pulled out the red gem and handed it to Hisum, who was standing next to him. "Here, I promised, and you have kept your word. It's yours."

Hisum held the jewel for a moment, seemingly hypnotized by it. Then he remembered himself, and the jewel disappeared from sight into the folds of his robe. "You honor us with your trust. Let us go. The sooner we get moving, the farther we can go before it gets too hot."

It was indeed a trusting gesture, and Reirig was a bit surprised by it. In most cases, a traveler like this wouldn't pay his guards until they arrived in Makara; paying them up front was just asking his escort to run off at the first sign of trouble. But then again, Ferochi had given the gem to Hisum, not Reirig. Perhaps he had realized that Hisum's honor wouldn't let him desert Ferochi, even if Reirig had been tempted to do so.

The three of them headed out the gate. Reirig found himself holding his breath as they did so. He wondered any of the guards would recognize the high priest and try to seize him. But none did, and soon they were out in the sands. The city grew smaller and smaller behind them until it disappeared entirely into the haze of shimmering air and gently blowing sand.

There were no roads in the desert; the shifting of the sands quickly destroyed any attempt to make a trail. But there were landmarks, and those of the desert tribes could recognize them easily. If even the landmarks failed them, the tribesmen had memorized the position of the sun and mastered the trick of using it to keep themselves moving in a straight line. Whatever difficulties arose, Reirig had no doubt that he and Hisum could navigate the path to Makara. But he still grew more and more uneasy the further they got from the capital. He heard the old woman's warning echoing in his head: *he means nothing good.*

As they walked Hisum explained the route that they'd be taking to Ferochi. "By the time that the sun has fully risen, we should have reached the Traveler's Market; we'll rest there until evening, then walk as far as we can in the time that the light holds out until we need to make camp in the desert. It's a pity that it's a new moon, and we can't take advantage of the cool of the night to walk. As we near the end of our journey, the moon should grow brighter, and we'll be able to make progress by its light, but right now, we'd kill ourselves if we tried to walk through the desert in darkness.

"Tomorrow, we should be able to spend the day at the caravan gather point near Shadowbird's Rock; there's a well there, and usually some people we can trade with for food. Past that, though, our way gets harder. We know of a few places where we can shelter during the day, but sometimes we'll simply have to find what shade as we can and pray that Sumer does not send his hottest weather."

"Mmm hmm," Ferochi said. Reirig was a bit surprised; he would have thought that Ferochi would have had more of a reaction to the invocation of a deity other than his own. But then, he would have expected Ferochi to take more of an interest in this conversation in general. Ferochi seemed indifferent to the details Hisum was sharing, details that would mean the difference between life and death. *I guess he really is just a decadent, self-centered, Riverlander who assumes that his servants—that would be us—will take care of everything.* But next to that thought was another warning from the old woman: *no weak or cowardly man could become High Priest of Ar.* Did that apply to decadent, foolish ones as well?

Yet Ferochi's indifference to their route suggested that he wasn't planning what Reirig most feared, an ambush somewhere along the way. If he had been, surely he'd be trying to steer them to where his allies were waiting, suggesting shelters near those points, wouldn't he?

If he's not planning an attack along the way, then when we get to Makara, perhaps? Reirig couldn't rule it out, but he wondered if the old woman's warning had driven him mad. The old had wisdom but could become to set in their ways.

The woman had obviously had some run-in with the priests in the past, and perhaps that led her to see a threat that just wasn't there.

These thoughts continued to run through Reirig's mind as the sun grew higher and they approached the Traveler's Market. He did his best to focus on the place ahead and any dangers that they or their client might face there.

As they got close to the market, Reirig heard shouts, stamping feet, and the whinnying of horses. There was something going on there. Reirig tensed. "Wait here," he told the other two. Cautiously, he approached the market. There was no way to sneak in this part of the desert—men were obvious against the flat expanse—but he remained alert and ready to run, trying to observe as much as possible before he was noticed.

The cause of the commotion quickly became obvious. The Shining Prince's soldiers were there, at least a company of them. They were going from stall to stall and tent to tent, speaking to the people there. Reirig was too far away to hear what they were saying, but the way they moved made it obvious that they weren't there to shop.

"What are they doing?" Hisum said in a whisper.

Reinig turned to see his two companions had come up next to him. "I thought I told you to wait."

Ferochi wasn't listening. He was watching the soldiers. "They're after me. They must have heard about my escape and tried to prevent it."

"We can't go there." The soldiers hadn't noticed them yet, but it was only a matter of time. "We need to find somewhere else to shelter today."

"Are there other shelters?" Ferochi asked.

Reinig considered. "There's the remains of the old Sumersal village, but that's almost six hours' walk. There's the caravan gather point we were planning to stay at tomorrow, but that's even further. We're just going to have to take our chances and hope that there's some place to camp."

"And what are our chances? Really? Will we find shelter before we die of the heat?"

Hisum said, "Reirig and I are clever, and we know some tricks to surviving in the desert. Our odds are probably less than even, but they're better than they would be if we went into the market full of soldiers."

Ferochi seemed to think about that. "No. *Our* odds are not better in the desert. *Mine* would be. Those soldiers are after me; they care nothing for you. I cannot ask you to go to your deaths." Without another word, he started to run into the market. When he was about twenty yards away, he screamed, "For the Lord Ar!"

At first, Reirig and Hisum had been too stunned to do anything. It wasn't until Ferochi started screaming that they had a chance to react. Hisum started forward, and just in time, Reirig grabbed his friend and pulled him back. "It's too late!" The soldiers had heard Ferochi's cry and almost a dozen of them were charging towards him. Reirig and Hisum couldn't help Ferochi, and there was no point in dying for a man who was already doomed. All they could do was watch as the inevitable played out.

As the first couple of soldiers reached Ferochi's position, the priest reached into his robes and pulled out something. Reirig was too far away to see exactly what it was, but from the way Ferochi moved, it seemed likely it was some sort of knife or dagger. He slashed at the soldiers, and one stumbled backwards. Another soldier, however, dodged Ferochi's strike and drew his own sword. He struck Ferochi with the flat of his blade. Reirig expected the priest to fall, but Ferochi surprised him. He staggered, but he got back up and charged at the soldier again. He lunged with his dagger, the soldier parried with his own blade, and then the rest of the company was on him. Reirig soon lost sight of Ferochi in the melee. Shortly thereafter, there was a cry of triumph. The crowd parted, and Reirig saw two of the soldiers dragging an unconscious figure in a brown robe. Reirig couldn't tell if the man was alive or dead.

The soldiers took the body over to where a number of horses waited, threw him over the back of a brown gelding, and tied him there. The soldiers mounted their own horses, then rode off in the direction of the capital, carrying their prisoner—or the corpse of their enemy—with them. The entire thing had taken less than five minutes from the time that Ferochi charged to the time the last horse cantered out of sight.

May Sumer send his heat to roast them in the desert, Reirig thought, but he didn't really believe that it would happen: the soldiers were in for an uncomfortable ride, but their horses were desert-bred and would cover the ground back to the capital in a few hours, before the day became truly unbearable. That, plus the fact that the soldiers undoubtably had extra waterskins on those horses, meant that they'd make it safely back—unless Sumer *did* directly intervene, and Reirig doubted he would do that. Not to avenge the priest of another god. Not even to avenge the honor of two of his followers.

Reirig put his hand on Hisum's shoulder. "We should head in to the market and get some water."

"But—"

"I know. But we won't change anything by standing here and roasting. Let's go."

Hisum followed, but he refused to raise his eyes. Reirig understood; his own shame was no less. He and Hisum had failed, and failed in the worst possible way. Guards were supposed to sacrifice themselves for their charges, not allow their charges to sacrifice themselves for the guards. And adding to Reirig's shame were his own thoughts, his doubts and fears about Ferochi's intentions. All those doubts had been directed towards a man who'd given his life for his companions, a man who'd proved to be anything but a coward.

The two tribesmen went into the market, found a spot in the shade, and sat to drink from their waterskins. They remained in silence for a while, and then Hisum said in a low voice, "What about the jewel, the one that he gave us as payment? What do we do about it?"

"Well, we can't precisely give it back—"

"Don't you dare suggest that we keep it! We didn't do the job he hired us to do. We barely even started it. We have no right to this."

"Keep your voice down. This isn't the sort of thing we should be shouting about."

Hisum nodded. He said, more quietly, "I'm sorry for losing my temper. But we can't keep it."

Hisum was right, of course. *But the man is dead. And that ruby could bring so much money back to our village!* He imagined returning the village wearing a fine robe of white linen, with gold bracelets on each wrist, walking in front of a giant cart filled with dried dates and figs, piles of cloth, dolls and wooden toys for the children, luxury their people could only imagine. He and Hisum would be heroes. And all they had to do to make that vision a reality was to take a gem that belonged to a man who could no longer make any use of it. All it would cost them was their honor.

If it were Reirig's own choice to make, he might very well take the jewel and accept the dishonor. But it was obvious that Hisum was not going to accept that, and Reirig had no desire to fight with his partner. Besides, Hisum had possession of the gem. "I suppose we need to return the gem to his fellow priests. He claimed it was a relic of their temple. They would be the rightful owners."

Hisum nodded. "But how do we find those priests? Given what just happened, I can't believe they'll be anxious to talk to outsiders."

"Perhaps we can find some of them at the tavern where we met Ferochi. That old woman recognized him as a priest, perhaps because she had seen others."

"Maybe, but she didn't seem eager to help them. We might have better luck if we went on to Makara. If the High Priest was trying to get there, then there are probably others from his temple as well. They may even be worshipping openly."

"It's possible, but Makara is a long way. Is it worth making the trip just to give up the gem?" Reirig sighed. "We can't go to either place right now. Let's think about it during the day and decide what direction to go when twilight comes."

Hisum nodded again, and the two settled in to wait. Reirig did his best to sleep, putting the shame and horror of the morning's events out of his mind. Hisum, however, seemed more uneasy. He would sit and rest beside Reirig for a moment or two, then stand up and start pacing. He would pause, pull the gem from his pocket, stroke it for a moment, then return to pacing before sitting down to rest again. Then, the cycle would repeat.

At last, he turned to Reirig. He held out the jewel. "Will you take this?"

That was the last thing Reirig expected him to say. "Why?"

"Because.... Just, please. Take it!"

Hesitantly, Reirig removed the gem from Hisum's hand. Hisum breathed a sigh of relief, leaned back against a nearby wall, and in a few moments, was sound asleep. Reirig smiled fondly at his partner, then returned his attention to the jewel. He knew that he ought to put it away—there were a lot of greedy people in the Traveler's Market, and it would be better if none of them saw the jewel—but he could help running his hands over it, fingering its facets, and staring into its blood-red depths. Again, he saw that vision of himself dressed in finery and distributing treasures to the people of his village like some sort of benevolent god. His people would all be happy. His tribe would prosper, become powerful, be able to take over the neighboring tribes, and perhaps even challenge the Lands by the River for their wealth. His name would be honored forever among the Sumerai, revered even, as the one who had changed them from a poor desert tribe into an empire. All he had to do to make that dream come true was hold this priceless jewel and say, "You are mine!"

Abruptly, Reirig stood up. He started walking back and forth to distract himself. It was hard to daydream when moving in the oppressive heat. But hard or not, he kept thinking about the gem. He wanted to look at it again, so he pulled it out and stared at it. It was so beautiful. The way it shone. The way the light reflected off of each of its dozens of facets. It's color, the perfect crimson of blood just come forth from the veins. Perhaps Reirig shouldn't sell the jewel. Perhaps he should just keep it for himself. He would never see such beauty in anything else….

Reirig shoved the gem back into his pocket, out of sight and out of temptation. He kept walking. He was growing hotter and more miserable but no less obsessed with the jewel. At last, he sat down, overcome with the need to rest. He was still thinking about how much could be his if he just claimed the jewel as his own. He *needed* to get rid of these thoughts, so as soon as he felt up to it, he rose once more. As he started to walk, he thought that maybe the temptation was too much for him. Perhaps he should wake Hisum and give the gem back to him.

As he started to move towards Hisum, however, it struck him what he'd been doing: sitting, pacing, staring at the jewel, then pacing again. *I'm doing exactly what Hisum was doing.* It could be a coincidence; anyone who held that gem would recognize its value and feel the weight of its temptation. But Reirig didn't trust coincidences.

He removed the jewel from his pocket and put it on the ground. From his other pocket, he removed a pipe and some of the rough bark of the lorol bush, one of the few plants capable of growing in the desert, and one sacred to Sumer. Reirig put the bark in his pipe, lit it, and as he breathed the fragrant smoke, said a prayer.

"Great Sumer, who fled the shadows of the Lands by the River for the clear air of the desert, who shuns the darkness and embraces the light, who battles the lying demons, open my eyes now and let me see the truth about this jewel of the supposed god Ar."

Reirig picked up the gem and again stared into its depths. Once again, he saw the vision of wealth being delivered to his village, and the crowds calling his name. But the man standing in front of that wagon wasn't him. It was a tall, broad-shouldered man who reminded Reirig a bit of Ferochi. There was something about his eyes that drew Reirig's gaze. They were dark, and the longer Reirig looked, the darker they became. It was as if nothingness had taken solid form and taken up residence within those eyes.

The vision shifted. Again, Reirig saw his tribe conquering the neighboring villages, then marching towards the Lands by the River. But now Reirig could recognize the scene for what it was: they weren't conquering for the Sumerai tribe, they were conquering for the man with the empty eyes. They were conquering for the darkness.

"Reirig?"

Reirig looked up from the jewel to see Hisum standing in front of him. Reirig returned the jewel to his pocket, dumped the ashes out of his pipe and put it away, and turned his attention to the sky. The sun was touching the western horizon; he'd been absorbed in the visions most of the day.

He said to Hisum, "Let's go."

"It's not quite twilight yet…."

"It's cool enough. I want to leave."

Hisum led the way through the market towards the west side and started into the desert. Reirig followed at first, but as they got further away, he realized they were off course. He grabbed Hisum's wrist.

"Where are you going?"

Hisum was clearly confused. "Back to the capital."

"We were going to Makara."

"That was when Ferochi was alive. Now that he's dead, you said you thought it was better to go back to the capital to try to return the gem."

"I've changed my mind. We're going to Makara."

"Why?"

Reirig growled. "Are you questioning my orders?"

"Yes." Hisum planted his feet in the desert sand and turned to face Reirig. He shook his wrist free of Reirig's grasp. "You gave good reasons why you didn't want to go to Makara. Now, you're saying that you do. I'm your partner, not your servant, and I will not blindly follow you to Makara unless you tell me why you changed your mind."

Reirig opened his mouth but found he had nothing to say. There *was* no reason he now wanted to go to Makara. He still thought returning the capital gave them the best chance of returning the gem with the least amount of trouble. "You're right. Let's go back. Under no circumstances. We must press on to Makara."

"What?"

"If you want to know why, I'll tell you. Makara is where we can sell the jewel for the best price. We'll use that money to buy weapons, then start recruiting our army. Our people will be the core, of course, but we'll need more."

"What are you talking about? We decided that we need to give the jewel back to the priests."

"You decided that. I'm deciding differently. That jewel represents the greatest wealth our people have ever held and it's—" Reirig stopped with his mouth open. His lips were trying to say *mine*, but something in him couldn't say the word.

Nor do I want to. I agreed with Hisum. We are not thieves, and our honor won't let us keep payment for a job we didn't do. And that was before I saw the vision in the gem. Now, I want it even less.

Hisum's eyes grew wide. "Reirig, behind you!"

Reirig tried to turn, but something stopped his movement. He found himself facing forward again, and his knife was in his hand. "We're going to Makara. If you defy me, the punishment for disobedience is death."

Hisum was still looking behind him. "It's that man, the man I thought I saw in the gem. He's here!"

"Did you hear me? We're going to Makara!" Reirig took a deep breath and found his voice. "Hisum, I don't know what's wrong with me. Run! Get back to the village. Save yourself!"

"No." Hisum drew his own knife and charged. He slashed, not at Reirig, but at something behind Reirig. Instinctively, Reirig raised his blade to parry. *No, you idiot. He's not attacking you. Whatever enemy he's after, it's your enemy too.* But Reirig couldn't help himself. He found himself striking back at Hisum, trying to drive his partner away from this thing behind him, the thing he couldn't look at. The two men battled: slash, parry, attack, repost. They were evenly matched: Reirig was the better fighter, but Reirig wasn't truly on his own side. He knew that Hisum was in the right here, and he wanted to surrender and let Hisum do what he needed to. But something inside him wouldn't let him do that.

Hisum kicked at Reirig's knees. Reirig dodged the blow but lost his balance as he did so. Hisum took advantage and lunged. Reirig found himself on his back in the sand. He tucked his knees under himself, moved to a squat, and then leaped into a backflip, bringing himself to his feet facing Hisum again. This was a good fight, and his blood was up. It was getting hard to remember that Reirig was fighting against his will. Instinct was taking over, and he wanted to win.

Then say the word. Claim the jewel, say it's yours, and we can fight as one. Together, we'll be unstoppable.

Reirig bared his teeth. There was no "together," not in his own body. He was his own man, a son of Sumer, a warrior of the Sumerai tribe, and he accepted no one's control. He dropped to his knees to avoid Hisum's next blow, then reached into his robe, pulled out the jewel, and threw it as far as he could.

Instantly, it was as if he had been released from bondage. Reirig's mind was his own, as was his body. He turned his head, and there he saw the man from his vision, the man with the eyes of darkness. The man moved his hand as if to lift something out of the ground. He seemed surprised when nothing happened.

Reirig scrambled away from the figure. "Who are you?" he asked.

The man grinned. "You know."

He did. "Ar."

"My servant did well. He kept his promise. And I will keep my promise to you. Take the jewel, claim it as your own, and I will make your people the rulers of this land."

"Never. We are the children of Sumer. We do not make deals with demons."

Hisum had paused, but now he seemed to recognize that Reirig was no longer controlled. He charged again at the figure of Ar, and this time, he reached his target. The figure staggered backwards. Hisum slashed at his arms, and black blood oozed out.

Hisum attacked, stabbing again and again. Ar was a pathetic fighter, now that he no longer had Reirig as his puppet. But even though Hisum was winning the battle, Reirig could tell that it wasn't enough. Though Ar appeared stumbling and bleeding, Reirig recognized that his essential being was untouched. They needed another weapon. Reirig pulled out his pipe again, filled it with the bark, and lit it. He stood up, walked next to Ar, and blew a mouth full of smoke in his face. Ar backed away from the smoke, and this time, Reirig believed he had suffered real injury.

"Remember what the old woman told us," Reirig shouted to Hisum. "Ar is one of the demons that Sumer fought. Use what's sacred."

Reirig continued to blow the smoke at Ar, driving him backwards, towards the gem. In another moment, Hisum had lit his own pipe and was moving to assist. Soon, Ar was standing on the gem, Reirig in front of him, Hisum behind him, both of them blowing the sacred smoke. Finally, Ar took the only route of escape remaining to him—back into the gem.

Reirig picked it up and tapped his pipe so that the ash covered the jewel. He put it back in his pocket. Hisum let out a breath. "Is it over?"

"I think so," Reirig said. "Ferochi was indeed brave, though in the service of evil. His mission was to deliver that cursed gem, the vessel of his god—

or demon, rather—to us. Once he'd done that, he no longer cared about anything else. That's why he sacrificed his own life; what happened to him didn't matter as much as letting us get away with our supposed payment."

Hisum shuddered. "And then that demon tried to possess you."

"And probably would have, except for one thing: it needed me to claim the jewel as my own. Until I did that, it couldn't completely control me. And I fear that I might have, if you hadn't convinced me after Ferochi's death that we couldn't. Ferochi assumed that we barbarians would be only too eager to take the jewel when given the opportunity. He underestimated your honor. I owe my very soul to that honor, my friend. Thank you."

Hisum accepted the compliment, then said, "What do we do now?"

Reirig considered. "Ar was hoping to escape. He really didn't want to go back to the capital, so I think that's just where we should take him. I'll keep the gem covered with ash as we go, which should keep the demon from trying another possession." He thought for a moment. "But just to be sure, I think we should keep our pipes lit on the journey back."

By the time the sun set, Reirig and Hisum were back in the capital. Hisum said, "I could use a drink. Do we want to go back to the tavern where our friend, the old woman, is?"

"Sounds good. I could use a drink too. For that matter, we should probably buy her one. She tried to warn us, after all. She knew what a snake we were dealing with." Reirig paused for a moment as a thought occurred to him. "I have just one errand I need to run first. It's on the way."

The tavern was on the other side of the river, and Reirig and Hisum caught one of the ferries that moved the city-dwellers across. Reirig waited until they were above the deepest part of the river, then dropped the blood red jewel. For a second, it reflected the torch light, and Reirig saw a malevolent red glow. Then, the jewel disappeared into the depths. Reirig imagined it reaching the bottom and embedding itself in the mud where it—and the demon that it held—would be forgotten.

Ilium's Vengeance

By Seth Taylor

Flames rose higher than the mighty walls and temples. The scent of blood and smoke filled the air. Screams and wails ripped through the air as a people was put to the sword. That was Scamandrius's first memory. The burning of Troy.

He had been told it had once been a beautiful city with mighty walls, shining temples, and prosperous people. But Scamandrius never saw Troy in its glory; he had been far too young when the city of his birth was laid low and destroyed by the combined perfidy of the Achaeans and treachery of the Gods. All he remembered was flames and slaughter as the great city of Troy had been put to the torch.

Even its name was gone. Troy was the ugly name that the Achaeans had given to their rival on the far side of the sea. An ugly, rough name from an ugly and rough people. The people who had lived there called their city Ilium. A beautiful lyrical name that matched the beauty of the city itself. However, history was written by the victors, and in the case of the Great Siege of Ilium that had been the Achaeans. They had hung their own ugly name on the corpse of their longtime rival and no one else had been interested enough to say otherwise.

Scamandrius vowed that they would pay for that. Pay for it all. The rape and ransack, the arson and pillage, the murder and desecration. All of it would be extracted pound by bloody pound from the Achaeans and the gods who had supported them.

That vow was what had brought him to this wine-dark sea.

Waves lapped rhythmically against the side of the boat. It was not one of the great galleys of the Achaeans. In the decades since the fall of their city, the survivors of Ilium had only been able to claw back a small piece of their former glory. They had not the wealth for fleets of sturdy galleys or armies of chariots all crewed by men with the finest armor and weapons of bronze. No, not anymore. All the diminished and impoverished people could spare was a dozen poorly armed men in a fishing boat. The vessel was old and at the end of its usefulness. The men were mostly youths born after the fall raised on stories of revenge but lacking any of the formal training of their forebears. Their arms were mostly repurposed farm tools, axes, sickles, and knives. Though there were some bronze spearheads and arrows which had been scavenged from the ashes of Ilium. They wore no armor, only simple breechclouts on the warm summer night. It was a poor excuse for a raiding party and an even poorer vessel for the revenge of murdered Ilium. The days when the fallen winterbourne warriors of Ilium could strike fear into the hearts of their enemies were long since gone.

The inexperienced crouched within the low hull of the boat. They chattered nervously, sharpened weapons, or clutched some totem representing a family member lost to the Achaeans. Their anxiety was a palpable thing, a vibration about their frames and a quaver in their voices. Such was not the same for the two figures standing in the small craft's bow. They were still and confident in the night. One a veteran, the other the son of the fallen Ilium's greatest hero.

"Is tonight the night?" whispered Polydamus. He was the oldest man in the little band. So old that, as a young man, he had fought in the great war against the Achaeans. During the fall of the city, he took a blow to the head that had crushed his right eye and left him insensate upon the ground. That blow had saved his life as he was mistaken for dead and spared the mass slaughter of his people.

"I believe so," Scamandrius stood in the bow of the boat and looked out over the black water at their target. The night was dark except for the light of the stars, but the small shrine blazed with the light of torches. "The winds and tides are with us, and the night is moonless."

"As you say." Polydamus hesitated before continuing. "Are you sure this is the right course of action, my lord? Killing Achaeans is all well and good, but this…this risks the wrath of the gods."

Scamandrius did not answer right away and let the silence between them fill with the lap of the waves and the rustle of the rest of his men readying themselves for combat. At last, he turned to look at his lieutenant in the dark. "It is said that I resemble my father."

"It is true, my lord." Polydamus's tone indicated just how unexpected he found the change of topic. "You do possess many of the same qualities as Prince Hector. You have his height and his solid build, his dark eyes, and general features. Though your lighter skin and hair you took from your mother."

"So, I have been told, many times." As always, the son of Hector spoke with a voice that sounded like it belonged to a talking bear, even though he spoke quietly his voice seemed to vibrate the whole boat. "I had to be told such things about my own parents because I have no memories of them. I was barely more than an infant when Achilles killed my father and dragged his body behind his chariot." Scamandrius spat over the side of the boat, the sound was oddly loud upon the calm sea. "I do not even remember when my mother gave me to one of her maids to hide in my family's tombs. What I do remember is smoke and fire as our city burned around us. I remember the screams when the Achaeans found the maid who had hidden me and dragged her from the tomb. They did not find me though. I was hiding under the corpse of one of my ancestors, and I remember the smell of ancient rot and my own fear. I was lucky, the maid had taken her own son into hiding as well, and the Achaeans thought the poor child was me and flung him from the city's walls, thinking they had ended the line of Priam and Hector." His hands tightened on the ship's railing, and the wood creaked under the pressure.

"Your survival was celebrated by all of the survivors of Ilium," responded Polydamus.

"All two hundred of them. Those who did not follow the traitors Aeneus and Antenor." Scamandrius gave a bitter laugh. "Much like my own family, the people of Ilium were butchered, tortured, and enslaved. My point is that while Achaean hands may have wrought this evil upon our city, it was the will of the Olympians that drove them to it. They sat up there on their mountain, laughing and making sport at our suffering. Treating us as pawns in some petty game between them. We prayed to the Olympians and gave them tribute and sacrifices, the same as our enemies. Yet, in the end, they withdrew their protection and drove Agamemnon to expunge us from the world altogether, and he nearly succeeded. Those who call themselves gods owe us a debt in blood. A debt that we will begin collecting this night after forty long years."

"As you say, Astyanax."

"I told you, don't call me that. That name died with Ilium. I can't be the high king of a city that only exists in our memories. Only king of the dead."

"As you say. I'll go see to the lads."

"Make sure their weapons are sharp and they have their masks on." Polydamus moved away, leaving Scamandrius standing in the bow.

Since he was a small boy, Scamandrius had never felt truly alone. He felt like there was always somebody standing behind him, just out of sight. Though he could not prove it, he knew that it was the shade of his father. The ghost even spoke to him. When it guided and mentored him the voice was soft, and he was not sure if he was hearing Hector of Troy or his own intuition. When the voice exhorted him to vengeance it almost became audible, albeit to him only. Scamandrius gave up praying to the gods that betrayed his people a long time ago; he prayed to the shade of his father instead.

"Hector of Troy, help me avenge your murder and the murder of our people. May my courage hold fast, and my arm stay strong. May the blood of our enemies water the ground this night." He whispered the prayer so that it was not even audible to the others aboard the small boat. He then saw to his own weapons. As the captain of the small party, he had the best weapons. The bronze dagger at his belt and bronze tipped spear he carried were salvaged from the final battle with the Achaeans and likely older than himself. Those he handled with a familiarity borne from experience. The sword was a different matter. Most of the swords of old Ilium had been taken as spoils by the covetous Achaeans, but this one had escaped their notice. It was the only sword that the survivors of the murdered city possessed. This night would be the first time in decades that it would be unsheathed in anger.

Scamandrius tightened his hand around the hilt of The Last Sword and breathed deeply through his nostrils before turning to the rest of his small band and raising his voice only slightly. "To the oars, but quietly now. We make for the beach."

Normally, rowing towards shore on a night as dark as this one was an errand for fools. Navigating a path through the hazards that abounded shallow waters was a difficult enough task in the light of day. At night it was far too easy to ram the boat into a submerged rock, sandbar, or the shore itself. Scamandrius had scouted this area very carefully in advance of this raid. He knew that the cove near the shrine was a gentle, sandy thing with few rocks of any sort. Any vessel could sail into the cove at low tide and gently beach itself on the soft sand at the bottom and then float back out to sea when the tide rises. On this moonless night, it was the lights of the shrine that guided his boat right into the cove.

The boat slowly ground to a halt on the unseen bottom in a susurrus of wet sand on wood. They were still over a hundred yards from shore.

"Stow oars," Scamandrius spoke so quietly now that his deep voice was more perceptible as a vibration through the wood of the boat than sound. "Remember to lower yourselves into the water. We don't want any splashing about to alert our hosts." The son of Hector heeded his own words and slipped over the low side of the boat and eased himself into the warm, summer waters of the Aegean. The water only came up to his waist, and he pushed himself through the warm sea with his powerful legs. He made for shore, still using the flames of the shrine to guide him.

Behind Scamandrius, his men also quietly slid over the side of the boat though few did so as gracefully. He approved. The priests at the temple were busy with their ceremony and were secure in the knowledge that nobody would risk the wrath of their god by harming them. But other things stalked the dark and glided through the black waters. Scamandrius hoped that his men's clumsiness would not draw the attention of those creatures of the night.

He stepped onto the beach after wading only a hundred yards or so. A light breeze struck the wet, lower half of his body creating a chill counterpoint to the otherwise warm night. The captain waited on the beach for the rest of his men as they too emerged, dripping and shivering from the sea. He did a quick headcount, twelve still. Nobody was lost to Poseidon or one of his children during the crossing.

"Quickly now, while the priests are distracted. Make sure you keep your masks on. We do not want the gods to know who defied them this night. Dolon, Nestor; lead the way through the bush." Scamandrius could barely see the nods of the two boys in the dark. They were both shepherd lads who spent their days guarding the sheep and goats on the hillsides above Ilium. Their duties had taught them to be as stealthy in the bush as the wolves that stalked their charges. Even on this dark night, he had faith that the pair of lads could find their way through the strip of brush and trees that separated the shrine from the beach.

Under the direction of their guides, the raiding party glided through the small coppice like ghosts. In a brief moment of fancy, Scamandrius felt as if he could see the spirit of his father gliding through the trees alongside him. Intent on wreaking a vengeance of his own from beyond the grave with weapons of shadow and starlight. Was that his sire's shade at his side or just an odd interaction of the shadows of the trees and the firelight from the shrine? As soon as he looked at the apparition directly though it disappeared.

Perhaps it was just an imagining conjured by his vengeance-soaked mind. His personal ghost had never manifested itself physically before. It merely spoke to him when he needed it to, which it did once he reached the edge of the firelight.

STOP

Scamandrius gave a signal to his men to stop in the form of a bird call. It was of a type that was relatively common and active at night. Their enemies were not likely to recognize it as anything more than that, but his companions had been listening for it. All dozen came to a silent halt within the pure blackness of the wood while their captain listened to the dead.

His father had never spoken so clearly before. Perhaps the nearness of blood spilled in righteous revenge was giving strength to the shade. Or maybe the words he had for his son were just that important.

LOOK

Compared to the darkness of the moonless night, the clearing in front of the shrine blazed with the intensity of the sun. The clearing was surrounded by torches and a great bonfire burned at its center. Everyone within it stood out like an actor on the stage of a play. Three priests of Selene at their goddess's altar, their white robes stained with the blood of the sacrificed, calling upon the mercy of their goddess and imploring her to return the moon to the sky. As they did every month. At their feet were two corpses of young men. Likely slaves taken in some raid or another. Their throats had been slit and their bodies prepared to be fed into the bonfire's flames. Besides the priests, there were half a dozen acolytes, most of whom were tending the fire though two were dragging a third sacrifice from the shrine to the altar. Most importantly to Scamandrius, there were four temple guardsmen arrayed around the clearing. They wore heavy bronze cuirasses and helmets and carried fine spears. So far, there was nothing that he had not anticipated and planned for. Nothing that should have caused his father to shout from beyond the grave.

LOOK

At the repeated command, Scamandrius redoubled his scan of the shrine and its surroundings. What had bothered his father so? Surely there must be something that was agitating the shade. What could Hector see that he could not? See. That was when he realized that he had made the mistake of a novice raider. He had looked directly into the illuminated area and allowed his eyes to be dazzled by the flames there. The area beyond the firelight was as sticky and black as pitch and blinded him just as effectively. It was only through luck that he caught a hint of movement within the infinite shadows of the night. Something was there.

What was lurking just beyond the firelight? Whatever it was, it had not been anticipated nor planned for. Scamandrius was sure that his band of raiders could defeat the four temple guards, the priests, and the acolytes.

They had the element of surprise and the vengeful ghosts of Ilium on their side. Their mysterious guest though could be a servant of the Olympians. Some monster beyond their collective ability.

Scamandrius opened his mouth to order his men back to the boat when his eyes lit upon the third and final sacrifice who had just been hoisted upon the blood-stained altar.

She was like no woman he had ever seen.

The sacrifice was, of course, young and beautiful. What was less common was her locks of fiery red hair which rivaled the flames of the bonfire. Scamandrius had never seen hair like that. He had heard stories of people with red hair living in the far northern lands, but most of the people living by the sea had hair of black or brown with a few rare blonds scattered amongst them. It was said that his aunt, the famed Helen, had blond hair like golden sunbeams which was one of the reasons her beauty was still the stuff of legends. Yet, even Helen of Troy had not adorned her head with a crown of tamed fire as this young woman had.

Scamandrius knew then that he would risk all: his life, his men, and even the vengeance of his people to save that beauty from the priest's dagger. Perhaps he had more in common with his Uncle Paris than with his own father.

The girl was stretched out upon the altar. Acolytes gripped her ankles and wrists, holding her down though she bucked and kicked wildly. If not gagged she likely would have been screaming as well. The girl had spirit. The head priest stood above her; his dagger lifted to the moonless sky as he called his final entreaties to his goddess. His voice was high and wavering, filled with religious fervor, and grew in volume as he reached the crescendo of his prayers. He then gripped the tool of his grisly trade in both hands and prepared to drive it down into the unprotected breast of the fair maiden he wished to offer up to his deity.

The world seemed to pause.

The inevitability of the ceremony had been interrupted, and everyone stared at the spear that had seemingly sprouted out of the chest of the priest. Even the high priest seemed stunned and stood, still as a statue, for a long moment before coughing up blood and falling to the ground. Only then did every head in the clearing rotate to look in the direction the spear must have come from. It had been a mighty throw and the spear had arced through the clearing, over the bonfire and altar, and embedded itself in the high priest's chest before Scamandrius could even contemplate his actions.

"Kill them all," Scamandrius commanded as he drew his sword. "No mercy."

His men responded with lusty cries and charged into the clearing. The two temple guards closest to them were unprepared for a dozen armed men to come boiling out of the brush. They could not get their shields or weapons up in time and were knocked over and killed with blades thrust between the chinks in their bronze armor. The two guards closer to the shrine had the time to lower their spears and turn to face the threat. Between their helmets, cuirasses, greaves, bracers, and shields they presented a solid defense of bronze. They would not be killed as easily as their brothers.

The acolytes charged the intruders from Ilium with a fanatic's fervor. Clad in nothing more than white tunics and bearing little more than burning brands and ceremonial knives as weapons, they threw themselves at the raiders. They were cut down for their trouble.

One acolyte charged Scamandrius directly. The son of Hector easily stepped out of the way of the flaming branch that the crazed man carried and then used his sword to cleave his opponent's skull to his teeth. The acolyte fell to the ground in a lifeless heap. His fellows quickly suffered a similar fate under the spears and knives of the Trojan raiders.

The surviving priests did not attempt to emulate the crazed charge of their subordinates. They retreated behind the pair of temple guards, loudly shrieking for their goddess, Selene, to help them.

Their prayers were answered.

From the deeper shadows next to the shrine, something moved. A patch of darkness shambled forward into the firelight. The shade of Hector shouted a warning that only Scamandrius could hear.

DANGER

"I figured that much out for myself," muttered the captain of Ilium as the servant of the Olympians moved into the light.

The ruddy glow of the bonfire glinted wetly off an eye the size of a grown man's fist. That eye was alone in a head the size of a man's torso. That head was nearly twelve feet off the ground, perched atop a body of lumpy muscle-covered bronze armor.

The raiders from Ilium stopped their charge at the sight of the monstrosity.

"Cyclops!" shouted Polydamus. "Form up." The old veteran's voice carried a note of panic. It was not every day a man encountered a monster, much less one ready for battle.

The one-eyed giant eschewed a helmet, likely because no human could reach his head, but did wear a bronze cuirass that covered its whole torso. It also wore greaves on its shins and bracers on its forearms. Those minor pieces of armor were the size of a shield of a mere man. In its hand, it carried a club that looked as if it had been carved out of a whole olive tree. It stopped once it was fully within the light and grinned, revealing teeth the size of a boar's tusks. The two surviving temple guards moved back to flank the monster, and the three priests moved behind it. The raiders had pulled back into a tight knot with their weapons bristling outward in a defensive hedge. The lone surviving sacrifice huddled on the altar that sought to claim her life and appeared unable to move. The tableaux held for several long moments before the cyclops began speaking.

"You think my mistress, Selene, knew not of your coming." Despite its brutish appearance, the cyclops spoke Achaean as one with culture and education. His voice was as loud and low as the rumble of thunder in the mountains. "She had a warning that raiders would arise from the sea to molest her servants and tarnish her rituals. While she did not believe that anyone could be so brazen or foolish, she sent me to punish any transgressors. It pleases me to carry out my mistress's commands." It raised the tree trunk in its hand and leveled it at Scamandrius. "I would know who you are before I dispatch you."

The captain of the raiders had not pulled back into formation with his men and instead stood forward and alone in front of the gods' monstrosity. He knew that he should be scared, terrified, but he felt the presence of his father at his back. Hector of Troy was lending him his bravery and wisdom this night.

"I am one who challenges the authority of the Olympians. One who does not bow to their genocidal whims. That is all you need to know, one eye."

"A heathen then. It will greatly please my mistress when I kill you." The cyclops brought his massive club down to smack against the meaty palm of his offhand. "Look upon your doom, people of the sea." The monster stood, posing for the men of Ilium, confident that his mere bulk would be enough to strike fear into their hearts. His arrogance made him vulnerable.

ATTACK

Scamandrius heeded the urgings of his dead father and darted forward. His sword, the Last Sword of Ilium, held low and ready.

The cyclops raised his club high into the air to bring it smashing down upon the impudent human. Except, Scamandrius was already too close.

The Trojan ducked under the whistling menace of the club and stayed low as he dashed towards the monster's legs. He did not bother to attack the armored bulk of his foe's body or try to reach the unreachable eye. Instead, he aimed for the small slices of vulnerable flesh that peeked above the bronze of the greaves and below the thick, studded leather of the cyclops's kilt.

The Last Sword of Ilium was old, but bronze was ageless, and Scamandrius had kept its edge as keen as the day it was forged. It easily sliced through the one-eyed monster's thick skin and bit deep into the meat of its leg. The beast roared in pain and fury as its crimson blood sprayed through the night air.

Scamandrius continued his forward dash, barely avoiding the outstretched and grasping fingers of the enraged cyclops. Ahead of him, the two priests quailed backward and fled into the illusory safety of their shrine. Only when he was beyond the reach of his foe's club did he stop and turn back to face the enraged creature.

"It seems you have much the same vulnerability as Achilles, one-eye. Methinks you are not his equal as a fighter, however."

"You dare!" roared the cyclops. Gone was the erudite diction of a measured and cultured man. Only the rage of a monster remained. "I will bite your head off!" It lurched forward, the cut in its leg had slowed and unbalanced it, but still it stood. The club raised for a swing that could kill a bull.

"Kill the last two guards," Scamandrius shouted to his men. "Leave this monster to me."

The captain of Ilium flicked the blood from his sword and braced himself. He thought to charge at his opponent. To try and replicate his previous attack. His eyes tracked the end of the cyclops's club as it rose into the air. He would need to get the timing just right…

INSIDE

The shout of the ghost stopped Scamandrius before he could charge forward. He hesitated for a split instant. He did not think it wise to enter the shrine, to hamper his own movement. Yet, it was equally unwise to ignore the advice of the greatest warrior Ilium had ever known. He backed up hastily towards the shrine as the end of the cyclops's tree-sized weapon plummeted down at him.

The wisdom of Hector's warning became immediately apparent when the whistling arc of the one-eyed giant's club was interrupted by one of the shrine's marble columns. Chips of marble and splinters of olive wood scattered through the air. The cyclops staggered backward as his club rebounded and nearly bucked out of its hands.

Scamandrius seized the opportunity and lunged forward to stick the point of his sword in the meat of the cyclops's right thigh. The monster gave a fresh bellow of pain and swung its club back around to smash the impudent human. The son of Hector danced backward to the cover provided by the shrine. Once again, his foe's weapon collided with a column rather than him, though this time with far less force.

The cyclops gave a frustrated growl and bared his misshapen teeth. "You fight as a coward, heathen."

"You fight as a child, monster." As he spoke Scamandrius looked beyond his opponent at where his men were battling the two remaining temple guards. The guards were skilled and well-armed, but they were outnumbered. Each fought six raiders and was surrounded. They would not last long. Scamandrius just had to keep the one-eyed beast distracted until then.

"Is that so? Then act the child I shall." The monster tossed his club to the side and dropped to his knees which merely put his head only nine feet above the ground instead of twelve. It then crawled forward, its massive hand extending towards Scamandrius. "Hiding in my mistress's house will not keep you from me."

Scamandrius backed away from that grasping hand, back through the portal into the shrine itself. Let the cyclops try and grab him in the dark. He would lop off his fingers one at a time.

DANGER

The ghostly warning nearly came too late. Scamandrius threw himself to the side as a dagger cut through the muscles of his left shoulder. If he had not moved, then it would have surely pierced his heart!

The captain of Ilium shouted in pain and whirled to sever the hand that held the dagger. The priest screamed and clutched at the stump of his arm. The second priest paused in his own strike; his face contorting in horror as his compatriot's blood splashed over him. Trust a man who reveled in the blood of the helpless sacrificed to shirk at blood spilled in honest combat. Scamandrius lunged and drove his sword into the priest's chest, ending his miserable life. He then silenced the shrieking of the wounded priest with a cut to his neck. The priests of Selene were useless in a fight…but they were useful as a distraction.

The hand of the cyclops closed around the Trojan's leg and jerked him off his feet. The Last Sword of Ilium flew from his grip and clattered to the stone. Scamandrius tried to regain his weapon but before he could the monster dragged him from the shrine and hoisted him into the air.

"You thought you could escape me!" boomed the cyclops as it dangled Scamandrius in the air like a fish pulled from the ocean or a rabbit from its burrow. It held the man at the end of his monstrous reach in the air above its head so that he was looking down into his one-eyed countenance.

Scamandrius grasped for the last weapon at his disposal, the bronze dagger. He ripped it from his belt and tried to stick the creature's massive hand, but its hide was too tough for the small weapon. Each of the monster's fingers was as big around as a man's wrist and his grip was as hard as stone. The dagger was a puny weapon to injure such a thing. The cyclops winced when struck with the dagger, but it did not drop the man from Ilium.

"It will give me great pleasure to remove your head from your body." The cyclops opened its mouth revealing jaws of ivory teeth that could have belonged to a herd of wild boars. The mouth opened wider and wider, wide enough to fit around a man's head. It then lowered the Trojan down into the awaiting maw.

Desperately, Scamandrius drove his dagger into the monster's hand but barely broke the skin each time. Again, and again. He might as well have been trying to kill a bear with a fishhook for all the good it did him. The cyclops did not even appear to notice, so intent it was on biting the troublesome man's head off.

It did notice when Polydamus stuck his spear into the back of its knee.

The cyclops roared and dropped Scamandrius to the ground. It then spun and struck Polydamus with a back-handed blow that sent the old soldier spinning off into the night.

Scamandrius picked himself up off the ground and gave his head a shake to clear it. He then cast his eyes about the clearing in search of something, anything, that he could use as a weapon. His eyes lit upon the great bonfire which still blazed away at the center of the skirmish.

ROPE

It was only at the shade's direction that Scamandrius noticed the rope lying at the foot of the altar. It had been used to secure the sacrificial victims while the priests went about their bloody work. The red-haired girl on the altar was still bound, likely the reason she had not tried to flee. Scamandrius intended to put it to a far more noble purpose.

The cyclops had removed the spear from his leg and had turned to confront the rest of the raiders. The others were not as bold as old Polydamus and instead of charging the monster they hurled spears and stones at it. Avoiding the reach of its long arms and massive hands. But, like the now dead priests, they did serve as a fine distraction.

Scamandrius ran towards the cyclops's legs with the rope. While the beast was preoccupied, he threw an end of the rope around its leg and tied a quick slipknot. Having to spend years fishing for his food had given him a knowledge of knots that he could never have gained as a prince. He then backed away from the giant, towards the bonfire.

"Perhaps if you had two eyes you could see that you have yet to kill me!" Scamandrius threw a rock at the cyclops and struck it on the side of the head.

Either the shouted insult or the rock got the monster's attention, and it turned away from the nuisance of the raiders to their captain. With a roar, it lunged towards Scamandrius with both arms outstretched. It obviously intended to rip the man apart with its bare hands. In one massive step of its left leg, it had cleared half of the distance between them.

Scamandrius danced backward around the blaze. He hoped fervently, though he dared not pray, that the plan worked. He doubted that he could survive falling into the monster's grasp a second time.

The cyclops pursued the Trojan…until the rope around its right ankle drew tight. The monster stumbled when the line between its leg and the heavy altar snapped taut. Stumbled…right into the roaring menace of the bonfire. The cyclops was big and tough. Even without its armor it likely could have shrugged off dozens of wounds that could be inflicted by mere men. With its armor, it was likely as hard to kill as any god. However, its bulk and armor did not protect it from the fire. The creature screamed as it crashed in amongst the burning logs; it sounded like a dozen pain-maddened horses. The impact scattered embers and bits of flaming debris across the clearing. Almost immediately the air was infused with the scent of burning flesh.

That was a smell that Scamandrius knew intimately. It brought him back to that day that he had been but a toddler, fleeing the wrath of the Achaeans.

It seemed fitting that the start of his vengeance, of Ilium's vengeance, should be accompanied by such a smell.

BURN

Apparently, Hector's shade thought much the same.

The cyclops tried to escape the pyre, but it had been built big and hot. Meant to fully consume three corpses. As it tried to push itself back to its feet, the raiders thrust their spears into the fire. Stabbing the creature in the arms, shoulders, and neck. Its blood spilled out onto the coals and flashed into smoke. Twice the cyclops attempted to save itself and twice it fell back into the blaze as the combination of heat, wounds, and exhaustion took its toll. The second time it fell it did not get back up again. The horrible screaming stopped, and the great monster lay dead.

Scamandrius did not have long to revel in his victory.

"Captain," shouted Dolon. "Polydamus is dying!"

The son of Hector left the body of his foe to burn and rushed to the side of his second in command.

The old soldier lay crumpled at the base of the tree. Either the blow from the cyclops or the impact with the tree had broken something within the old man and blood ran freely from his mouth. His eyes still fluttered open though as Scamandrius knelt beside him.

"My lord," his voice was weak and clotted. "Were you victorious?"

"I was. Thanks to you, old friend." Scamandrius clasped one of Polydamus's hands in his own. It felt cold and limp; the life already fled from it. "It was only through your bravery that the monster dropped me. Otherwise, it would have killed me."

"What kind of second in command would I be if I allowed my captain to be eaten?" Polydamus coughed weakly and yet more blood spilled from between his lips. "I should have died long ago with all of my brothers. Perhaps the fates kept me alive long enough so that I might serve Ilium one final time in saving its prince?"

"Perhaps so, perhaps so." Scamandrius squeezed the old man's hand fiercely so that Polydamus might feel his touch as his life fled the mortal bonds of this world into the next. The last survivor of the winterbourne warriors of Ilium died with a slight smile on his lips.

Scamandrius stood and wiped his eyes with the back of his hand.

"What now, captain?" asked Dolon who stood just behind him.

"Gather the riches of this place. The gold and jewels of the shrine, the weapons and armor of the guards. Even the torn and stained vestments of priests will have some value in the right markets. Remember, this was not just an act of vengeance. Our struggling people will need these riches if we are ever to rebuild. Also, ensure that all of the priests, guards, and acolytes are truly dead. We do not want anyone left alive to tell the Olympians of our attack."

"Yes, my lord. But what of the sacrifice?"

Of course. The sacrifice. The beautiful girl who had started all of this when Scamandrius had risked his life and the lives of his men and even the vengeance of his people to save her from the sacrificial dagger. She still lay, bound upon the altar. Miraculously untouched by the chaos which had boiled around her. He walked over to her and looked into her eyes. Even in the firelight, it was easy to see that her eyes were the vibrant green of grass in springtime. Scamandrius had never seen eyes like that before. Those green eyes gazed back defiantly. The woman had spirit. Despite being bound and gagged she still was not broken.

"You will be alright." Scamandrius gently removed the gag from her mouth. "My men and I will not harm you."

SELENE

Scamandrius reflexively raised his eyes upwards at the ghostly warning. He scanned the black sky for any hint of the moon. For any sign that he had drawn the attention of the goddess. But the sky was empty apart from the cold and distant light of the stars. Even the goddess of the moon could not force it to appear in the sky outside of its appointed time. It was only when he looked back at the girl that he understood the warning for her eyes now glowed with the same pale light as the full moon.

He threw himself backward just before the girl's snapping teeth could rip out his throat. Silvery laughter followed him.

"You are fast, heathen." The sacrifice sat up and those glowing eyes swept across the clearing and the remains of the battle. Her voice was strained, as if ill-suited to the throat which held it. "I thought to punish you for what you have done to my servants and my holy place." The slender body tensed and the ropes confining her limbs stretched and creaked but ultimately held. "It appears that my vengeance will have to wait. This vessel has not the strength to break these bonds."

"I would have thought a goddess intelligent enough to wait until she was untied." Scamandrius picked himself up off the ground and stood before the gaze of the moon.

"This vessel had been prepared by my sacrificial rites and its contact with my altar, but she is not a believer. I cannot possess her the way I could one who is truly mine. You are lucky, heathens." Selene raised her voice so that all of the men of Ilium could hear her. "I will kill all of you for the insult you have done me this night. Know that every time the moon is in the sky my baleful gaze is upon you. Know that I will find you and wreak my vengeance upon your homeland. Think on your homes and hearths, your families. Think of all of them as blackened cinders. Such will be my wrath." As she spoke her voice grew louder and harsher until it was a primal scream.

Many of the men quailed before the pronouncements of the goddess. Even Scamandrius felt the goddess's power weighing heavily on his mind. Yet he still stepped close to the vessel and raised his eyes defiantly. "You are welcome to try." He then leaped forward and shoved the body of the red-haired girl off the altar. She crashed to the ground. As soon as she left the altar, the light of the moon died in her eyes. They reverted to the previous, bright green and the girl cried out in confusion as she looked around the clearing. "The goddess is gone. You are yourself again." Scamandrius was not sure how much the girl understood of his words. It was obvious that she was not one of the peoples of the Aegean and likely did not speak Achaean. She still must have understood the intent of his words for she gave him a hesitant nod. Scamandrius then cut the last of her bonds and helped her to her feet.

Scamandrius looked about at his men who were all staring at the girl with fear and trepidation. "We knew the risks of baiting a goddess in her own den. Yet we came anyway, for the vengeance of our murdered city and the remains of our people. We have won a great victory here this night. As for the goddess's vengeance? Bah!" He made a gesture as if he were throwing away a piece of rotten fish. "With what can she threaten us? Our home has already been reduced to ashes and our city slaughtered. Are we to quail now that she would give us that which we have already received? She also knows not who we are. With our faces covered and bearing no sign of any nation, we look like just another band of brigands to her. The gods are not omnipotent, despite their airs to the contrary. Our people have learned that the hard way. Come, let us gather our spoils and leave this place. Soon we will be toasting our victory here amongst the ruins of our home…and planning our next attack."

The men took heart at his words and went back to gathering the loot. For his part, Scamandrius made sure to recover his sword though now it was not the only one his people possessed. The girl followed him into the shrine like a lost puppy. As he picked up the blade, he heard a spectral whisper.

AGAIN

"Yes, father. We will do this again and again until our vengeance is slaked and our people reborn."

GOOD

The voice of Hector was fading, but Scamandrius could still hear it above the clamor of his men…and so could the girl. She shot him a sharp look, her green eyes flashing in the dark.

"You speak to the dead?" Her Achaean was slow and halting but her meaning was clear.

"The shade of my father speaks to me, yes. You can hear the dead?"

"I am a…priestess of my people."

"Where are your people?"

"I do not know. Take me with you. I can show you how to speak more with the dead."

Scamandrius rocked backward. Could he commune with his father beyond single-word warnings in the heat of battle? Could he truly benefit from the experience of the greatest warrior of Ilium who had ever lived?

"What is your name?"

"Sindrun."

"I will take you with me, Sindrun. Fate placed you in my path for a reason. You will help my people attain our vengeance."

The girl with the fiery hair nodded. "And mine."

His brown eyes locked with her green ones, and he recognized the same fire burning within them. In time, they would both have their vengeance upon the gods.

Strength of Leadership

By A.R.R. Ash

Valrok crested a hill overlooking a swarded descent that led to an unwalled town built along the coast of the sparkling blue-green water of a fjord. He had never before traveled this far north, into Nordgard, an ungoverned region along the fringes of the trackless tundra. Valrok took a moment to appreciate the air—clean, fresh, and quiet compared to the miasmic, cacophonous atmosphere of the cities to which he was accustomed.

The brief season of the sun was turning cold and the days short, and the gentle smoke and light from hearthfires already burned in the structures below the descending sun. Single-masted dragon ships sat moored along the wooden piers.

Yes, he could remain here for some time before those pursuing parties would find him. And, by then, he would be long gone.

Valrok hefted his gunny sack over a shoulder and put a hand to the scabbarded blade at his waist to keep it steady as he descended. The slope near the crest was of higher grade, and Valrok stutter-stepped until he reached the gentler incline halfway down the hill. From there, the walk was easy, across an expanse of planted fields and on to the packed-dirt streets of the town.

What sort of town had no wall? Not even a rampart or palisade? Valrok shook his head at the quaint naivety of the place.

"Hail, stranger!"

Valrok turned his head toward the speaker to see a man, hand raised, attired in breeches and fur coat. Then he glanced back over his shoulder and looked about in the likelihood the man addressed another.

"Welcome!" the man said and went back on his way.

Valrok stood shaking his head. Who addressed strangers in such a manner? In the southern cities, such behavior, at best, would have marked the man as soft-skulled. More likely, it would have earned him a dagger between the ribs and his belongings dispossessed.

The air was brisk, yet a number of fur-clad townsfolk were about, all looking at Valrok with wide eyes and facile smiles. Even among the cosmopolitan cities of the south, Valrok's physique often drew attention to him, but this level of attraction was unnerving, and he put a comforting hand to the hilt of his longsword.

At sudden, hurried movement to the side, Valrok spun, the sound of metal sliding along metal as he began to pull his blade from its scabbard. Yet he paused, nonplused, sword still half-sheathed, at the unexpected sight. A woman, her head hidden within a fur-lined cowl, hurried toward him holding a cloak out before her.

"You'll catch a death of cold, young man," she said as she approached.

Valrok could see that she was not quite old enough to be of his mother's age, yet too old to be an elder sister.

"Take this," she said, her nose and cheeks ruddy. "It'll warm you."

As if the cloak still possessed the maw of whatever beast from which it came and might clamp its jaws upon him, Valrok reached out hesitantly for the cloak. He glanced at the woman's hooded face for any sign of malice or deception but was met with only an ingenuous smile.

Though he would never admit to feeling the chill, his light tunic did nothing to protect against the cold. Fortunately, he had exchanged his kilt for warmer trousers. His scraggly mop of black hair and months-long growth of beard, tied into two plaits, served to insulate his head and face. Donning the cloak, fitting snuggly over his burly frame, the fur was soft and warm on his skin.

"Thank you, good woman," Valrok said, wariness still clouding his tone. He reached to his waist to pull a coin to pay for the cloak.

"Oh, no, young man!" the woman said, throwing up her hands and taking a step back. "I cannot accept payment for a gift."

A gift? Who gives a gift to a stranger? What sort of mad place did he find himself? Perhaps he would be better off quitting the queer town and facing his pursuers.

Valrok cleared his throat. "Ah, well, I thank you once again." With a nod, he continued on, searching for an inn or boarding house and studiously avoiding eye contact with any of the blatantly staring townsfolk.

The town had no apparent design, structures seemingly built as the need arose in whatever empty space could be found. An animal enclosure sat beside a brewery, which pressed up against a smithy, which rested along a private residence. Still, the buildings, some of multiple stories, were all of solid, stone construction.

"Ah, that'll do," Valrok said to himself as he spotted a longhouse just ahead. Smoke rose from three chimneys, and flickering orange light seeped through the shutters. As he entered, the close heat of the interior was as much a physical barrier as the door to the structure.

Patrons sat carousing around long tables that ran the length of the building. Yet when Valrok entered, all talk and laughter ended, beer sloshed onto tabletops as the ascent of mugs was abruptly halted, and all turned their eyes to him. Valrok stopped, again putting a hand to the hilt, and surveyed the crowd. A strange observation then struck him: no one was armed. Indeed, he had not seen a single sword, battle axe, war hammer, or long dagger since entering the town.

One never went about the southern metropolises without an open weapon and several others hidden about one's person. If it was not a town of soft-skulls, perhaps it was a town of magic-casters. Valrok tasted a bitterness in his mouth at that thought.

Valrok continued to the far end of the longhouse, where a balding, shirtless man stood behind a bar. As if the hair atop his head had migrated, the man's chest was covered in a thick carpet of gray hair, and his physique showed the sagging muscle of age.

He glanced at Valrok's blade, then smiled. "What'll ya have, stranger?"

Valrok grunted. "Your strongest stout."

The man nodded, placed a pitcher beneath a keg, and filled the vessel with a dark liquid.

"Blood stout, made with the blood of the snowmen from the northern mountains."

Valrok moved to retrieve a coin, but the barman shook his head. Rather than argue—he wasn't certain how he might earn more funds in this strange country, so he would take every opportunity to conserve his coin—Valrok nodded in thanks and moved to an empty space along the table's bench.

By this time, the drinking and talking had resumed, and nearby patrons raised their mugs in a silent health to Valrok. He raised his pitcher in turn, then put it to his mouth. The drink was nearly as thick as honey and had a bitter, metallic taste, but it was strong. Setting the much-reduced pitcher on the table, Valrok wiped his mouth with the back of his hand.

After a second quaff, heat kindled in his chest and head. That, combined with the warmth of the fires and the bodies, had Valrok removing his newly acquired cloak. At the sight of his thick biceps, which barely fit through the armscyes of his tunic, the revelers nearest him gasped and raised their mugs again.

Grunting in nonunderstanding, Valrok asked, "Are you always so friendly to strangers?"

The man nearest Valrok's left said, "Rethgar Halfjutunn's going to be in for a surprise." Beer dripped from the tips of his long, scraggly, dark blond beard.

Valrok's brow bunched as he asked, "Rethgar Halfjutunn?"

The man across the table from the one who spoke guffawed and added, "Aye, but Earl Hjorn Naadfadir's gonna be even more surprised." His light brown beard was stained darker in patches by the meaty stew he ate.

Valrok's further inquiry died on his lips when he smelled the savory aroma of the stew. His stomach rumbled, though the sound was lost to the din of the longhouse. "Where can I get something to eat?"

Beer Beard craned his neck toward the bar. "Gertha, a bowl for our friend!"

After but a brief wait, a matronly woman in an apron brought a steaming bowl and several rolls of brown bread.

As soon as the bowl hit the table, Valrok set to eating in earnest, heedless of the scorch on his tongue and palate. The tender meat fell to pieces in his mouth without the need to chew. He lowered the pitcher he had drained and was about to call for another when Gertha set another before him.

For the remainder of the night, each time he reached the dregs of his pitcher, he found another brought to him before he could ask. As the surfeit from the hearty meal filled his belly and the tingling warmth of the stout spread from his head to the tips of his extremities, Valrok thought that, mayhap, he might have judged too harshly the hospitality of these northerners.

Valrok snorted himself awake and coughed. He lifted his head from the sticky tabletop and ran a hand over his mouth and double-braided beard to wipe away the drool and spilled stout. His mouth tasted of old beer. With a start, he recalled where he was and slapped his hands to his waist, ensuring his purse and blade were still there. They were. Valrok glanced around the now-quiet longhouse, his neck aching from having slept slumped over on the table. A few others lay on the floor or hunched over in their seats, though most had gone.

His head throbbed and hurt all the more as he tried to bring the events of the night to mind. He saw flashes of a young, dark-haired woman behind his eyes, though he could remember nothing of any conversations he might have had. Hands flat on the gummy tabletop, Valrok pushed himself up, pausing briefly to allow the wave of nausea and dizziness to pass.

With slow, testing steps, Valrok walked some small distance down the table, where a mug still held a quaff's worth of wheat-colored beer. In a single gulp, he downed the stale contents and belched; the daggers in his head retracted a bit. He had certainly felt worse, like that week-long celebration he'd had with the corsairs over the taking of the prince's treasure barge. That had been a fete.

The noise of a growing commotion outside reached his ears, and Valrok hurried from the longhouse as quickly as his wobbly legs would allow. There, he saw a man of impressive size and sinew, attired in a cloak of white fur and wearing about his neck a golden torc that ended in twin dragon heads. He was surrounded by a company of other men, all of whom spoke simultaneously and loudly. Yet only the torc-adorned man was armed as far as Valrok could discern.

When the man spotted Valrok, he held up a hand, and the others fell silent. With eyes intent on Valrok, the man began walking toward him.

As the man did not grasp his blade, Valrok refrained from reaching for his, though he did stand straighter and swell his chest.

The man stopped two paces from Valrok, yet said nothing for several moments, rather eyeing Valrok up and down. Despite the man's size, Valrok stood slightly taller and with more bulk.

Anger and anticipation of a challenge burned away the vestiges of Valrok's grogginess. With a growl, he said, "Explain yourself."

The man released a throaty sound of his own. "I go to negotiate the terms of the battle, and you think to undermine me in my absence?"

Valrok's eyebrows shifted downward in confusion. "Battle? Terms? What nonsense do you speak, man?"

"Do not feign ignorance! You are here to challenge me."

"Challenge you?" Despite the morning chill and having left the cloak he'd been gifted in the longhouse, the heat of anger rose up his neck. "I'm merely passing through."

"Then why would you come armed? Don't deny it!"

Valrok shook his head. "Deny what?"

The man smirked. "Or is it that now you see me, you fear to face me?"

A rumbling came from deep in Valrok's throat. "Fear you?" he shouted. Valrok put a hand to his blade.

The man gave a bark of vindication. "I knew it! Very well, then." He took several steps backward, dropped his cloak to the ground, and, removing his torc, handed it to a woman who stood nearby. He drew his blade. "I accept your challenge, stranger."

Though Valrok understood nothing of the foolishness the man spoke, a fight he understood. He drew his own sword, holding the large weapon with two hands.

Excited murmurings and conversations broke out among the townsfolk, who encircled the two. Valrok glanced at the eager faces of the watching crowd.

"As is the law," the man said, "the contest ends only when one combatant requests quarter or is unable to continue."

Valrok grunted, shrugged.

The man nodded and, raising his sword, moved toward Valrok. Steel struck steel with a grating clang that rung in the cool air of late morning; sparks flew and died before reaching the ground. Valrok accepted the vibrations that traveled up his arms and brought his sword around for a swing from the side.

Again, a metallic clash sounded when the man sent his blade out to block. As the two continued, the proof of their exertion was shown in the whisps of their breath in the chill. In short order, Valrok grew hungry and bored with the contest, and he decided to put an end to it.

Stepping forward after a parry, Valrok smashed his forehead into the man's face. Amid a spray of blood, the man staggered backward, and Valrok raised his sword to crash the pommel into the man's temple.

The man fell, bonelessly, to the ground, his eyes rolling backward, somehow he maintained consciousness and managed to mumble, "Yield."

With a grunt and a shake of his head, Valrok scabbarded his blade, turned, and returned to the longhouse in search of food and drink.

Valrok was shoveling cold stew, bread, and potatoes into his mouth when the man entered. His defeated opponent had dried blood along the side of his face and around his nose and mouth, and he walked a bit unsteadily, though his eyes were focused.

After a brief glance at the man, Valrok returned his attention to his meal.

The man came to stand across the table and in silence for some time while Valrok ate. When Valrok paused to quaff his beer, the man said, "Well fought, stranger." He set the torc on the table, near Valrok.

Valrok glanced at the item. "What's this for?"

Face bunched in confusion, the man answered, "You bested me. Leadership of Heimstead is yours."

Valrok swallowed without chewing. "Leadership?"

The man shook his head. "Of course. Why else would you come armed? Except to challenge for leadership."

Valrok took another draught to give himself time to think. Given the hospitality he'd received thus far in the town—apparently called Heimstead—he could become accustomed to such treatment, rather than having to fight and steal for survival. At least until his pursuers came calling.

When Valrok didn't respond, the man said, "I'm Hjorn Naadfadir."

Valrok grunted and said around a mouthful of food, "Valrok." He returned his attention to his bowl.

From the periphery of his vision, Valrok noted Hjorn shrug then turn to depart, leaving the golden torc. In going, Hjorn said, "I'll await you outside."

Valrok finished his meal, downed the remainder from his pitcher—lines of beer trickled down either side of his chin—and retrieved the torc. Too small to fit around his neck or to wear as an armband, the piece became a bangle on Valrok's forearm. Stepping outside, he found himself besieged by townsfolk, waving hands and parchment and raising their voices to be heard over one another.

"What of my claim to the land?"

"Two goats have gone missing."

"If we do not sail soon, the northern seas will become impassible."

"When will Rethgar Halfjutunn come?"

"I've heard the trolls have returned to the eastern mountains."

Valrok stood surrounded by the clamoring throng, pressing him from all sides. From habit, one hand found the hilt of his blade, while the other began moving townsfolk aside.

"Everyone! Everyone!" Hjorn's voice sounded above the din. "Allow Earl Valrok a moment to settle in, and I'm sure he'll be pleased to hear your petitions." Nudging through the press of bodies, he created a path, through which he drew Valrok.

Once Hjorn had extricated Valrok, he began leading the larger man to a two-story building of gray stone. "Come."

"What is this madness?" Valrok asked with a backward glance at the townsfolk.

Hjorn smiled. "You are the earl of the town now. They look to you for leadership."

"Bah! They sound like squawking, squabbling children."

Hjorn nodded knowingly. "Such is the burden of the wise leader."

The two entered the structure, and Valrok found himself within a single, large room filled with tables of varying sizes and a large desk near the far wall. To the right was a wooden staircase. The smell of smoke and whale oil filled the space.

The woman who had given Valrok the cloak upon his arrival sat at a small table to one side. She stood and nodded in welcome. "Greetings, Earl."

Valrok grunted.

"This is Sigghild Hearthstone. She is your amanuensis," Hjorn explained.

Valrok narrowed his eyes in suspicion. "My what?" *She's not unattractive…*

"Oh, ah, she will schedule your meetings, scribe your letters, assist—"

"Enough," Valrok interrupted, his heart falling. He had not experienced such a sense of hopelessness and whelming when he'd alone faced an entire tribe of trollkin.

"Do not worry," Hjorn said, flashing a wide smile. "I'm sure you'll make a fine earl."

By but the second day of Valrok's listening to the petty complaints and never-ending requests of the townsfolk, Sigghild's primary duty had become to ensure that Valrok's pitcher remained full. For his part, Valrok had taken to clearing the large pine desk, behind which he sat, of all paperwork and laying his longsword across its top. Whenever a petitioner annoyed him—which was frequently—his expressive black eyes and countenance would darken. He would lay a hand atop the sword and clear his throat. More often than not, the individual abruptly realized that the matter at hand was not as pressing as previously thought.

Other than the endless supply of beer, leadership of the prosperous trading town was not at all as Valrok had envisioned it. Rather than concubines and feasts of succulent meats and spices from far off lands and battles against monstrous invaders, he faced armies of clamoring townsfolk who were armed with mounds of parchment, all looking to him to make decisions on property boundaries, trade tariffs, even the appropriate recompense for a jilted bride. Such tedium could only be some form of Infernal punishment. He had more than half a mind to abscond in the night and take his chances with his pursuers. At worst, they only wanted to kill him.

"You said Knoke had only to pay one head in tax, yet you charge me two." The thickly bearded shepherd jabbed a finger toward his earl.

Valrok's face scrunched in his trying to recall the previous conversation; indeed, he tried to recall the name Knoke. For all he knew, this man fabricated the story to trick him. He glanced to the pitcher at the side, then scowled. It was empty. He transferred that scowl to Sigghild. Which damnable god had he offended to be forced to endure such torture? The list was surely long. Valrok began to extend his hand toward his sword.

"He comes. Rethgar Halfjutunn comes," Hjorn said as he entered the building with a breathless scout. A gust of biting wind blew in with them and threw the door to slam against the wall.

The shepherd forgotten, Valrok stood, barely daring to hope that the interruption would provide some break from the monotony. He had heard the name before, though had yet to learn anything more. "Who?"

While the scout's breathing steadied, Hjorn said, "A rival earl who has been taking every town in Nordgard, in effort to make himself king."

Valrok's heart leaped in thrill, as if being absolved from punishment. Never had he heard such welcome, wonderful news. He retrieved his sword. "Gather the town! We must build defenses."

Sigghild and the scout merely looked at Hjorn, their expressions neither fearful nor excited, but confused.

"Valrok, may we speak?" Hjorn asked.

His blood stirred and eager to prepare for conflict, Valrok's response was clipped, "What?"

"Have you not been curious why you've seen no others armed during your time here?" Hjorn spoke in the patient tone of a teacher leading a student along a path to reach the correct conclusion.

Valrok shrugged. "It is strange, but—"

"We have eliminated war in Nordgard."

Valrok fell silent and froze so fully that one could be excused for believing he had been bewitched. So foreign to him was the concept expressed in those words that they might have been spoken in another tongue. "But…but you said…" His face fell in an expression that, on any other, would have been called sadness. The former earl might as well have said that they'd eliminated air or ale or ate only vegetables.

"War has been eliminated," Hjorn continued, "not battle or conflict. Our contests are settled by single combat between the leaders of each side."

Slowly, movement returned to Valrok. He breathed in relief. "So, I still fight?"

Hjorn nodded. "Otherwise, what purpose does deciding leadership by combat serve? Nothing about physical prowess or skill in arms would indicate strength of leadership. The ability to wield a blade does not prepare one to negotiate trade agreements, any more than swinging an axe or war hammer readies one to understand the incentives provided by different systems of taxation or the need of various public works. Hefting the largest rock does not grant one the vision or rhetorical skill to inspire populations to greater heights. No, if the strong wish to hold power, regardless of competence, this system allows us to preserve life and conserve resources."

Valrok, however, had stopped listening to the explanation as a second wave of relief enveloped him. He would still be able to fight. His body stiffened as sudden understanding struck him. "That was why the townsfolk greeted me as they did. They believed I came to fight for the town against this conqueror."

Hjorn again nodded. "I had just come from negotiating the terms of the combat with Rethgar. A fight to the death. If he wins, Heimstead would join his growing kingdom. If I—you—win, you assume control of his holdings."

Valrok's lips turned upward, and his heart beat faster in his powerful chest. "I will defeat this Rethgar."

"Do not be overconfident," Hjorn warned. "Rethgar Halfjutunn is not a mere man; he is a half-giant. He stands half again your height, his sinew is as steel, and he wields a sword as long as you are tall."

Valrok waved a dismissive hand. "Bah! I have fought and defeated giants, not mere half-giants. I was swallowed by a colossal snake and cut my way out through its belly. In the gladiatorial arenas of Sybbia, I battled all manner of man and beast."

Hjorn inclined his head. "As you say."

"I believe he will be here in one week's time," the now-breathful scout said into the break in the conversation. "He is to fight the earl of Svellheim in two days."

Despite his bravado, Valrok understood the benefit of foreknowledge of an enemy. "I wish to lay eyes on this Rethgar before he arrives."

The scout said, "I can show you."

"Then let us go," Valrok said, sliding his blade into its scabbard with the scrape of metal.

"Now?" the scout asked, face and tone evincing confusion.

"Of course! Nothing is to be gained by procrastination," Valrok said as if scolding an errant student. Now that he had an enemy to battle, Valrok was filled with energy and activity.

The scout nodded. "Very well."

A brief while later, Valrok and the scout rode eastward upon fresh mounts under the deepening chill of the falling sun, their coats drawn tightly around their bodies. Only then did Valrok recall that he had left the shepherd standing, unanswered, in the office. They rode in silence, enjoying the quiet and solitude of the road. The wind and clop of hooves faded into the background of Valrok's awareness, like sounds so constant and steady that they became inaudible.

By morning, they arrived at Svellheim with time enough to procure drink and a first meal at the longhouse. Not long after, the streets teemed with townsfolk as they congregated to await the fight.

Svellheim's earl was a man of lean muscle, armored in leather and a steel cap with a noseguard, and armed with longsword and wooden round shield.

Rethgar strode into town as if it were already his, and Valrok could see him looming above the gathered watchers as he approached. The crowd broke like a wave around a sea stack from his path.

Valrok growled deep in his throat. Now he understood why Hjorn had goaded him into a fight: Hjorn had not wanted to battle Rethgar and wished to pass the burden onto Valrok. No matter; he would end his opponent as he done so many before.

Rethgar wore no armor or clothes, other than a breechcloth. A dull green fur, like that of a troll, covered his entire chest, arms, and legs. Small tusks protruded from his lower jaw, which extended slightly beyond his face. He might have been half giant, though his other half was likely not human. In one hand, he held an oversized sword as Hjorn had mentioned, and in the other he wielded a battle axe that would have been as a halberd in the hands of another.

As the two faced off, the earl of Svellheim did his best to stand straight in the face of that enemy, though he still shook noticeably.

Rethgar rumbled, "To the death," and swung his axe downward at his opponent.

The earl made the mistake of blocking with his shield. The blow split the wood and shattered the arm behind it. Howling, the earl fell to his knee, and Rethgar thrust his blade with such force that he transfixed the man, ending his pain and screams in an instant. When Rethgar retracted his blade, Valrok could see through the hole left in the chest, like a tunnel, and the body crumpled.

The crowd was silent.

In his rumbling voice, Rethgar said, "I rule Svellheim. If any wish to challenge me, step forward."

If anything, the silence only deepened, as if the very wind and animals decided they didn't want their sound to be mistaken for a challenge.

"Very well," the voice boomed. "Then bring me food and drink." Rethgar began walking toward the longhouse, though Valrok was certain he'd not fit through the door.

The scout was ashen, but Valrok grinned and slapped him on the back. "Fear not. I've faced and prevailed over worse. Come, let's return."

As they rode, Valrok vibrated with the excited anticipation of a worthy fight. However, his exultation was tempered by the knowledge that, once he won, he would be cast back into the drudgery of leadership.

The thought of the piles of parchment had him more afeard than the coming battle.

When, two days later, the two arrived back at Heimstead, Valrok nearly fell from his mount when he saw who awaited him. He pulled up on the reins and alighted to look upon one of his pursuers, the pinched face of the Ebon Seeker. The short, thin man wore a black cape and a rapier upon either hip. A bulky, scarred thug stood to either side of him.

"Don't look so surprised, Valrok," the Ebon Seeker said, hints of amusement in his tone. "I can track a rat through the sewers. Did you really believe you could long evade me?"

Valrok had known that he would be found eventually by one of the parties sent after him, and he'd thought it likely that the Ebon Seeker would have been the first. Yet he hadn't thought he'd be found so quickly. He put a hand to his hilt, and the movement shifted his cloak. In that movement, he noted the Ebon Seeker's eyes track to the torc he wore upon his arm.

Valrok couldn't help but smile at the solution to his problems. Presently, with one thrown bout, he could free himself from the toil of leadership, and Rethgar Halfjutunn would rid him of one of his pursuers.

"You failed to uphold your bargain and deliver the item from the Transmogrifier Ushar," the Seeker continued.

Touching a finger to the torc, Valrok said, "Seeker, surely this trinket would cover the coin I owe your employer, including the cost for your services."

With seeming effort, the Ebon Seeker pulled his gaze from the item. "Perhaps…" he said in exaggerated nonchalance, so as not to appear too eager, though Valrok saw the avarice in the man's eyes.

Valrok's smile widened. "Now, if you would just be so kind as to challenge me for it…"

The End

The Amulet of Souls

By Michael K. Falciani

H'bare sat in his wooden stool, the wool cowl of his cloak pulled neatly over his head. The swarthy warrior took pains to stay hidden within its shadowy depths. He sat alone in the dark confines of the Wild Onion, a seedy inn that lay as far from the center of the city of Sarish as he could find.

A serving girl, a lass of perhaps seventeen summers, placed a wooden bowl in front of him with a dull thud.

"Another?" she asked, giving his empty mug a nod.

"Aye," he answered, knowing there was a long road ahead of him.

The girl made to leave and hesitated, giving him a hard look.

"You *can* pay?" she frowned, narrowing her eyes.

A silver coin, triangular in shape, danced across the back of H'bare's fingers. The girl's face softened, and her frown vanished.

"I'll be back," she sniffed, picking up his clay mug, moving to the rear of the inn.

H'bare grunted and lifted a steaming spoonful from the bowl and began to eat. The meal was common fare, stewed goat, mixed with brown rice and zucchini. It was overcooked, barely fit for consumption—but it was warm and filling, just what he needed before his exodus from the river valley.

As H'bare's spoon scraped the bottom of the bowl, the serving girl returned. She held a mug of tepid beer in one hand and a wooden tray stacked with figs in the other. It was his turn to narrow his eyes, this time in curiosity.

"Compliments of the house," she winked, her blue eyes dancing playfully.

H'bare's face softened, and he lowered his head with a slight bow.

"My thanks," he exhaled, giving the girl a brief smile.

"Try one," she invited, motioning to the fruit.

He pressed his lips together and extended a hand forward, lifting a greenish-orange fig from the tray. As he did, his arm froze. A tiny sliver of a tattoo on his wrist, a silver khopesh, slipped from underneath his sleeve. His eyes flashed at the girl, and he knew he'd made a mistake.

"It's him," she snapped, looking across the room at the tavern owner. Her voice had gone cold, bereft of the warmth displayed moments ago.

The barrel-chested proprietor lifted an iron cudgel from behind the bar, glowering at H'bare. A dozen or more patrons, each wearing hard looks upon their faces, stood, carefully eyeing the cloaked figure.

"Brin, step away," the owner barked, gripping his club tightly.

"How can you live with yourself?" the girl hissed, whisking away the tray of fruit from the table. "Coward."

H'bare's eyes went flat, taking in the room. These were not his enemies, yet he knew they hated him, misplaced as their feelings might be.

He stood, deliberately placing another spoonful of food in his mouth.

"Leave it," one of the patron's ordered, fingering a knife at his belt. "Turncoats like you don't deserve to eat."

H'bare snorted and chewed his food slowly. He placed the spoon in the bowl, filling it with the last of the stew.

"I said leave it," the patron repeated, angrily drawing his knife, stepping forward. "A yellow-bellied deserter…"

In the blink of an eye, H'bare kicked out with his leg, catching the angry patron in the chest. Everyone heard the snap of breastbone as the knife wielder folded under the attack, dropping to his knees in agony.

The eyes of the entire room moved from the man on the floor, to the dark cloaked figure standing impassively in front of them.

H'bare finished his meal, setting the spoon in the now empty bowl. The swarthy warrior lifted his mug and drank its contents in a single swallow. Not a soul moved—each watching him intently.

He placed a fist to his chest, belching softly before picking up his belongings from where they lay on the stool next to him. H'bare strode across the room until he stood in front of the now cowering serving girl.

"Keep it," he said softly, flipping the triangular coin in the air toward the owner.

The innkeeper caught the coin, deftly pocketing the money. "You need to leave," the barrel-chested owner threatened, his voice lacking conviction.

"Indeed," H'bare snorted, reaching for the tray held by Brin. In no hurry, he grabbed a handful of figs, popping one in his mouth.

The crowd flinched, as the man turned and walked toward the door. H'bare opened it and exited, leaving the door swinging wide behind him.

"Sheep, the lot of you," came his parting words, floating through the doorway.

Zahra felt inside her pouch for the fifth time in as many minutes. Her fingers grazed the edge of a polished silver amulet that housed a mystical ruby the size of a man's thumb at its center. A jolt of magic pulsed through her every time she touched it.

"The Amulet of Souls," she thought to herself, retracting her hand again. She could scarcely believe she had managed the seemingly impossible task of stealing it from under the nose of its owner. Pursuit was eminent; the eldest daughter of the pharaoh knew she needed to leave the city as soon as possible.

At the thought of her father, the girl fought back tears that threatened to blur her vision. She had watched from a hidden cubby as Kadira, sorceress of Upper Valasca and first counselor to the pharaoh, had drained the soul from her father using the amulet. The incantation had been short, the results, swift and deadly. A red mist had surrounded Zahra's father, his feet rising more than a foot off the ground to where he hung helplessly in the air. With a quick flourish of her scepter, Kadira swept her rod through the mist, gathering its magic to her. The pharaoh's powerful frame, moments before healthy and strong, collapsed to the floor, a dried husk, devoid of life. Kadira, an older woman of more than fifty summers, absorbed his life's essence into the ruby of the amulet. The sorceress had pulsed with power. A heartbeat later she looked up, now appearing only a half score of years older than Zahra's eighteen summers. Afterward, Kadira had spoken.

"The power of the amulet belongs to me!"

Zahra, a firm believer that the sorceress was more loyal to her own agenda rather than that of the pharaoh, was not surprised.

Blinking back tears, the princess gathered her thoughts. No one, not even the sorceress, could wear such a powerful artifact for long. Zahra fled silently from her place of concealment. She raced ahead of Kadira and gained access to the secret hallway that ran adjacent to the magicker's room. There, Zahra waited, only seconds ahead of her father's killer.

When the sorceress entered, she lifted the amulet from around her neck, its ruby flashing in the candlelight. Kadira pushed a small latch on the backside of her bedpost. Doing so opened a small compartment, hollowed out on the near side of the bed. The sorceress placed the amulet inside the compartment and gently pushed it back into place. From her vantage point from the peephole in the hallway, Zahra could not make out where the sides of the compartment began, and the those of the bed ended.

The sorceress left the room and locked the door behind her, secure in the knowledge her artifact was safe.

Moments after her departure, Zahra entered the room and stole it.

Now on the run, the princess raced through the streets of Sarish. Her father had once told Zahra if something happened to him there was one person she could trust. An old friend, far removed from the politics of Valasca's three kingdoms. A shamanistic holy man, named Karg El'Jardan. Unfortunately for Zahra, Karg lived nearly one hundred-fifty miles away in the Oasis of Kali. It was located on the other side of *Kathban Albahr*, a desert wasteland known as the Sea of Sands. It was one of the harshest environments in the three kingdoms. Surviving a trip across would be difficult under the best of circumstances.

Zahra bared her teeth in determination. *"The hell with the danger,"* she thought to herself. *"Kadira will answer for her treachery."* Long suspecting betrayal, the princess and her father had quietly plotted against such a possibility.

Zahra held tight to the pouch and raced onward, heading toward a stablemaster located at the edge of the city.

The dilapidated building smelled of rotted fruit and camel dung. Tufts of sand wafted in the evening air, covering every nook they touched with a thin layer of dirt. Behind the building was a large pen housing a trio of the ugliest birds H'bare had ever seen. The former guard mused to himself, wondering at the purpose of such animals. With leathery red heads and bodies the size of a large dog, none looked fit for flight.

Dismissing the creatures, H'bare stepped through the doorway of the stablemasters chambers less than an hour until sunset. It was dim inside, but oppressively hot. The room housed only one small wooden desk and a matching chair of buttonwood. On the walls were hooks and shelves scattered haphazardly about. They were laden with saddlebags, coils of rope, tack, and harness—all manner of things that might be needed by those who wished to procure a mount.

In the chair was a woman, lean of build, she sported sharp eyes filled with greed. Ama was not the finest stablemaster in Sarish, but she was the most discreet, especially for those wishing to make a quick getaway.

H'bare dropped the veil he'd placed across his face and gave the woman a knowing look.

"I thought I might be seeing you," she rasped, standing from her place on the far side of the desk. She moved around to the front and leaned in. The two kissed one another on the cheek in a formal greeting.

"You heard?" He raised an eyebrow, moving a step back.

"The whole city knows," she snorted, snatching up a wine skin from the desk behind her. "I thought, perhaps, you'd left by now."

He grunted and gave a quick shrug of his shoulders.

"Did you hear? The sorceress has put a bounty on your head."

"I'm not surprised," H'bare drawled.

Ama gave him a tight grin. "Every merchant in Sarish, every citizen up and down the Adrar River Valley will turn on you for what she's offering."

"Not you," he said, his hand coming to rest on the hilt of his khopesh.

She raised one of her eyebrows and widened her grin. "No?" she asked. "Why not?"

H'bare relaxed. "Two reasons," he explained. "The first is because you want someone official to carry your…wares, across the Sea of Sands. I can do that."

"You left the service of the king," she pointed out, taking another drink from the wineskin. "You're no longer employed by the crown."

"This says I am," he replied, reaching under his robes, pulling out a tightly rolled parchment, handing it to her.

Deftly, Ama unrolled the papyrus sheet and scanned the contents.

"Where did you get this?"

"From the pharaoh."

Ama looked at him closely for a moment and handed the parchment back. "The other reason?" she asked.

"I'd kill you," he answered, rolling the papyrus tightly, tucking it away.

Ama broke out in harsh laughter. "You've some camel sized balls on you swordsman, I'll give you that."

The swarthy man did not flinch at her amusement, knowing the wares she wanted smuggled across the desert were worth a fortune.

"Do we have a deal?" he grunted.

She looked at him for a long moment before extending her hand. "Alright," she agreed. "Wait here."

Ama was gone for less than a minute. When she returned, she was carrying a tightly packed leather satchel, cracked and worn with time.

"Best you leave immediately," she said with a grunt, tossing him the satchel. "I've a single camel in the stables. It was meant for another, but she has not arrived. I doubt…"

Ama trailed off as a woman, short in stature, stumbled into the room from outside.

"Ama," the girl panted, her breath short and labored. "Thank Dourne you are here. My mount… have it…brought around…I must be off…quickly!"

"Who is this?" asked H'bare, frowning at the girl's sudden appearance.

Ama's eyes widened. "The other rider I was telling you about," she answered. "You're late…mistress."

"Late, and in a hurry," the girl gasped again, still trying to catch her breath. The newcomer moved the veil covering her mouth enough to wipe the sweat from her face.

"You already promised the mount to me," H'bare growled, looking at Ama pointedly.

"Yes, well, perhaps we can come to…another arrangement?" Ama stammered, bowing her head in apology.

Glancing back at the girl, H'bare jolted with a start. She had moved her veil enough to where he could see her face.

"Highness?" he asked, stunned to see the princess in such a state.

Zahra looked at his dark countenance in the fading daylight.

"The deserter," she accused, staring at him, her expression like stone.

Before either could speak again, the distant tromp of heavy feet could be heard coming from outside.

Ama stuck her head out the doorway and swore. "Jora's balls, what have you two brought down on me?" she asked harshly.

H'bare shot a quick look at Zahra who returned one just as hot.

"Who is it?" the black clad warrior asked.

"A squad of soldiers. Looks like the Guards of the Silver Tree."

"Shit," H'bare cursed, as the princess grew pale.

"Get out of here, both of you!" rasped Ama, moving outside. "I'll stall them as long as I can."

"You still want me to go?" H'bare asked, surprised.

"A deal is a deal, now go!"

"I'm not…" the princess began.

"Curse you, Foxclaw, take her with you!" Ama continued, ignoring the princess. "You're both going to the same place! You owe me for this!"

"What is she talking about?" Zahra asked with a gasp. "You deserted my father in his time of need, and now you are leaving Sarish?"

"There's no time to explain," H'bare growled, grabbing her by the arm, making for the back door.

"Unhand me," she hissed, unsuccessfully trying to free herself from his grip.

The swarthy warrior ignored her protests and dragged the princess out the backdoor, leaving the sound of Ama's sarcastic banter with the guards behind them.

Night had fallen, and the two crept from the confines of a narrow tunnel, exiting the city. H'bare had paid another of his triangular coins to a bedraggled man hidden at the tunnel entrance. The unsavory fellow, almost certainly one of Ama's employees, reeked of stale sweat and rancid beer. He had guided them through nearly a quarter-mile of a dark, underground passageway.

Once clear, H'bare led them west, each step taking them further from the Adrar River Valley.

"I didn't need your help, you know," the voice of the princess snarled from the other side of the camel.

H'bare kept walking, his feet crunching softly in the hard-baked sand.

"Deserter," Zahra barked, stepping in front of the camel, only inches from H'bare. "I said…"

"I heard you," he grunted, glancing at the princess.

"Then acknowledge me," she snapped, her chin jutting out angrily.

Again, he ignored her, keeping a steady pace.

"Are you listening?"

H'bare stopped, and turned to look at her, his eyes dangerous.

"The whole god-forsaken desert is listening," he hissed.

"Then say something!" she shot back. "You are walking along over there seemingly without a care in the world. What are we going to do?"

"I'm thinking," he replied. "I knew exactly what I was going to do before you happened along. Get across the Sea of Sands as quickly as possible."

He rubbed the side of the camel absently.

"The mount is well equipped, with enough food and water to make it to the Oasis of Kali," he reasoned.

"What's the problem? We can still…"

"It is well equipped for *one* person, not two," H'bare spat in frustration. "Now I'm saddled with you, the pharaoh's daughter—who has somehow brought down the wrath of his sorceress upon us."

Zahra said nothing, though her eyes widened.

"Yes, Zahra, I know who the Guards of the Silver Tree serve. I should cut your throat now and rid myself of the added burden you bring."

Zahra's hand moved to the knife at her waist. "You will not touch me, traitor."

He snorted and started walking. "I don't need to touch you to kill you girl."

Zahra glowered at him as he moved away. A fit of rage washed over her, and the princess launched herself toward him. With a scream, her fist struck his back, bouncing off the leather cuirass he wore hidden under his black tunic. "If you want to kill me, then do it!" she shrieked, striking at him again. "What's wrong with you? Aren't you man enough to follow through on your threats?"

"Will you be silent!" he raged, cursing his luck.

"I will not be silent—not on the word of a coward who left his service on the eve of battle!"

H'bare spun, sweeping his foot under Zahra's legs, knocking her to the ground. Immediately he was on top of her, his hand firmly clamped over her mouth muffling her screams.

"Enough," he snarled, his voice a harsh whisper. "You will bring every raider in the desert upon us with that racket!"

She stared up at him, her eyes still angry.

Taking a deep breath, H'bare exhaled slowly.

"I did not desert my company," he explained. "That lie was told when I refused to fight in the battle with our *allies* to the north. The lands of Suladar have been at peace with Upper Valasca for decades. Their soldiers are brave, but no match for your father's elite warriors of the Ivory Hand."

He paused and let out a small sigh. "I signed on to fight, yes, but I have no wish to be a butcher—so the general revoked my commission. Your father, a wise ruler, heard my argument and stayed his hand, choosing to negotiate rather than fight. That bitch Kadira circulated the rumor I'd deserted, blaming *me* for the lack of conquest she'd promised the southern pharaohs."

He removed his hand from her mouth and leaned back, drawing away from her. "That is why I am no longer part of the Ivory Guard."

She stared at him, her eyes surprised.

"I didn't…that's not what I was told," Zahra stammered.

The warrior sighed and looked back at her. "The real question is, why is Kadira after you?"

"What do you mean?" Zahra asked a bit too quickly.

H'bare eyes flattened. "I've no time for games, highness. She would never come after you so openly. The pharaoh would protect…"

"My father is dead," she hissed, cutting him off. "Kadira killed him. I watched as she did it."

H'bare looked at her, his eyes unblinking, hearing the truth in her voice. "How?" he asked, craning his head back the way they had come.

Sitting up, Zahra removed something from her pouch. "With this," she said simply, holding out the amulet.

Stunned, H'bare stood, momentarily unable to speak.

"What, in the name of the gods, possessed you to steal *that*?" he asked, his voice soft, filled with astonishment.

"It's the source of her power," Zahra answered.

"I *know* it's the source of her…" he sputtered, his face in shock. "She will chase you to the end of the three kingdoms to recover that artifact!"

"That's why I'm taking it to someone who can help me get rid of it."

H'bare began to curse under his breath. "Sands girl, she will send her entire retinue—two hundred strong! Who do you know that can help against that?"

Climbing to her feet, Zahra brushed herself off as best she could. "My father told me of someone—Karg El'Jardan, a great man, whom he said I could trust with my life."

Instead of being soothed, H'bare looked apoplectic. "Karg? He sent you to Karg?"

"You know him?"

"Oh, I know him." H'bare sounded sick. "Everyone in the three kingdoms knows him."

"You see? He *is* great."

H'bare shook his head. "The only thing he is *great* at is moving products all around the world," he said, pointing at the satchel Ama had given him. "You need a carton of pipe weed from Jaborandi; he's your man."

"My father must have trusted him for a reason," she faltered, absently touching her pack. "Does he use magic?"

The former guard rolled his eyes and shook his head. "He knows some magic, yes—but it will not avail him against Kadira."

"Why not?"

"Because she's the most powerful caster in the three kingdoms!"

There were a few moments of silence between the two as each considered the other's words. It was Zahra who broke it.

"Well, I trust in my father. I'm going to the Oasis of Kali—unless you know of some secret path we can use? Are you going to help me or not?"

H'bare stared at the princess for several heartbeats before stepping toward the camel. "I am going to have to alter the plan," he reasoned with a sigh. He glanced up at the stars overhead and shifted the mount to the northwest.

"You're going to help me?" Zahra asked, her voice tinged with surprise.

"I have to," he muttered striding quickly across the sand.

"Why?"

"Because I swore to serve the crown highness—you are the heir."

"I thought you left?"

"That was before…it doesn't matter. I serve you now princess. Besides, I need to get this," he motioned to the satchel on his back, "across the Sea of Sands—else I'm going to be on the run for the rest of my life."

"What's in that?"

"Believe me princess, you don't want to know."

Zahra hesitated, and then ran, catching up to H'bare, walking close by his side.

"Thank you," she murmured, looking at him in the pale light of the moon.

"Hmmmpt," he grunted.

"What's the plan?"

H'bare quickened his pace. "We walk northwest for most of the night. I know a place that has water. It adds a bit to our distance, but we can gather enough to last another day, if we are lucky."

"If we are lucky?" she questioned.

He snorted again. "Yes, if the Savlar Raiders aren't about."

"If they are?"

H'bare loosened his khopesh in its baldric. "Then we die."

They marched long into the night, stopping every two hours for drink and rest. They spoke little, both focused on the task at hand. Less than an hour until dawn, H'bare called for a halt, his eyes searching the darkness ahead.

"Wait here," he whispered, rubbing the neck of the camel.

Ahead of them was empty wasteland, an endless flat of pale sands.

"Why are we stopping?" Zahra whispered, peering into the darkness.

"We're close," he answered, cocking an ear ahead of them.

"To what?"

Glancing at her, he kept his head steady. "There is a narrow strip of soil ahead, one that is fertile enough for plants to grow on."

"We're miles from the Adrar River," she argued.

"There's a vein of water that runs close to the surface nearby. It flowers all manner of grasses in the days before summer."

"How do you…"

"Quiet highness," he chastened softly. "Other desert dwellers know of this place. If the Savlar are close, we need to be wary."

Zahra pursed her lips and nodded in understanding. Together they waited for more than a quarter of an hour, hearing nothing but the silence of the night. Finally, H'bare nodded in satisfaction and began to move forward once more.

"Stay close to me," he whispered. "I didn't hear anything, but it pays to be cautious."

"I don't understand," she muttered, drawing up next to him. "Even if there *is* grass growing—how are we supposed to get the water?"

He gave her a sniff. "You will see."

They walked another half mile when each could hear the low buzz of insects close by.

"What is that?" Zahra asked.

He nodded in satisfaction. "A hive of bees. We are close."

"The presences of bees means we are close?"

H'bare grunted his affirmation. "Aye. Bees don't fly at night. But they can fly a quarter of a mile to and from water," he explained.

"So, there's a pool close by?"

"Not a pool," he answered reaching to the camel.

H'bare took two pieces of cotton fabric from one of the saddlebags. He handed one to Zahra and placed the other over his shoulder. "Not long now," he murmured.

"How can you tell?"

"Can't you smell it?"

Zahra inhaled deeply and understood what he'd meant. The faint scent of spring flowers touched her, and she smiled, despite the gravity of their situation.

"How did you know?"

H'bare shrugged and moved forward once more. "I have been through the Sea of Sands many times. I have learned a few of its secrets—observe."

Stopping at the edge of the field, he bent down and pointed to a lump of grass. "Water gathers on the blades as the heat of the day dissipates. If you are careful, you can gather it with this."

As he spoke, the swarthy warrior removed the fabric from his shoulder and brushed it along the blades of grass. Finished with the first clump, he quickly moved to another, repeating the process. By the time he got to the third, he had gathered enough water to squeeze it from the cloth into his mouth. A steady stream descended until the cloth ran dry.

"Where did you learn that trick?" Zahra gasped.

"As I said, I've been through the desert many times. I watched and learned from those more experienced than I. Now, enough talk. Drink your fill. We will replenish our supply and move on. Keep an eye out highness. The Savlar may be about."

For the next half hour, the pair moved among the grasses gathering as much water as they could. It was a tedious process, but they were able to refill the entire waterskin after drinking it dry. The camel grazed on the grass, its water efficient body getting all the liquid it needed one mouthful at a time.

As the light of dawn began to rise over the eastern landscape, they continued to the northwest.

"I thought Kali was to the southwest of Sarish?" Zahra asked.

"It is," H'bare answered from his place atop the camel. "However, we'll need to find more water on the way. I know a place where we can do that, but it lies in this direction."

"What place is that?" she asked suspiciously.

He looked down at her grimly. "The Rifts."

Zahra felt her heart sink in her chest.

Two hours past sunrise H'bare called for a halt. There was no shade to be found, but the pair unraveled their headwraps and used hooks fastened to the saddle to create a minute amount of shade. While cramped, they were able to keep out of the worst of the sun. H'bare allowed only a mouthful of water each as they wolfed down a tasteless meal of dried goat meat and cheese.

Despite the heat, Zahra was tired and quickly drifted off to sleep. H'bare stayed awake, knowing the path he was taking them on was perilous. He looked in every direction as far as he could. Satisfied no one was within a mile's radius, he closed his eyes, knowing the camel would stir at any approaching danger.

Three uncomfortable hours later he woke to see the princess staring at him.

"That's unsettling," he said with a start.

"So is traipsing across this desert with you," she quipped back.

He gave a grunt and sat up, looking again at the landscape.

"Did you sleep well?" he asked.

She frowned. "Not really. I had a dream. It was quite unpleasant. I kept seeing the ruby in the amulet. It was pulsating with light."

She shook the thought away, unsettled by the memory.

"It is a fell thing," H'bare agreed. "The sooner we are rid of it, the better."

"What's your plan?"

H'bare rolled onto his side and took out his Kukri, a foot-and-a-half long knife with a curved blade. Using the rounded pommel, he sketched out a rough map in the dirt.

"This is us," he began, making a divot in the sand. "We need to get to Kali, over here on the coast," he pointed, marking a spot southwest of their position. "The issue we have is our water supply. We must continue northwest into the Rifts. There are caves located at the bottom of those canyons with pools of water in them if you know where to look."

"Sounds easy enough," Zahra said with a nod.

"It won't be," he warned. "Where there is water, there are other living things that are after it. The Rifts are filled with Savlar Raiders, along with other creatures I'd just assume avoid."

"If it's so dangerous, why are we going?"

H'bare sighed. "Because it is the only route available to us. If we'd ridden straight across the Sea of Sands, we'd have run out of water halfway. Should we survive the Rifts, we can make our way southwest and arrive at Kali in good order. Besides, I don't think Kadira will risk chasing us into those canyons."

"You think this is our best chance?"

"I do."

"Then what are we waiting for?" Zahra began to stand, but a hand from H'bare stopped her.

"Patience," he explained, biding her to sit down.

"Why?" she asked in irritation. "I'm hot and sore. The sooner we move, the better. We are wasting our time here."

He shook his head and gave her a wry smile. "Your training is in politics highness—that is your strongest arena. If you move at the wrong time in the marbled halls of the palace, you can die. It is the same out here."

"What do you mean?"

H'bare put away his Kukri and sat, his legs crossed under him. "You say you are hot and sore? At the moment we are not exerting ourselves. We're seated in this little patch of shade, resting. To move now would exhaust both our water supply and our strength. We'll wait as we did yesterday, until dusk approaches. After that, we'll walk all night, conserving our energy and our water."

"How will you know where to go?" she challenged, painfully aware of her inexperience.

"The stars will be our guide," he answered, glancing overhead.

"You…you used the stars to navigate your way?"

H'bare gave her his first smile. "Yes, highness. It's an old custom."

Zahra blinked, taking in his dark eyes. "I would like to learn," she said, looking determined.

He gave a soft chuckle. "If we survive this, I will teach you. For now, let us rest. The sun will set in a few hours. I will instruct you on a few tricks I've learned from our Savlar counterparts."

"You've learned from the enemy?" she gasped.

He flashed her an even bigger smile and spread his hands apologetically. "Enemies, friends, it all depends on your perspective."

They started off an hour before sunset. They had walked less than a mile when the princess turned her nose in the air.

"What is that god-awful smell?" she asked, wrinkling her face in disgust.

"I thought it was you," came H'bare's bland reply.

Zahra's frown turned sour. "Your humor is as revolting as your beard," she snapped.

The warrior gave her a grin. "There's a dead rat in one of the saddlebags—placed there moments before we left."

"Why?"

H'bare shrugged. "No idea, but Ama put it there herself, so—I assume she has her reasons."

"Well, it stinks to high heaven," huffed the princess, moving forward to remove the odiferous animal.

H'bare stopped her with a raised hand. "Leave it alone."

"I'm not walking across the Sea of Sands with the stench of death lingering every step of the way!"

"Walk in front of me then," he suggested, waving his hand forward. "Best keep an eye out for horned vipers and spitting cobras. They love to hide in the sand."

She stared at him, her eyes narrowing in anger. "You are a terrible travelling companion," she grated between clenched teeth. "The camel makes for better company."

"She doesn't mean it," H'bare said, rubbing their mount on the neck. "She's just grouchy."

Despite the smell, they made good time. In all, they travelled nearly forty miles, as H'bare pushed them hard through the night. They took turns riding the camel, each trying to conserve their strength.

More than two hours after dawn, the dead rat revealed its purpose.

Zahra was seated on the back of the camel when a shadow appeared on the ground nearby, growing larger with each passing second. Realizing the danger, the princess screamed in surprise and leapt from the camel's back as a large tuft of black feathers landed behind her.

"By the sands—what the hell is that?" she shrieked from her prone position on the sunbaked earth.

Turning at the noise, H'bare squinted his eyes and grunted in surprise. "A turkey vulture," he reasoned. "That's what the rat was for."

Standing on the camel's haunch was one of the large, ugly birds he'd seen at Ama's.

"What?" Zahra asked, still in shock.

"Turkey vultures have a keen sense of smell," he explained, helping the princess to her feet. "They can pick up the scent of carrion from a long way off."

"By the Sands of Aranor, why did it drop on us way out here?"

H'bare looked at the bird who was trying unsuccessfully to dig into the bottom of the saddlebag. Reaching forward, he drew out the rat and flipped it to the ground. The vulture swooped down and began devouring it raucously.

"Ama wanted to send us a message," H'bare said, looking closely at the foot of the vulture. Wrapped around its leg was a tightly wrapped parchment. Quickly, he removed it and unrolled it so they both could read the contents.

Guards of the Silver Tree make for the Oasis of Kali, two hundred strong led by Kadira herself. They will be waiting for you when you arrive. They left the morning after you did. Ride hard, else you will not return home.

A

"Damn," H'bare muttered, scanning the contents again.

Zahra's shoulders drooped in defeat. "They will be waiting for us. What can we do?"

H'bare did not answer right away. He pulled down his veil and took a drink of their ever-shrinking water supply. "What would you advise, highness?" he asked, offering her the skin.

"I want Kadira to pay for what she's done," Zahra answered swiftly. "If we continue through the Rifts, is it possible to find our way into the Oasis without being seen?"

"I couldn't say for certain—however, I do believe they won't be looking to the north. If we are careful, we might have a chance. That's if we manage to survive whatever lies in the Rifts."

Zahra drank from the waterskin, her mind weighing the possibilities. "I will do what you think is best," she said finally.

H'bare shook his head. "No highness. While I have my own opinion, I am your servant in this. I will advise, but the decision must be yours."

The dark-eyed girl pursed her lips in thought. Unconsciously she felt for the amulet in her pack. "We will go into the Rifts," she said with finality. "I will see this artifact to Karg or die in the process."

"I will be with you," he said, leading them away.

They spoke little that day, each occupied with their thoughts. H'bare noted that Zahra was more withdrawn during daylight as they rested in the shade. She'd kept her pack close, never letting it or the amulet out of her sight. It was concerning to the swarthy warrior, who suspected the artifact was having some insidious effect on her. However, more daunting was the prospect of entering the Rifts and getting out alive.

They were off again an hour until dusk. H'bare knew they would get to the Rifts by sunrise if they pushed hard. The waterskin was only a third of the way full. He knew they needed to find more water or risk dehydration.

As dawn unfolded, the Rifts came into view. Rocky and jagged, they cut deep into the desert floor. It took the pair more than an hour to arrive at the entrance leading down into the ravine. Once they did, both stood in shock.

The decapitated heads of a dozen raiders were propped up on wooden stakes sharpened to a point. Men, women, and in one case, a child, had been killed, displayed here at the entrance of the Rifts.

"What...who would do such a thing?" Zahra asked when she could find her voice.

H'bare walked up to the first, studying it intently.

"This is one of the Savlar," he whispered, looking past the head, down into the canyon. "A week old, at least."

"I thought the Savlar ruled here," Zahra questioned, staring into the lifeless eyes of the child.

The ground that led to the entrance was littered with prints, none of which H'bare recognized. Kneeling, he lifted a six-inch-long barbed tail, as black as the night was dark.

"What kind of creature could have a stinger that large?" Zahra whispered, her voice awed.

"A Scorpious," H'bare answered grimly.

"But...those are creatures of legend. Surely you are mistaken?"

H'bare looked at the girl, his face deadly serious. "We, unfortunately, are going to find out."

The Rift was a series of canyons that stretched across the northern part of the Sea of Sands for nearly fifty miles. Descending hundreds of feet beneath the surface of the desert, little was known about the canyon's depths. Even the Savlar kept to the upper reaches, far from the dangers lurking below.

The pair skirted along the southernmost face at the bottom of the cliffs, thankfully out of the sun. There were signs of human habitation along the way, though none of it was recent.

After two hours of travel, they came upon an opening in the rock face near several adobe shelters built against the canyon walls. More of the unidentified footprints could be seen on the ground—made far more recently than those encountered near the canyon's entrance. H'bare called for a halt, looking warily into the cave.

"This is the cavern I've been to," he said softly, lowering his veil. "There is a spring not a quarter mile inside."

"Do you hear it?" Zahra asked, rubbing at her pouch. "They are coming."

"What do you…" he began, before drawing both his Khopesh and Kukri.

A woman of perhaps forty summers crawled from the cave entrance. She was dressed in tattered wool linens, caked with grime. Her eyes, a mass of red and white puss, had been savagely gouged out. She was bleeding from an ugly wound across her abdomen. Only her blood-soaked hand kept the entrails from spilling out.

"By the gods, what happened to you?" H'bare demanded, his voice in shock.

"You are…from the empire?" she rasped in question, blood bubbling from her mouth.

"Yes," H'bare answered, lowering his weapons, kneeling next to the woman.

"The Demon Queen is stirring," she gasped, struggling to sit up. "The Scorpiki have been called. Caerhael's Tear cries out to them! You must not…" she coughed hoarsely, choking on her blood. She fell back to the ground, the breath rattling in her throat for a final time.

"May your journey to the havens be in peace," H'bare said, touching his forehead in reverence.

"What did she mean?" the princess asked, her eyes wide. "Caerhael's Tear?"

"I don't know," H'bare grunted, rising to his feet. "We've travelled many miles since last night. We need food, drink, and rest. Come Zahra, we will find all three at the spring."

"What of her?" Zahra asked, pointing at the still form of the woman.

The warrior sighed and put away his weapons, leading the camel through the entrance. "I will bury her while you rest," he answered as his form was swallowed by darkness.

Zahra slipped a hand inside her pouch and touched the cool metal surrounding the amulet. "I hear you my queen," she purred, lifting the artifact from her pouch to stare at it lovingly.

"Highness, come on."

The princess gave a cruel smile and followed her companion.

As good as his word, H'bare found the small spring of fresh water he had spoken of. A faint magical light, cast long ago by an unknown Salvarian mage, illuminated the cave.

H'bare and the princess were able to drink their fill and replenish their supply of water. The camel drank deeply, satiating its hunger by licking clumps of lichen off boulders saturated with condensation. Much to their surprise they found a second camel in the back of the cave sporting a shallow wound across its leg but looked otherwise hale.

"Eat something highness," H'bare suggested, tossing the bag toward her. "You need to keep up your strength."

Catching it easily, the princess nodded and took out a piece of goat cheese.

"Best to bury the woman at the entrance now," she said, biting into the cheese, chewing it absently. "Afterwards, you can rest here with me."

H'bare gave her a questioning look before shrugging and started toward the entrance.

"Take the camels with you," she ordered, leaning up against the cave wall.

"Why?" he questioned, turning around.

"I can still smell dead rat, and wet camel is just as revolting," she mumbled from around another bite of cheese.

H'bare raised his hands to keep her from explaining. "I'll take your word for it." Grabbing the reins of both mounts, he led them back to the entrance of the cave.

Alone, Zahra dropped the bag of foodstuffs and reached into her pack. Fingers trembling with anticipation, she hung the Amulet of Souls around her neck.

Satisfied the woman had been put to rest, the warrior took a long drink from his waterskin. H'bare put it away and wiped a trickle of sweat from his brow. He patted a last bit of dirt with an old bronze shovel he'd found nearby in one of the structures. So far, all had gone according to plan. If they could just leave the Rifts without incident…

"They are coming," said a voice, breaking his chain of thought.

H'bare whirled, searching the canyon. Seeing no one, he stood, wondering if he'd imagined it.

"It's not your imagination," the voice said.

"Where are you?" the warrior asked, looking at his surroundings again.

"I am thousands of miles away and We've little time, they are coming!"

"What are you talking about?" H'bare asked aloud. "Who's coming?"

"The Scorpiki! They are nearly to you now."

"By the sands," cursed H'bare, making to run back into the cave.

"No!" the voice shouted. *"She's put Caerhael's Tear on already. Zahra has become a vessel to the Blood Queen."*

"The amulet?" A cold fear hit H'bare in the pit of his stomach.

"Yes. Zahra's not herself while it's around her neck. Listen to me, for I've little time to explain. Hide yourself, and the camels. Let the Scorpiki take her. They will go to their temple below ground. Once there, you must remove the amulet from around her neck. Free of it, the amulet will lose its hold over her. Keep it in your possession. Then, you must ride as quickly as you can to the Oasis."

"But… Kadira is there, with an army of her soldiers. How will I…"

"You are the Foxclaw," the voice said. *"Clever and daring. The Scorpiki won't let you escape so easily, not with the Blood Queen in their midst. Use them and rid the desert of its scourge."*

"Who are you?" H'bare muttered, moving to the camels.

The voice hardened with determination.

"I am Tyberion of the Red Sun."

Despite the heat of the canyon, the warrior felt a chill run down his spine.

H'bare moved the camels into the small adobe hut with little time to spare. Outside he could hear a clicking noise of what sounded like scores of creatures moving along the hard stone of the canyon floor. Unable to peer out the doorway from his place behind the mounts, the swarthy warrior waited, not daring to breathe.

Moments passed and the creatures footfalls drew to a halt. As time dragged by, H'bare eased his way past the camels, and peeked out the doorway.

At least a dozen big-bodied creatures' stood at the entrance of the cave. Larger than the camels beside him, each was surrounded by the chitinous shell of a scorpion. Huge claws were fixed upon appendages extending from either side of the creatures' torsos. Eight legs, four to a side, supported their weight from underneath. Mixed in colors ranging from deep black to a dusky gray, the creatures stretched nearly ten feet in length, ending at the tip of a cruel looking barbed tail. Affixed atop the thorax was a human-like head, covered in bronze scales.

"So, the legends are true," whispered H'bare, shrinking back inside.

He did not have to wait long. Within moments another scorpious came out of the cave, the princess riding boldly upon its back.

"To the summoning chamber," H'bare heard Zahra say in a voice that was not her own.

"What the hell?" H'bare wondered aloud, watching as the scorpiki rode off.

"Caerhael has possessed her body," answered the voice, returning once again.

"Who is Caerhael?" H'bare demanded.

There was a pause before Tyberion answered. *"The queen of demons, left here on Quasa. Follow them—not too close, but near enough that you can see them enter the opening to the undercity."*

"This is suicide," H'bare grumbled, leaping atop his camel.

"*We will see*," came the ominous reply.

H'bare followed as closely as he dared for nearly half a day, always keeping a respectful distance as the scorpiki moved at a pace close to his own. Two hours until sunset he saw the group disappear into the left side of the canyons. H'bare crept up to a massive stone opening that sloped down into the earth. Carved atop the entrance was a reptilian eye surrounded in flame.

"*You must leave your mounts here*," Tyberion's voice warned. "*Let them rest while you are inside. You will have to push them hard to make your escape.*"

"You seem to be awfully confident I'm going to make it back here with the princess in tow," H'bare grumbled.

"*I have cleared most of the path, warrior. Only a single guard will stand between you and the chamber of summoning. It is a half mile descent. I wish you luck, Foxclaw.*"

"How am I supposed to snatch the princess from inside the middle of hundreds of scorpiki?"

"*You will know the time.*"

H'bare loosened his khopesh from its baldric. "That's not really helpful," he growled, tethering the camels to a rock close by.

As H'bare made his way downward, he took in his surroundings. The tunnel was nearly twenty feet wide and half again as tall. He decided no less than four scorpiki could walk side by side with room to spare. Small, magical floating spheres illuminated the tunnel at various intervals along the way, evidence of a magicker in their midst.

The minutes passed, and H'bare began to slow. From ahead he could hear the footfalls of the scorpiki walking upon stone. He slowed his pace, knowing he was close.

Seeing a brief movement out of the corner of his eye, H'bare threw himself to the side of the tunnel in the nick of time. A huge claw flashed beside him, taking a swing at the spot where his head had been a moment ago.

"Sands!" H'bare cursed, drawing both his khopesh and his kukri with a steely rasp. Moving quickly, he blocked a second attack and stepped inside the creature's range. He slid under the monster's chin and thrust upward, taking the brute by surprise, driving his kukri into the creature's throat. Thick blood oozed out of the neck as the demon-spawn gave a chittering cry of rage.

The scorpious reared upward and brought it's left arm down striking H'bare hard on the shoulder. The swarthy warrior grunted in pain, feeling his shoulder pop out of place. H'bare drove his kukri deeper into the creature's throat until its hind legs collapsed. Withdrawing his blade, H'bare let the monstrosity fall and stumbled to the side of the tunnel, dropping his khopesh from fingers numbed with pain.

Fearing he only had seconds before more of the creatures arrived, H'bare took a deep breath and slammed his shoulder against the tunnel wall, popping the dislocated arm back into place.

"By the gods, that's a bitch," he panted, sinking to the ground.

"*The time is at hand,*" pulsed Ty's warning. "*You must get to the chamber now!*"

H'bare gritted his teeth in pain and pushed himself to his feet. Gingerly, he picked up his weapon and stumbled his way down the tunnel.

The former soldier slipped into the underground chamber and ducked behind a pillar that extended upward further than he could see. He looked at a raised dais nearly one hundred feet away from him and stared in awe.

Standing inside a blood washed pentagram stood Zahra. Around her neck the ruby amulet glowed with a fierce light. An amber radiance washed over a sea of scorpiki, illuminating hundreds of the creatures in the confines of the vast stone chamber.

Zahra, her voice inhuman, began to speak.

"*Egredere, mater quasa! Ostende nobis potentiam tuam! Amplius lava super nos magicam tuam et hanc terram ut tuam vindica! Cape hoc vas tuum!*"

The ruby began to glow brighter, enough to where the shade-loving scorpiki were forced to turn their gazes away from it.

H'bare knew this was his chance.

He ran past the demon-spawn and bound up the steps to the top of the dais. Too late, Zahra noted his presence as he stepped over the pentagram, tearing the amulet from her neck.

"No!" shrieked the alien voice coming from Zahra's throat.

The moment he removed the amulet the light faded from the room, leaving it unnaturally dark after the brightness preceding it.

"Come on!" H'bare hissed sharply, dragging the now confused princess behind him.

"Where are we?" she asked, a tinge of fear in her voice.

"Believe me princess, you don't want to know!"

Tearing past the scorpiki, the pair ran up the tunnel before the hundreds of subterranean creatures could ascertain what had happened.

Minutes later the exhausted pair burst out from the cave entrance to see the two camels look lazily over at them.

"Mount, Highness," H'bare ordered, struggling to climb atop his camel.

"What of the amulet?" she demanded. "It's mine—I demand you return it to me!"

H'bare looked at her in bewilderment. "Are you insane? That fell thing will not touch you again!" He slipped the amulet safely inside the saddlebag that once housed a dead rat.

"It is mine!" she shouted, stomping over to him. "The power of the amulet belongs to me!"

She froze a half-step from H'bare, realizing in horror those were the words Kadira had used after killing her father.

"I...what has become of me?" she gasped, faltering.

H'bare looked down upon the princess with sympathy. "It isn't you Zahra. Your heart is pure. It's the magic of that amulet. Its power has overcome your judgement. I will see you bear that burden no longer."

Zahra made to speak again, but a shake of the head from H'bare stopped her. "Mount highness. We must leave this place, else..."

From inside the cave came a clattering of chitinous footsteps.

"Now girl! We must ride!"

Inside the length of a heartbeat, Zahra was atop her camel and the two began to lope away. Only seconds behind came a mass of scorpiki, boiling out from the tunnel, racing after them through the sharp stone canyons of the Rifts.

The chase was long and arduous. At first the scorpiki had stayed close, their chitinous footfalls echoing throughout the canyon. However, those large, bulbous bodies were not built for speed. Inexorably, the long-legged camels were able to outpace them. Still, with Tyberion's warning fresh in his mind, H'bare did not let up. Even when dismounted he led the princess at a swift pace. They broke free of the Rifts a good three hours past nightfall and still they raced onward.

As the night dragged on, their stamina began to wane. By now the pair had been on the move for nearly a day and a half without rest. It was with great relief when they stumbled into a place H'bare had been looking for. Old ruins, once inhabited by a tribe of Savlar, had been reduced to a smattering of worn-down stone buildings.

Finding solace inside one of the more solid structures, the pair sank to the ground in exhaustion.

"Thank you," came the tired voice of Zahra from where she lay, leaning up against what remained of a wall. "You saved my life."

"We're not out of danger yet," H'bare responded, taking a long drink of water.

"How far to the Oasis?"

H'bare passed the skin to Zahra, glancing up at the stars. "No more than ten miles," he responded.

The princess drank slowly, savoring every drop. "What of Kadira?" she asked. "Have you given my father's murderer any thought?"

"*You are the Foxclaw*," he heard Tyberion's voice echo in his head once again.

"I have," he answered aloud, knowing what he must do.

"What's that?" she asked, laying her head down to rest.

"Tomorrow, we rid Valasca of its greatest enemy," he answered, laying next to her.

Zahra drifted quickly off to sleep, while H'bare made his peace with what he knew he must do.

They woke at dawn the next day. The princess was surprised that H'bare was in no rush to leave. When they did start toward the Oasis, it was at a comfortable walk.

"Are we not in a hurry?" she asked, anxiously looking behind her.

"Not yet," he answered, saying no more.

Two hours passed when they found themselves climbing the last rise into the Oasis. That was when they saw the sands of the desert kick up in the distance behind them.

"They are close," Zahra muttered, standing on top of a dune.

"I know," H'bare answered, his voice calm.

"Shouldn't we…" Zahra began, her eyes still searching behind them.

"Not yet," he answered, rubbing absently at his injured shoulder.

From inside the green of the Oasis a mere hundred yards away, a small army rode out, emblems of a silver tree proudly displayed on two-hundred shields.

Sitting on a horse in front of them was Kadira.

"You have stolen what belongs to me," she shouted, her voice carrying across the sands.

"You murdered my father," Zahra spat in hatred, her dark eyes flashing dangerously.

The sorceress smiled. "Now it is your turn, princess," she sneered, waving to her guards.

"Kill them both. Bring the amulet to me."

Her soldiers drew their weapons and began to ride forward.

"It has been an honor to serve, highness," H'bare said, smiling at Zahra, pulling out his kukri.

"What are you…"

"I did not tell you all of it," he interrupted, looking at her close. "Had I stayed in the palace, I may have thwarted Kadira—but I left. Because of that, the pharaoh is dead."

"There was no way you could have known."

H'bare's face hardened in determination. "I'll not make that mistake again. "You have a pure heart, princess. You will make a great pharaoh."

"H'bare, what are you...."

"Please," he continued, drawing the amulet from the saddlebag. "Make certain my name is cleared as a deserter."

"I don't under..."

"Hee ya!" H'bare shouted at the top of his lungs, striking the flank of Zahra's camel with the flat of his blade.

The mount bleated in surprise and lurched forward, racing toward the Oasis.

H'bare put the amulet around his neck and charged down the hill, his kukri held high overhead. "Come my children!" he shouted, beckoning to the sands behind him. "Let us cleanse this land!"

As he pointed at the Guards of the Silver Tree, dozens of massive scorpiki crested the dune behind him, enthralled to follow whoever wore the amulet.

Kadira's guards, expecting the attack of a single rider, were stunned at the terrible force that materialized in front of them.

The scorpiki, now fully committed, raced past H'bare and slammed into Kadira's army, spilling human blood onto the desert sands.

H'bare gave a high-pitched whistle, stuffed the amulet in his waterskin and threw it toward Zahra where it landed only a few feet away from her.

"Remember me!" H'bare shouted, giving his princess a sharp salute. Turning back to the battle, he drew his khopesh and entered the fray.

The fight raged for several minutes, H'bare and the scorpiki cutting a bloody swath through the guards, making their way toward the sorceress. Dozens of fights broke out around them as the swarthy warrior fought his way toward the Sorceress of Valasca. As he drew close, Kadira raised her scepter of polished bone, unleashing her magic. H'bare was hit with a mystical force, one strong enough to knock him flying off his mount. He crashed to the ground, only inches away from his desired target.

Kadira's personal bodyguard leapt toward him, their iron blades hacking savagely at the former soldier of the pharaoh.

A raging scorpicous, already bleeding heavily from its torso, bowled its way into the group. All of them went down in a bloody heap of fleshy arms and chitinous legs.

Moments later, the fighting ended. Kadira's guards, killed to a man, littered the sands of the desert around her, their blood mixing with that of three score fallen scorpiki. Hand wrapped around her scepter, Kadira strode past them all with nary a glance. Instead, she stopped in front of Zahra who was holding the waterskin containing the amulet.

"Did you really think you, alone, could defeat me?" Kadira asked. "I am surprised you made it this far. Now, give me the amulet, else your passing will be one of excruciating pain."

As she spoke, the sorceress raised a hand in front of her, a ball of green fire building in her palm.

Zahra bowed her head in resignation.

"You are right, sorceress," the princess admitted, her voice bone weary, filled with defeat. "Save for one thing."

The princess looked up, a dangerous smile on her lips.

"I am not alone."

From behind Kadira, H'bare's khopesh swept toward the sorceress. Eyes wide, Kadira sensed her danger a moment too late. Slicing horizontally, the steel blade cut the magicker's neck clean through. An eyeblink later, Kadira's severed head dropped to the ground, rolling lifelessly in the sand.

Lying on the ground next to it inside an old waterskin, was her prize, the Amulet of Souls. Unknown to Zahra, the magic faded from it.

H'bare, covered in a swath of wounds, dropped to the ground as the life drained from his body.

Zahra cried out and ran to him, falling to her knees, knowing he could not survive his injuries.

"You did it," she whispered, stroking the hair matted to his head.

H'bare flashed a pained smile. "*We* did it," he gasped, coughing blood.

"Don't go," she pleaded, her voice desperate. "I'm your pharaoh. I order you not to die."

H'bare's face filled with a serene tranquility. "I will always be…bonded to you, majesty. It was my…honor to serve."

The blooded warrior let out one last expulsion of breath and passed peacefully into the afterlife.

Heartbroken, Zahra held him and wept.

A Horse Like Starlight

By D.J. Swift

Urzka, the witch of the Anni, rode a handsome stallion so white that it glowed even in the overcast afternoon. From the moment Andras first saw its gently arching neck, long legs, and graceful gate, he wanted it more than he had ever wanted anything in his life. Safely hidden within a copse of trees, he watched her thunder past, resplendent in her dark silks and fine white furs, and surrounded by two dozen Anni mounted archers. Her long black hair billowed in the frigid autumn wind. A single, faceted jewel the size of a robin's egg hung between her dark brows on the silver band that rested across her unlined forehead. The jewel, sometimes green, sometimes blue, sometimes almost black, cast unearthly light in all directions.

All the stories had said she was beautiful--her beauty was the only thing soldiers from old had remembered about her. But that shining white horse stood out from among the other drab mounts in every shade between dun and brown. It even outshined Andras' own fine mare. The horse was fit for a king. And yet, the Anni witch rode on its back.

Andras watched the horde of Anni invaders disappear into the golden horizon, dust churning in their wake. After forty years of peace, the Anni had returned, and the witch rode among them.

"Why did you not kill her when you had the chance?" Gabor asked over his cup of ale. "You saw her. You know what she has done to our people in the past. Yet you didn't kill her."

Andras bristled at the reprimand from his younger friend. He was two years older than Gabor, and in this instance anyway, at least twice as wise. "She was surrounded by the full force of an Anni scouting party, more than twenty strong. I'd wager you wouldn't have tried killing her if you had been in my position."

Gabor scoffed. "I would have. And they never would have caught me."

Andras raised a brow at Gabor's confidence. "Unlikely. You know how swiftly they ride. They are born on horseback."

The witch always rode at the center of the company surrounded by the bulk of the force, and it was clear to Andras that they would protect her at any cost. Legends spoke of the enchantments Urzka wrought. They said that it was by her magics that the silk armor of the Anni became impenetrable, whether by bolt, arrow, or blade. They warned that she commanded the very dust of the earth so that it did not stir up, even when trodden upon by many horses. If the stories were to be believed, this was why the horde was able to surprise each town they came across.

Gabor snorted, pulling Andras from his thoughts. "Sounds like an excuse to me. You had a clear shot, and the world would be a better place had you taken it."

Andras shook his head. "No, it was not the right time to kill her. But now that they are here, we must do something about her."

"Do you think the king would reward us if we captured or killed her?" Gabor asked.

"I do."

"And they were riding southwest, you said?"

"Toward Krieg. I'm certain of it. My father sent his fastest rider to warn the city, but we do not know if he will arrive in time. I did not see any sign of the rest of the force. Father rode north to inform the king that the Anni have returned and that the witch is among them."

"I wonder why we haven't heard anything about their return until now?"

"Two reasons alone, my friend. Either they killed all whom they encountered, or they avoided being seen by people altogether."

The outer reaches of the land were desolate and sparsely populated, even after the grants issued by King Vajda, awarding fiefs to knights willing to build defensive walls and castles. It was possible that no one had yet seen the invaders. But Andras thought it was more likely that the Anni had simply slaughtered everyone in their path. It was their way.

Gabor shook his head. He, too, knew the stories of Urzka's craft. "Your father has left, then?"

"Before dawn this morning."

As Gabor leaned forward over his cup, his golden locks spilled over his broad shoulders. He had a gleam in his eyes that Andras recognized. "What is to stop us from going out after the witch ourselves?"

Andras grinned. "Nothing at all."

They left before dawn. The guard at the gate let Andras pass when he told him he was on the king's business. Of course, it was only true in the strictest sense. While destroying the witch would help the kingdom in the impending invasion, King Vajda had not specifically expressed a desire that Andras kill the witch himself. Sometimes it was easier to ask forgiveness, having carried out a great deed, than to ask permission. He had no intention of showing his face back at Csendorvar Castle until he had done for his father a mighty deed that would bring glory to the Erdoszi family.

In the days of his grandfather, during the past invasion, none of the towns or cities had been walled, and only a few castles had stood in the way of the onslaught. But under the rule of King Vajda the Good, the whole nation had undergone a campaign to build walls around the major towns and cities. This time they would not be easy victims of Anni arrows. Only Urzka and her dark magic stood in the way of a sure victory against the invaders from the east.

Gabor met Andras in the trees near the river a mile south of the castle. Dawn grayed the horizon as they turned their horses toward Krieg, twenty miles southwest. As they rode, the only thing Andras could think about was the witch's shining white horse. He imagined himself sitting astride that great stallion beside the king. Not even the king had such a fine horse. And what magnificent foals it would throw. That alone would enrich his family.

They pushed their mounts hard for hours. At last, Andras and Gabor emerged from the heavily wooded southern road. In the distance, Andras saw several columns of dark smoke rising high up in the sky. He wheeled his mount to a stop beside Gabor.

"Smoke," he said, pointing to the sky.

Gabor gave a solemn nod. "It comes from Krieg."

"No doubt. But it means we are catching up with them. I'll wager they are still pillaging."

"But how did they get in?" Gabor protested. "The walls are tall, and they are no more than twenty mounted archers."

"The burning is not from within Krieg. They are razing the land all around it. And you must never forget the stories we heard in our youth. The witch may be beautiful, but during the last invasion, she used her dark powers to destroy entire towns, slaughtering every man, woman, and child who resisted her. We will learn more as we approach the hill. But let's lead our horses for now and keep to the trees to stay hidden from their eyes."

The town of Krieg nestled against a hill, crowned with a low tower, and surrounded by a stone wall. Farms spread for two miles around the city walls in all directions. The two young men trekked along the edges of the wood searching for the Anni until dusk.

"Look, I see some of them," Gabor whispered. He nodded in the direction of a large farmhouse, newly aflame. A dozen or so mounted warriors surrounded the house. Andras was too far away to hear their words, but they sounded angry.

"Do you see any of our people among them?" Andras asked

"No. And I have not seen anyone all day. You?"

"No one. Let's hope that it is a sign that the word arrived in time for everyone to escape behind the walls."

"Indeed."

"Let's follow them. Perhaps they will lead us to their camp." And to the white horse. But Andras kept that thought to himself.

The two young men did just that, keeping themselves concealed within the woods. Their chain mail rang softly, but the troop of Anni continued bickering with each other and the bridles of their horses rang so that Gabor and Andras went unnoticed. Andras knew only a few words of the Anni tongue, but from the few words he made out, they seemed angry not to have found any prisoners.

As the sun settled into the horizon, Andras feared they would lose sight of the warriors in the dark. But before he could express that concern to Gabor, the Anni encampment came into view. Andras held up a hand.

"Let's leave our horses here. We will come back to them with our spoils."

They tied their mounts to limbs where they could browse and crept forward to the edge of the forest. Andras spotted a sentry. They waited until the man's back was turned to them and he walked away before going any further. At the edge where the encampment met the woods, the two stopped.

"Which tent is hers?" Gabor asked.

They both looked at the tent in the center, a yurt made from white skins and hung with dark draperies fringed with gold.

"It has to be the one in the middle," Andras said.

Gabor nodded his agreement.

"But I don't know how we get into it," Andras said. He was beginning to feel a moment of doubt that his excellent plan might not be, however much he wanted the witch's white horse.

"I don't know. They seem interested in whatever's coming out of that great pot over the fire over there," Gabor said, gesturing to the massive campfire with the tripod and black pot suspended above it.

"Must've worked up an appetite with all that pillaging," Andras said dryly.

"I think we may be able to use the tents themselves as cover. The sentry certainly isn't very diligent," Gabor said.

"That's a bit odd, don't you think?"

Gabor shrugged. "Maybe it is. But maybe they didn't get much food from this raid."

"How many of them do you see? Aside from the witch. I don't see her. She must be in the tent."

"Sixteen," Gabor said. "No wait, seventeen. There is the sentry."

"There were twenty of them."

"Maybe they lost a couple in the fighting. Maybe they have more than one sentry."

"I'm most concerned about the latter possibility."

"Nowhere to go but forward," Gabor said, grinning.

Andras returned the grin. "You're an idiot. Let's go." He crept forward in the dark, his dagger in hand. Though his heart raced in his chest, he felt almost giddy for what he was about to do. Father would be proud of him.

They hunched low to the ground and hurried to the shadows of the first tent. There, they caught their breath and watched for movement. Most of the Anni men seemed unusually taken by the prospect of a hot meal. Andras would have felt sorry for them, had circumstances been different. But despite the distracted state of their enemies, Andras knew that he and Gabor must avoid drawing attention to their presence. They crept forward, from tent shadow to tent shadow until they found themselves outside the witch's tent.

Go in? Gabor signed to Andras.

One at a time.

I enter first.

No. Me.

Gabor rolled his eyes but refrained from arguing with Andras further.

Andras drew a deep breath and listened at the door. But all he heard was the distant guttural chatter of the Anni and the sound of his own heartbeat in his ears. He drew back the flap just enough to let his eyes adjust to the low light of the single lamp near the back wall. The pile of furs near the lampstand must be the witch's bed. He stepped inside.

The tent was empty. Instinctively, he had known this even before he entered. But as the flap fell closed behind him, he felt that emptiness to his core. Something was wrong. Moments later, Gabor cried out from the other side of the door. Andras turned to reach again for the flap, but it was already beginning to open. He stepped back into the shadows beside the door. His hand instinctively went for the dagger on his belt.

Thin, wrinkled hands and thin arms wrapped in faded furs pushed Gabor into the tent. Whoever it was had Gabor's arm shoved up behind his back in a shoulder lock and held a knife firmly against the skin of his neck. Andras raised the dagger in his hand. As the figure stepped through the doorway, Andras slammed the pommel down on the back of his head. The figure dropped to the ground.

It was no man.

The witch did not look as she had just two days ago when Andras had seen her, wild and beautiful in her silks and furs, with her black hair whipping around her in the wind. Gone was her smooth, unlined face, eternally youthful--at least if the stories were to be believed. Course gray hairs had replaced her dark ebony locks. He saw her scalp beneath the thin hairs, pale and spotted. The jeweled silver headband was still on her forehead, the dark stone dangling askew. He yanked the circlet from her head and took a quick step back as if she might grab him. But she lay as still as death on the ground, the back of her head smashed in and leaking darkly from the wound inflicted by the rounded point of his pommel. Truthfully, she was almost dead. Andras did not see any rise or fall from her breathing. If she was not dead now, she soon would be.

Gabor rubbed his neck. "I didn't hear her sneak up on me," he whispered.

"Tie her up," Andras said. "Until we can figure out what to do."

"We're going to have to kill her," Gabor hissed. He glanced down at the old woman and the growing stain of blood on the back of her head. "I've never killed a woman before."

"You've never killed anyone before," Andras snapped. He shifted uncomfortably. He had never killed anyone before, either, but he was not about to admit it aloud. Not here.

Andras lifted the silver headband and stared into the dark, multi-faceted stone that hung from it. Though small, it was surprisingly heavy. The witch had never been seen without it, not for all these decades. It sparkled in the dim light of the lamp, casting dark rays of light across the tent walls. It was dizzying to behold.

Andras began to feel as if the tent was spinning. As the walls whirled around him, he felt like he had when he was twelve years old and had gotten drunk with the stable boys during the harvest festival. His father had beaten him soundly for bringing dishonor to the noble Erdoszi name. As Andras stared deeper into the gem, that sickening dizziness diminished. The depths of the gem's color reminded Andras of a deep pool of still water. As he gazed into the stone, he saw wriggling movement from within it. But when he tried to concentrate on just one of those wriggling forms, he felt sick all over again.

"You see it, don't you boy?" came a woman's voice. Or was it a man's voice? It was difficult to say. It sounded at once young and old.

Andras never looked away from the wriggling forms within the stone. "What are they?"

"Where did you come from, boy?"

"I'm almost twenty. Hardly a boy anymore."

"Silence, child. Who are your parents?"

Andras tried to concentrate on where the voice came from, but it sounded as if it came from everywhere all at once. "Are you Urzka, the Anni witch?"

There came a tinkling, as of silver bells. Andras realized it was laughter.

"Urzka was useful to me in her time."

"Who are you, then?"

The voice paused for a moment. "I had a name long ago. But it's been so long since I had to use it that I've forgotten it."

"What are you, if you are not Urzka?"

"Stare into those moving shapes, boy. See if you can catch one with your eyes."

Andras found himself obeying without a thought. "Why? What are they?"

"Power, boy. All the power you could ever want. And it's yours for the taking if you can catch one of them with your eyes."

Andras blinked. "I don't want power." He looked at the limp old woman on the ground and began to turn away from the gem. But as his head turned, his arm moved to keep the gem in front of his face.

"Everyone wants power," the voice said.

"Can't say that's ever been true of me. Power sounds like more work than I want in life."

"Look at those shadows. You can see them move, can't you? Can you catch one? Even a slow one?"

"It makes me feel sick to look at them. I'd rather not."

"What do you want, boy?"

He hesitated to answer. "The horse that shines like starlight."

"I can make you one of those. Just look into the gem."

"I don't want one that you've made. I want the one that lies out there, waiting for me. I will have that one."

The wriggling dark forms reminded Andras of grubs. Only these were beautiful. And though he tried to look away from them, he found it harder and harder to do so. One deep inside the gem seemed to be taunting him, whipping its small tail back and forth in a rhythmic manner until Andras was sure he could capture it with his gaze.

Something inside of him clicked.

All at once Andras discovered he could pull that small, wriggling streak of color toward himself just by the force of his will. It opened before him and stretched out wide. He willed it to turn over and over before his eyes.

"This doesn't look like power," Andras said dreamily.

"It is the beginning of power. But power must have something from which to draw its strength."

"What does such a small thing need?"

"Blood. You must feed it. Then it will be yours."

Andras recoiled. "Never. I am no witch, to feed my life source to the dark powers."

"They do not seem so dark, though, do they?"

Andras stared at the small moving thing, now under his control. "No, I suppose not."

"Besides," the voice cooed. "It would do you no good to feed it from *your* life source. You need it. Look around you. Is there another?"

Andras looked around the dark tent. The room once again felt as if it was spinning. But as his gaze came to rest on Gabor, he said, "There is Gabor."

Gabor mouthed something to Andras. But Andras could not tell what he was saying. And he found the effort needed to try to read his lips frustrating.

"Indeed. His life source will do," the voice purred. "And look, here is your knife."

Andras' right arm raised, his dagger in hand.

"But Gabor is my closest friend," Andras began. "I cannot possibly--"

"That makes the blood all that much dearer," came the voice. "Now let me feed."

Andras felt his body propelled forward as if controlled by something outside himself. He tried to shout to warn Gabor. But his lips would not open. As the blade arced through the air toward Gabor, Andras screamed through lips pressed tightly closed.

Gabor dodged the blade, mouthing words that Andras could not hear, his face contorted with anger and astonishment. The knife in Andras' hand slashed out again and again. Gabor dodged each clumsy parry. Andras continued screaming, even if his mouth would not open. Tears burned his eyes and streamed down his cheeks. He fought this dark power with all his strength. With all the force of his will, he pushed it away from him. But the darkness had taken complete control of his body and moved it by its own malevolent will.

"This would be much simpler for you if you would cooperate," the voice whispered.

Gabor glanced at the gem dangling from the circlet in Andras' left hand, then back at the knife in his right hand. When the next slash came, he sidestepped, grasped Andras' right arm, and pulled him forward, pinning the knife hand away from his body. Before Andras knew what was happening, Gabor tripped him, slamming him into the ground. As he struck, the jeweled circlet fell from his fingers. Andras moaned. Gabor jerked the dagger from Andras' grasp and threw it aside. Gabor rested his weight on a knee across Andras' midsection.

"What has come over you?" he hissed. "You could have killed me!"

"The gem," Andras wheezed. "Don't touch it."

Gabor shifted his weight some to allow Andras to breathe. "Yes?"

"It took control over my body," Andras said. "It would have taken over my mind, too, had I not fought it."

"We should destroy it," Gabor said.

"How?"

"Smash it with a rock?"

"I suppose it does not hurt to try," Andras agreed.

Gabor helped his friend to his knees. "There are rocks all over the ground in here. Let's use that flat one as a base."

Andras rolled to his knees. He felt as exhausted as if he had spent the entire day in the yard training with Master Ferenc.

"Do not touch it with your hands," Andras said. "Move it with the tip of your blade."

Gabor slipped the tip of his dagger beneath the stone and lifted it to the flat stone embedded in the dirt. Andras rose to his feet and hunted for the largest stone he could find. At the edge of the wall of the tent, he found one the size of Urzka's head. With arms trembling from the strain, he carried the stone to where the gem lay.

"I do not know what will happen," Andras said.

"We must try. It is too dangerous to leave around."

Andras' went to his knees. His arms shook as he lifted the stone to his chest. With all the strength he could muster, he smashed it down upon the dark jewel.

The world around him went black for a heartbeat. But in the next instant, brilliant light beamed out from the gemstone, bright as the full moon on a clear night. Andras gasped as gloomy light danced like shadows around him.

The threads of light formed a scene before him. He saw a slave girl, no more than thirteen or fourteen, being hauled around behind a man mounted on a fine white horse. Her wrists were tied in thick hempen rope, and he pulled her around behind him by that rope like an animal. His mount did not shine like starlight, but it was beautiful for a shaggy steppe horse, with its thick mane, muscular neck, and stout legs.

The scene changed, and the man was asleep in his tent beside the slave girl. She slipped from his bed, wrapped only in a coarse horsehair blanket. Four chests sat in the shadows of his tent. She went to the smallest and withdrew a small key from where it was hidden in her hair. With movements slow and quiet, she slid the key into the lock and turned it. The lid opened. Inside sat the silver headband with the faceted dark jewel. She picked it up, mesmerized by the dazzling light dancing around the walls of the tent. A euphoric smile spread across her face. She placed the circlet upon her head. It was too big for a girl as slight as her. But as Andras watched the silver band became small enough to fit her brow. Her skin, once filthy, became clean and pale. Her matted hair transformed into beautiful, black locks. The horsehair blanket became a silk riding robe and rich white fur mantle.

She walked across the room to the pile of furs where the man lay and knelt beside him. A blade glinted in the low lamplight. She drove it downward. When she arose, blood covered her hands. As she turned, she was looking into Andras' eyes. The dark jewel pulsed on her pale forehead.

Urzka.

Andras blinked in the dim light. Urzka's dead eyes stared at him from where she lay. His head throbbed. Gabor was leaning over him, shaking his shoulders as if to wake him.

"We must get out of here!" Gabor whispered. "Get up! Get up! I hear noise in the camp! They know we are here!"

Andras heard clamor outside, but his head was spinning. He felt like he had been too long in his cups. He rolled to his side and came face to face with the gem. It was whole, although the attempt to break it left deep white scratches across some of the facets.

"It didn't work," Andras moaned. "We will have to carry it with us and try to figure out how to destroy it later."

Gabor cut a leather pouch off the witch's belt. He dumped the contents on the ground and handed the pouch to Andras.

"Would this do?"

Andras took the pouch and fetched his dagger from several paces away. With the tip of his blade, he shoved the circlet into the pouch, tied the top securely, and shoved it into his own coin pouch on his belt.

"It will have to do for now. We must leave," Andras said. He felt so weak he was not sure he could run. But he had no choice. This was his last chance to reach the rope pen where the Anni kept their horses. That shining white horse awaited him out there, but he must get to his feet.

Gabor pulled him up and brushed the dirt and dead grass from him. He stuck the dagger back into Andras' sheath.

"Let's go," he whispered. Gabor opened the flap a couple of inches and peered outside. Silently, he motioned for Andras to follow him out into the night.

As Andras stepped outside, he realized that the camp was much larger than when he had first slipped into it. Urzka's tent was still in the dead center. Only now, he had at least eight times as much ground to cover to escape. As his eyes adjusted to the change in light, he could not figure out where the horses were penned. Around them, figures ran past, all confusion and chaos. But it was as if they were all blind. Nobody saw each other. They crashed blindly into one another as they scrambled about. And as they got back to their feet, they stopped to fight. No one noticed the confused figures of Andras and Gabor as they wandered back and forth searching for a way out.

As Gabor crept toward the edge of the camp closest to Krieg, Andras grabbed his shoulder. "Where are their horses?"

"How should I know? What would I want with those ugly things anyway?"

"The witch's horse. I want the witch's horse," Andras whispered. "That horse is mine."

Gabor sighed. "They are somewhere to the rear of the camp. We will have to go further into danger to get it."

"It does not matter. I will have that horse."

Gabor shook his head. "If you insist. Though I think this is a fool's errand."

"It is my errand. And you should watch your tongue. I will be your lord one day."

Gabor's shoulders slumped, but he turned toward the rear of the camp. "This way, *milord.*"

Andras scowled but followed his friend as he found a path through the clamor of the camp. He heard whinnying horses in the distance, and his hopes surged. Around them, tents collapsed as men collided with each other and broke out into brawls. Several tents caught fire, and the flames spread between tents pitched too close. All around them men screamed and fought. It was as if the whole camp had descended into madness. Andras watched with wide-eyed horror as the Anni beat and killed each other. At last, Gabor stopped and held up a fist.

"The white horse is there at the edge. You should be able to grab him with no trouble. I will steal another mount. Then let's ride to the gates of Krieg. It is our only hope for safety. After dawn, we may be able to return for our horses in the woods."

Andras nodded.

They trotted to the edge of the pen of horses, made from hemp rope strung between stakes driven into the ground.

"We will need bridles," Andras said. He glanced at the nearby tents. "We will have to steal them."

Gabor rolled his eyes. "Of course, we will. Come on, let's be done with this."

Andras scowled. Gabor's attitude was beginning to wear on him.

"Follow me," Andras said, taking the lead. "They keep them in their tents."

They jogged to the nearest tent, fifty paces away. It still stood, though no lights shined from within. A man ran by, shouting something in Anni. Andras did not understand any of the words. As soon as the man had passed, Andras stepped to the doorway and opened the flap.

"Hold this open, Gabor. I need the light."

Gabor held back the flap, and Andras stepped inside, sword drawn. Just as his eyes had adjusted to the near-total blackness within, he saw something move toward him out of the corner of his eye. He blocked the overhead blow with his sword and shoved the figure back. He lunged forward with a slash to the figure's midsection. The man crumpled. Andras brought the blade down on the man's neck with a final blow. He took a moment to catch his breath and look around the tent for any other figures in the dark. He saw none. But on the far side of the wall, he spied the shadowy forms of three saddle racks.

Hurriedly Andras and Gabor sorted through the saddles, pads, and until they each had usable tack for a mount. As chaos continued to consume the Anni camp, they calmly walked the stolen trappings to the horse pen. The horses stamped and whinnied, moving nervously through the pen. Andras searched for the white horse. He had a momentary fear that one of the Anni had the same idea as him and had stolen the horse while he had been searching for tack.

"Hurry up!" Gabor's whisper came from several paces away, somewhere in the throng of horses.

At last, Andras spied the stallion when it lifted its head high into the air. Andras pulled a small apple from his belt and approached. After a cursory sniff, it ate the apple from his hand. Then the horse allowed Andras to saddle it without fuss.

Gabor had a more challenging time saddling the dun he had chosen. It bit him twice as he tightened the cinches of the saddle. Before mounting their stolen horses, Andras cut the rope lines of the temporary pen. As the horses poured out of the corral, he swung himself up on the white stallion. It seemed to glow under the soft light of the moon. The stallion stamped and snorted, flicking its tail, eager to run. Andras turned him in the direction of the road to Krieg and kicked him into a run. They thundered across the steppe into the night. He had never ridden anything so swift, so sure, or so beautiful. He had never felt more alive.

As they galloped down the road to Krieg, Andras saw lights on the walls and the windows of the keep grow brighter. He glanced back to see if they were being followed, but all he could see was Gabor on his dun horse, keeping pace. Andras let his horse slow to a trot as they began to ascend the hill to the city gates.

"Something's wrong with your horse," Gabor shouted behind him.

Andras glanced back, and then down. "What are you talking about?"

"It's changing," Gabor shouted.

Andras looked down again but didn't see anything different.

The gates loomed ahead of them. Andras and Gabor both began to shout up at the walls for someone to open the gates. As they approached, the gates remained in place, though Andras could see men gathering above watching their approach.

Andras pulled the white horse to a stop on the bridge.

"Who goes there?" a voice called down to them.

"Andras Erdoszi, son of Lord Anton Erdoszi of Csendorvar Castle. I am accompanied by my brother-in-arms, Gabor Radovan."

"I know your father. But why are you riding Anni asses?"

Andras swallowed the first insult that came to mind. "We have come from the Anni camp. We are here to report the death of the witch Urzka. The camp was in chaos when we left. We freed their horses. The Anni were too busy killing each other to notice."

The command went out to raise the portcullis. As it went up, they were met by guards with lit torches.

"Welcome to Krieg. Lord Toth will see you."

As Andras rode through the gates, he became aware of the sniggering of several men in the crowd. Andras ignored them. They were no doubt laughing at the primitive saddles that he and Gabor had been forced to use to ride to safety. But he would like to see any of these fellows ride away as swiftly as they had managed bareback and without a bridle.

Lord Istvan Toth met them at the keep. He was still wearing full plate, and he wore a mantle of green velvet trimmed with mink. Andras only then noticed the chill of the evening and shivered.

Andras dismounted and bowed respectfully. "My Lord Toth, I bring glad news from the camp of the Anni."

"So, I have heard, Master Erdoszi. I hear that you have slain the witch Urzka with your own hand. Is this true?"

The stallion nuzzled at Andras' pockets just then. As he pushed its muzzle away, he noticed that the horse seemed shaggier than he remembered.

"Yes, my lord. She had captured my friend, Gabor, and I was able to sneak behind her and strike her on the back of the head with the pommel of my dagger. I thought she was a man, so I struck with great force and smashed in the back of her head."

"And I hear that the Anni are in chaos? We can hear the noise up here, but we were not certain of what was happening in the camp."

"Yes, my lord. I don't know why, but when she fell, it threw all into chaos. The whole camp suddenly appeared larger than it had, and men were running blindly, killing each other, destroying the tents."

"It was some effect of her magic, no doubt. Did you catch sight of that magnificent white horse of hers before setting the horses free?"

Andras gestured at his mount. "This is that same horse."

Lord Toth threw his head back and laughed. The knights and guards with him laughed, too. Andras glanced over at the horse and started with surprise. Instead of a gleaming white horse, he held the reigns of a pale dun with a deep brown erect mane tipped with cream. The stallion again nuzzled his pocket. Thick, shaggy, and stocky, this horse was not the graceful white steed he had coveted.

"Even her horse was a glamour," Andras said with a sigh. He patted the horse's neck, turning his face away from the lord of Krieg to hide the burning in his cheeks. Somewhere in the distance, Andras heard laughter like the tinkling of silver.

Lord Toth stepped closer to Andras and clasped his shoulder. "It's a fine steppe horse, even if it isn't white. I'd still keep him. What a story it will make. You know they will sing songs of this for years to come. Now join me in the hall. Tell me more about your adventures. Tonight, we will raise our cups to Andras Erdozsi, the witch slayer."

The crowd of men closed in around Andras and Gabor, slapping their backs. At once, everyone rushed to speak to them. With so many talking all at once, Andras could hardly hear any single person. Someone took Andras' mount as the crowd pushed the two young men up the steps of the keep into the great hall, where it would be dark, raucous, and smoky. Andras wished to be left alone. Yesterday, he would have reveled in the glory of this moment. But now he felt he would give anything for a quiet corner of the steppe pony's stall where he could sit and think. Alone.

For the briefest moment, he was tempted to follow after the horse. At the top step, he paused to watch a stable hand walk the stallion to the stables. Its shaggy, pale dun coat glowed softly in the golden light of so many torches. But that beautiful horse with its long legs, graceful neck, and white coat that glowed like starlight was gone.

Dragon's Blood

By Richard Cartwright

"**J**ust how much do you think she weighs again?"

"Enough that we will need two wagons to haul the pearls equal to her weight once we return Princess Melom safe and sound to King Jaxom" Replied his tall red haired partner," Why do you ask, Arthan?"

"Because the magic from yonder stronghold reeks of evil corruption even from here. Not to mention the fifty soldiers I've counted on the walls. Shator, I find it odd that the king hasn't sent his troops and warrior mages to storm the place to retrieve his daughter."

"Umm... about that." Shator's olive skin blushed nearly as red as her tightly braided hair. "The king has already sent two companies of warrior mages and fighters since the kidnapping. He decided that a small stealthy team might be a better approach."

"Two companies? I would have liked to have talked to them to get some idea of the layout." Arthan couldn't hide the irritation in his voice.

"Well... the only survivor died of some festering corruption that ate her alive. They cremated her body with mage fire. She was raving incoherently when they found her in the ruins of their camp twelve days ago."

"Are you talking about that big burn spot we passed this morning?"

"Yes, there were concerns about the corpses reanimating. Fire was the only way to be sure they stayed dead."

"I wish the king had approached you…us sooner. Having more than two days before the full moons would have been helpful." Arthan regretted not being there for the audience with the king's seneschal. This was only his second quest with the ginger Akhi sword maiden, and they were still getting to know one another. He knew that she had served King Jaxom as a guard for Princess Melom. Shator was reticent about why she left the king's service.

They had met in a tavern in Lapour some two months ago. She was looking for work and he needed someone to watch his back while he retrieved an enchanted daggoth horn from thieves that robbed the merchant which had hired him. She came well recommended, and he'd quickly discovered that she was the best fighter he had ever encountered. One of her contacts at the palace had reached out to her while he had been occupied at the healer hall getting his leg repaired from an axman's strike. If not for her blocking parry, the ax would have cut off his head rather than just laying open his leg.

"To be honest, we weren't his first choice. Or his third." Was the warrior maid blushing? Arthan thought.

"Let me guess. We're going to find more burn spots?"

"Possibly. They never found the second party."

"Or the third?"

"Oh no. The third choice turned Jaxom down flat and left out escorting a caravan across the Plains of Damnation. The job fell into our laps after that." Shator beamed.

Arthan reflected on this bit of information. Five years ago, he had taken a job helping protect a merchant train carrying perishable kava fruit from the port city of Salton to Lapour. The clipper ship had been delayed in transit. The trader had elected to exchange the four weeks of travel over snowy mountain roads from the coast to the capital, for a week through the desolate Plains of Damnation, to ensure the rare delicacy made it to market at the peak of ripeness.

Arthan was new to the kingdom of Subiti and anxious to make a name and fill his purse. His tall, muscular body attracted those in search of a warrior for hire but were put off by his magical abilities, following the old prejudice against warrior mages His dwindling coins decided him to sign on without considering why most of the other sell swords turned the merchant away.

A week later the few survivors had staggered through the gates of Lapour, cargo intact. The trader's surviving son had paid Arthan a bonus that had barely covered the costs of repairing his weapons and brewing the potions and elixirs expended to heal the injured and destroy the magical beasts that had come at them almost nonstop for seven days.

Today's older and wiser Arthan would gladly take the mountain road in high winter, barefoot, and naked than to trod the plains ever again. He took a deep breath and reminded himself to never again let Shator broker a quest without getting all the details up front, assuming they survived this one.

"Have you ever crossed the Plains of Damnation, Shator?"

"Of course not. Everyone knows you have to be desperate, stupid, or suicidal or some combination of the three to do that." Arthan gave her his best hard stare. For a hardened warrior, she blushed a lot.

"Shator, I know that you aren't stupid or foolhardy. We were well paid for the last quest, so you aren't desperate for coin. No one in their right mind would take this on. As far as I can tell, you're not crazy. There is something you're not telling me. If we're going to make this work, we have to be completely open with each other."

"You're right. My sword mother had taken service with Jaxom when I was ten, after the death of Melom's mother. I had just passed the trials and it was my first time away from the temple. I was Mels guard and playmate. We grew up together. We shared the same tutors, I taught her the basics of fighting and my mother tutored us both on the advanced arts of war. We were very close. I won't see her sacrificed at the full moons while I draw breath." She spoke with an intensity that went beyond loyalty to a long time employer.

"So, a sister of your heart?"

"Something like that." She said and pointed at the cliff face off to one side of the fortress. "Did you see that?"

Arthan had noticed the movement. The castle backed up against a sheer cliff that was pockmarked with cave entrances of various sizes. He had speculated to Shator that they might be a way in. Shator had agreed but was leery of the time it would take to find a connected passage in the multitude of openings.

"Interesting," He focused his mage sight to magnify his vision. The rock face seemed to rush towards him to the point he could make out three skinny, naked individuals each struggling with a barrel nearly as big as they were. The collars around their necks identified them as slaves. A fourth very well-fed man in a brown tunic with a red sash watched them. The trio took each barrel in turn and tipped it over the edge of the cliff that jutted from the entrance, spilling out their contents.

"Looks like a kitchen crew emptying the slops barrels," Arthan reported. The discoloration on that part of the rock face made sense now, along with the circling carrion birds that were now gliding in for a landing at the foot of the bluff.

Glancing back up to the entrance, the slaves were now dragging the barrels back into the cave. The last one in line, who appeared to be female, although Arthan could barely tell due to the emaciated state of the body, pushed their barrel at the overseer and ran faster than Arthan could have thought was possible for the slave's starved condition and threw themselves off the ledge, following the garbage. He and Shator looked at each other after the body landed.

"Slave's choice?" Shator softly questioned.

"Looks like. I've never seen kitchen drudges that thin. I'm not even sure if the leaper was male or female." Arthan replied. "Well, I think we have our way in."

"I sure hope that none of the guards look up." Shator huffed as she hammered in another hook in the rock face to tie off to.

The three moons were close to full and casting enough light that it would be easy to think the sun was rising. Much lighter and he could read a scroll, Arthan thought. Assuming one would care to, hanging off a sheer cliff face. He wondered again whether it had been a good idea to have quashed Shator's idea that they could escape by levitating to the ground from the cave entrance instead of the ropes they were setting up to rappel down. Given the malevolence and power he sensed from the castle, he suspected he might not have much magic left to aid their escape. The amulets that he and Shator were wearing, along with a third for the princess, protected them from the scrying spells that flowed around them like waves, never bouncing back and alerting the caster.

"Let's take a quick break at the mouth of the big cave above the entrance to the kitchens." Arthan had marked the large cave entrance more than five times as wide as the cave from which the slave had leapt to the freedom of death.

"Sounds good to me," Shator replied with a touch of strain in her voice.

Arthan swung his body into the mouth of the cave they had decided to rest in. Unlike the cave below, that one had no ledge to speak of. He stumbled a bit on some groves on the rock floor as he landed, crouching down to keep from pitching over. Shator had her pack at her side and was sipping from a waterskin, breathing deeply. He could make out a puzzled look on her face.

Looking down, he noticed the grooves that had almost tripped him up stopped just a few feet into the cave. They were a good two to three inches deep, in rows of five. He checked the urge to sneeze as his nose picked up a dusty, dry smell with.

"Shator, do you smell..."

"I do not smell. Or nothing a good flight through a thunderstorm wouldn't cure," rumbled a voice from the darkness.

"The Plains of Damnation are looking good right now," Arthan muttered as he cast a globe of red light, revealing a dragon. Shator gasped and Arthan heard the snick of steel drawn from a scabbard beside him.

"Dismal place. The beasts there taste terrible. Sheath your sword, maiden. I am hardly in a position to threaten either of you, even if I was so inclined."

He could count on the fingers of one hand how many dragons he had ever encountered. All from a distance and all while they were eating. This specimen looked like it had missed a few meals, Arthan thought. The dragon wasn't starved, but hardly well fed either. The collar around his neck and chain bolted into the wall, wasn't a good look either.

"What happened to you?" Shator interjected. "You should be able to break the chain easily."

"I was dozing on the top of a ridge near here when I was set upon by Davan and his warriors. They snared me in a net enchanted with dragon blood and powered by Davan, who had slain a dragon and drained his blood." Arthan thought the beast had actually grimaced as it continued." He had learned from my butchered brother that our blood quickly loses its potency if not consumed. I could have broken free had he not consumed so much of the murdered dragon's blood that he could bolster the enchantment. As it was, the power overload nearly killed him. Had I realized it sooner, I would have ceased my struggles and let him cook himself that day." The last came out in a snarl.

"Davan? I know of him. A mage of middling power. Hardly a dark master. Could Davan be an underling?" Arthan mused.

"He was, young mage. Until he found a dying dragon and lucked out *on how to extract his magic. Now he draws my lifeblood through this cursed collar."

"He can help us, Arthan. Can we free him?" Shator interjected.

"Help you how? Until I eat my fill, I will be weak, drained as I am. If you free me I pledge to do what I can to aid you, but right now that's not much," the dragon rumbled.

"We're here to rescue Princess Melom. Davan intends to sacrifice her when the three moons are full. I am known as Shator," she explained.

"Aye. The dark mage likes to drain and drink my lifeblood in front of me. To taunt me no doubt. He thinks the sacrifice will allow him to channel even more magic. The more of my blood he drinks, the curse worsens. The fool."

"Curse?"

"Yes, Arthan, I believe she called you? Anyone who takes dragon blood without permission is cursed. Any good in the drinker is gradually changed to evil. Any reason is converted to madness over time. Stolen power comes at a price."

"So, the more he drinks the more powerful and unhinged he becomes." Arthan came to a decision. "May I approach in safety, good dragon?"

"I am starving, but I have never eaten a human. Although, I might make an exception for Davan and his men. Approach without fear. I am known as Gethin. You have my word I will not harm you."

Dragons always kept their word. Arthan reflected. That knowledge emboldened him to step up to Gethin and examine the collar. Close up, he could feel the enchantments. Physically, the collar looked like it had been fused to the neck. It looked to be silver, which took enchantment far better than copper, and not nearly as expensive as gold. In addition to the ring that the chain was lined to, there was a second fixture that looked like an ale tap. Arthan pondered the incongruity till a flash of horrific realization that the tap was used to drain Gethin's blood. A magic thread led off through a dragon sized set of double doors at the end of the cave. *No doubt an alarm if the collar was broken*, Arthan thought.

"Gethin, I can free you. But there is a spell that I suspect goes back to Davan that will raise the alarm when broken."

"That can be useful, Arthan. The alarm is raised, and Davan and his minions will rush up here. We can slip in through the kitchen like we planned, with the advantage of the confusion of Gethin escaping."

"Shator, that's a good idea."

"I fear that I may be too weak to fly out of here. Davan drained a flagon full of me just today."

"Would food help? We have extra provisions with the horses. I have magic infused oatcakes," Arthan pulled out two brown biscuits from his belt pouch of holding and offered them to Gethin.

"Freshly killed meat would be best. But needs must"

Arthan felt a graze on his palm and the cakes were gone. Gethan was chewing and swallowing. If that's how fast a weakened dragon moved, Arthan had no desire to go up against one at full strength.

"More?" Gethin inquired. "They're quite good."

Four more biscuits later, Arthan was impressed by how much better Gethin looked. Still thin, but his hide had lost the dull pallor from earlier. The dragon stretched, flexing its wings as much as the cave would allow.

"I suggest that we stretch out for a bit and rest till deep night. That will maximize the confusion when we strike."

"A good plan, sword maiden. Except the girl will have been sacrificed by then," Gethin rumbled.

"What? But the full moons are not till tomorrow night." Shator snapped.

"Tomorrow is when the full moons are at their peak. The ritual requires the sacrifice at the start of the full moons. Tonight." The dragon craned his neck to look out the cave entrance at the rising moon. "From what I can see of Luxor, I would say about an hour from now."

Cold dread ran through Arthan. Rather than settling down for the night, people would be rushing about preparing for the ceremony. For a moment, Arthan considered freeing Gethin and withdrawing. The look of steely determination on Shator's face told him that she was going to rescue the princess or die trying. He could do no less.

"We best be about it." Arthan said with more determination than he felt. "Shator, have the ropes ready. I will break the collar and we will rope down to the kitchen ledge and locate the princess. One of the kitchen people should know where she's being held, assuming she has been fed."

Shator moved to the mouth of the cave as Arthan prepared himself to break the enchanted collar.

"Hold, young mage. Before you remove my bondage, drink from me."

"What? I have no wish to descend into evil madness."

"Ah, but you would not. I freely offer you the gift and power of my blood. You will gain power that you will sorely need in the coming conflict and suffer not the curse. Take it. Your food has restored me far more than I would have hoped. I can spare a drink."

"Gethin, you're sure about that? I'm just getting him broken in as a partner. I don't want him going all evil on me," Shator snarked.

"I am sure. Now hurry. Time grows short."

In the end Arthan drank directly from the tap, crimson fluid pouring directly into his open mouth, reminding Arthan of an incident from years ago where he had won a bar bet that he could drink directly from the keg for three minutes. He managed, but paid dearly later. Hopefully this night will have a better outcome.

The taste was nothing like he had steeled himself for. Gethin's blood was sweet like a distilled wine. He drank greedily. The rush of power was indescribable. He could gorge on oatcakes and not match the sensation that the first drop of dragon blood hitting his tongue caused. His body warmed like drinking a cup of hot liquid. He felt full. So full.

"Stop. Shator, turn off the tap." Gethin ordered.

The flow ceased. Arthan reached for the knob. Shator slapped his hand away hard enough to sting. The flash of pain restored his senses as he staggered away from the dragon and gathered himself.

"That was intense. Shator, thank you for stopping the flow. I don't think I could have." "Such is the danger of dragon blood. We have to move." Gethin urged.

Arthan broke the collar binding effortlessly. Gethin heaved a sigh of relief. "I go to regain my strength. I will aid you further if I can. Farewell and good hunting."

With that, Gethin moved to the entrance and launched himself into the sky, dropping from view. Just as Arthan wondered if the weakened dragon had joined the slave on the valley floor, Gethan soared up, briefly flying across Luxor and then out of view.

"Let's be about it, Shator."

Arthan and Shator crouched behind barrels in the pantry area at the other end of the tunnel from the ledge looking into the kitchen area proper. The same man who had overseen the work party earlier on the ledge entered carrying a platter of food. A similarly dressed woman was chopping

carrots at a work table. The two slaves from earlier were scrubbing pots. Other slaves were scattered around the area, heads down, engaged in preparing a meal. The women peered at the platter the man had set down on the other end of the table.

"She barely touched anything. "

"I suspect knowing that you're about to have your heart cut out and eaten before your dying eyes later tonight doesn't aid the digestion." The two cackled. Arthan looked at Shator. She nodded and pointed at the woman.

A knife grew out of the woman's neck, turning her cackle into a gurgle. Shator followed her throw to finish the woman off. Arthan cast a spell of paralyzation on the man. They needed him alive. The slaves watched the action unmoving, although out of the corner of his eye, Arthan thought he saw some smiles from the drudges. The man he froze started to sway. Arthan leapt forward and caught him before he face palmed into the table.

"Here, let me make you more comfortable, my good man." Arthan laid him across a narrow bench. Now, I have just one question for you, Where's the princess being kept?" The man stared at him, mute. "Oh, silly me." He touched the man's throat and head. The cook croaked.

"Davan will have you strung up by your tool for this!"

"He might. But if you don't answer the question, you will have no further need for your tool. Answer the question." Shator had joined him wiping her bloody blade over the crotch of the paralyzed man. She joined in the conversation.

"I haven't had plains oysters in a while." Tracing her knife tip around the cook's crotch.

"We don't have time for that right now." Arthan paused. "Tell you what. Tell me what I want to know, and I give you my solemn word on my magic that neither I nor my companion will harm you, provided that you tell me where the princess is."

"Davan will have me fed to the dragon in the cell next to the princess if I tell you!" "Right where all the guards are congregating." Shator muttered.

"Now see. That wasn't hard. Now how do we get there?" The captive cook looked puzzled for a moment and then realized his slip. He grudgingly explained the route. The nods of several slaves corroborated his explanation.

"Let's be off then." Shator motioned towards some of the male slaves who had an impressive number of whip marks in various stages of healing looking at the man sprawled on the bench, "I think these men have some unfinished business with the cook."

Arthan suspected that the slaves were ready to exact vengeance for past beatings. As he was about to wave them over, the cook cried out.

"You're not going to leave me to them are you? They'll kill me!"

"We should care, why?" Shator snapped.

"When I was leaving, I heard the guards saying they were getting ready to move the princess. I know where. Keep the men from harming me, and I will tell you where."

"Agreed. You have my word that none of the men shall harm you. So be it." Arthan laid magic into the words.

"She's being taken to the Bowl. It's open to the sky and the moonshine. An altar has been set up there. That passage with the fur over it. It opens out at the top of the bowl."

"Very good. Thank you for your help. Arthan turned towards the passage following Shator. "Wait. Are you going to leave me like this?"

"Don't worry. The spell will wear off in about a half hour. Hope you treated the female slaves better than the male ones." Arthan called over his shoulder as he exited the kitchen.

From the screams at his back, it sounded like the cook hadn't.

The three moons were casting more light than Arthan would like, so he was careful to stay as low to the ground as possible at the lip of what looked like an extinct volcano crater. Several cave mouths of various sizes pockmarked the flanks of the gently sloping crater walls. The flat center had flaming brazier marking each of the four main directions. Glowing lines connected each point of direction that in turn ran to glyphs of power surrounding a stone altar. A struggling woman was bound to the top of the altar. Her naked breasts heaving as she struggled to free herself from the lines of force that both held her to the surface and ran to the power glyphs that merged into one glowing cable that connected to a glyph of concentric circles positions to one

side of the stone table. Dark robed individuals in twos and threes passed through the largest of the cave mouths and joined the procession circling up and down the shallow crater, moving to the edge of the glowing circle, to almost the lip of the bowl and clockwise around the altar area and glyphs. Their hooded heads seem to be looking down. In prayer or watching their footing Arthan didn't know or care as long as they weren't looking up. He turned to the prone Shator beside him.

"See those glowing lines? They are siphoning the moonlight energy into those four glyphs shaped like pots capped with the symbol for a sunrise with lines radiating out. They store the energy for collection. The princess is the focus. In order for the moonlight to be a usable magical power it has to be converted by a living being."

"Why's that?"

"I have no idea. This is the blackest magic there is. The only reason I know anything about it is that battle mages are taught the basics with the goal of disrupting such abominations when encountered."

"Wait, I thought the triple full moon was a once a millennium event?"

"True, but less ambitious dark mages use the same set up for a double or even single full moon. More ambitious practitioners of evil try it during the day. They tend to be self-correcting."

"How so?" Shator asked, puzzled.

"Daylight is orders of magnitude more powerful than moonlight. The few mad mages that have tried it end up as exploded bits of charred flesh. The focus was left looking like a stick of charcoal. Uthor the Unhinged drew four thousand storage glyphs and made the attempt on a cloudy day at dusk. The two surviving observers agreed that his body flared and exploded two heartbeats after starting the ritual."

"So, you can disrupt the magical working? Without being turned into charcoal?" "If I can get inside the circle, absolutely."

Shator gave a tight smile, barely visible in the dark war paint that covered her pale face and skin.

"Follow me."

Arthan belly crawled after her toward the cave entrance the robed figures were exiting from. Once they got to the mouth of the cave, Shator gestured she'd take one side and him the other. Just as Arthan was in position, he heard footsteps and murmured voices. Looking to Shator, he saw her waiving "no". He tried to make himself one with the rock face.

Three robed figures passed into view, One hissed. "Be silent, you clucking hens. I won't have my reward diminished because you two aren't being serious."

"Yes, magister. Will the power gift flow into us or be contained in the amulets?" Another voice asked.

"It will be part of us. Now shut up."

Looking over, Arthan saw Shator point at the cave and then show two fingers. He understood now. The groups of three and groups of two alternated. The next group to exit should be a pair.

A few minutes later, Arthan again heard footfalls and the murmur of voices coming from the entrance. He tensed, Shator had her dagger out. Arthan shook his head no and made a casting gesture followed by tilting his head on his hands like a person asleep.

Shator had a questioning expression, followed by a shrug and a nod. She tensed as the murmuring voices became understandable.

"Did you see the melons on the sacrifice?"

Her name is Melom. But yeah, she's got some tasty looking melons."

With that, the pair came into view. Arthan cast sleep on both of them. As they slumped, he caught the one nearest to him before he could hit the ground. Shator snagging the other. She had a look of rage on her face Arthan didn't understand. Pulling the two away from the entrance into an adjoining cave mouth, the smell suggested it was used for a privy. A pair of flickering candles illuminated a sharp drop off.

"Perfect," Shator whispered and quickly stripped her body of the ceremonial robe.

Arthan followed suit, revealing a small crystal amulet hanging from the necks of the unconscious figures. Arthan could feel power emanating from the teardrop shaped objects. "Don't touch the amulets." he whispered, Shator nodded.

He had just poked his head through the hood of the thick robe to make out Shator rolling one of the bodies over the ledge. The splat sound that followed made Arthan wince at the thought of waking up in that. Looking at the second body with the sliced throat, he realized they wouldn't be waking up in this life. Shator slipped on her robe as she made her way to the entrance after sending the second corpse to join his fellow.

The robe Arthan had liberated from Davan's minion was just the right size to cover his armor, weapons, and belt of magic supplies. It itched abominably but he didn't dare scratch. He leaned over as they both peered out.

"Was it really necessary to kill them?" Arthan had no problem with killing his enemies in combat, but butchering his unconscious foes seemed wrong somehow.

"Hard to raise the alarm when your throat's cut. If anything would have woken them up the smell of that privy would have. Plus joking about Mels pissed me off." she muttered back.

The spacing of the parties played in their favor. They would have fifteen or twenty heartbeats of time to free Melom, irrevocably disrupt the circle, and start their retreat. Neither of the previous owners of their robes had been armed. Artham had sensed magic from both, but not mage level power.

The amulets they wore were a different matter. Artham wondered at their purpose. Then he saw it. Faint lines that had been invisible from the lip of the crater ran from each cowled figure to the circle. All of the minions were linked to the magic working. That must be how Davan intended to share his power. Or shunt excess power into his underlings to keep himself from frying, Artham thought wryly.

"We're coming to the edge of the circle. As soon as I cross the line, I will run to the mage circle and cut the bonds binding the princess. I have to stand in the target to disrupt the glyphs. Go to the other side and help her down and out of here. As soon as the working is wrecked I will be right behind you, covering your back. I should be done before they can react."

"Got it. I'll grab Mels while you destroy the circle. Then we get out of here. If those two we got the robes from were any indication, I don't think any of them will be able to stand up to our blades and your magic."

The lines flared as Arthan crossed the circle. He gestured at the princess and the bonds dissolved Shator scooped the princess up in a bridal carry as Melom kissed her in a way that was far more bridal than sisterly, part of him mused.

"I knew you would come for me, Shator. I just knew it!" Melon gushed out between kisses.

"Mels, we're not free yet. Can you run?"

"To get away from here, yes, the princess replied.

Even with the focus removed, Arthan felt a rush of power from the converted moonlight that Melom's body had already passed to the storage glyphs. He stole a glance behind him.

The princess and Shator were back-to-back just outside the circle. Shator had cleared an arc around her and Melom was doing a credible job with Shator's short sword protecting her back. The bubble also protected Arthan. He turned back and started the disruption spell.

"How dare you!" a voice thundered from behind him. Shator cursed. Arthan concentrated on the spell a few heartbeats till he reached a stopping point. He turned just in time to deflect an ice bolt aimed at his back. The caster was striding toward the altar, dark magic swirling around him. He didn't have the grace of a hand-to-hand fighter or swordsman although the mage carried the long curving blade of the desert peoples of the south. He looked fit, his body spoke of the sparring circle rather than the build of someone who fought for his life daily such as he and Shator shared.

The minions turned and bowed to the dark mage as one, ignoring Shator and the princess completely. They seemed to be mesmerized at the sight of the man, *Davan*, Arthan thought. For his part, Davan seemed to bask in the adoration as his due.

"Run," Arthan hissed, "Take the princess and go while They're distracted. I'll finish destroying the circle and catch up."

"No," Melon spoke up. "We stand or fall together. You'll never get past the crowd by yourself. We won't leave you to die at the hands of these fiends. Will we, cuddle bear?"

The idea of buff, no nonsense Shator as a "cuddle bear" made about as much sense as the melting look she was giving the princess. Davan laughed.

"Mage, I will let them go. Provided that you take Melom's place on the altar."

"I have a different proposal. You let us depart and you don't die today," Arthan responded, extending his shield to Shator and Melon. It would only stop magical assaults; their blades would have to do the rest.

"Enough of this banter." He pointed to Shator and Melon, "Guards. Kill them." Four figures arrayed around Davan threw off their robes exposing sword belts. They drew and approached the women. "I will deal with the mage."

The attack was pure energy meant to overwhelm him in one strike. Arthan discovered that he could feed the excess into the storage glyphs. His body warmed at the transfer. Smiling, he taunted Davan. "Is that the best you have?"

The clang of steel to Arthan's right told him that Shator was engaged. He stole a quick glance. The girls were still guarding each other's backs, Shator flowed like water, thrusting and parrying the two men pressing her. Behind her, Melon was following her lead in the dance of death. She was holding off the third guard who was cautiously pressing her. The reason for his caution was sprawled behind him. The body of the fourth guard lay about a foot from his severed head.

The whooshing sound saved Arthan, as he turned back to Davan and barely detected the three ice spears rushing toward him. Arthan gestured at the brazier closest to the dark mage and sent it and the burning oil flying at Davan. He deflected it, splattering a group of his minions, who were still motionless, with burning oil. They screamed briefly as the flames engulfed them before collapsing to the ground. Arthan saw the life force pulled from their bodies to Davan. The amulet transfers power in both directions, Arthan thought grimly.

Arthan pressed the attack, throwing loose rocks, ice bolts, and the occasional fireball, exploiting the power glyphs to wear Davan down.

And it was working. Arthan could see his foe struggling, sensing his magical aura weakening. A cry of triumph from Shator caused Arthan to glance toward her. One of her attackers was struggling to his feet while his fellow was contemplating the hilt of the sword that's bloody tip was sticking out of his back. Melom was slicing the throat of her opponent who was on his knees, blood pouring from the back of his knees. *Time to finish this*, Arthan thought.

A chorus of cries rose up from the minion as they dropped like minstrel show puppets with their strings cut. Thick bands of lifeforce flowed into Davan like a waterfall pouring off a cliff. He magically glowed like the sun. Arthan thought he could see steam curling from Davan. He had to be cooking inside.

Two giant outcroppings rumbled, like giant hands were trying to pull them from the crater wall. Arthan felt dread. He couldn't stop them. They would both kill him, Shator and Melom and allow Davan to bleed off the excess energy harvested from his fallen followers. Frantically trying to figure out a counter, he remembered Gethan's words.

"As it was, the power overload nearly killed him. Had I realized it sooner, I would have ceased my struggles and let him cook himself that day."

The question was, would the transfer cook him in the process, Arthan briefly mused. Deciding that being crushed or being cooked both ended in dying, he made his choice.

Tapping all the power glyphs, he channeled their energy into his own as he cast the same spell that Davan first attacked him with.

His body felt like it had been dipped in dragon fire, his nerves burning. After three heartbeats of agony, Arthan crumpled to the ground, spent and gasping.

"Are you alive?" Shator gasped as she cradled his head.

"I think so. That's as close to burning at the stake as I ever want to get."

"We may not be alive for long. Look," Melom snapped.

Davan was encased in power, screaming like a damned soul in the flames of the underworld.

"Get behind the stone altar. I've got nothing left and the magical backlash is going to scour everything around him. The stone of the altar may save you."

"Mels, grab his feet." Shator barked.

"No time! Leave me!" He thought he heard the flapping of wings.

The next thing Arthan knew a cloud of dust stung his eyes and absolute darkness enveloped him and the girls. Splats like heavy rain struck the leathery wings that Arthan could make out as the glow from them increased and then faded. Gethan pulled back from the trio, shaking his wings.

"I really need a bath now," Gethan rumbled.

The area was littered with charred bodies, some in pieces. The ground was scorched everywhere except for the area that the dragon had shielded. At the center of the destruction were two boots with blackened joints sticking out.

"Is that Davan?" Melom asked musingly.

"Yes. Those must be dragonhide boots. Dragonhide can absorb and reflect power. Once my magical energy was replenished, what was left reflected back," Gethan replied.

"Let's get out of here before the carrion birds or the survivors in the keep decide to investigate, Shator interjected: "Arthan, can you walk?"

"I think..." trying to rise felt like he had an entire village on his back. He sagged back to the ground. "Not."

"I can help with that."

"Gethan, you saved our lives. We're in your debt already."

"No bother. I am chock full of power now." He ran a talon across the pad of his other foreleg. Blood oozed out, the cut already healing. "Hurry, lick it before it's reabsorbed," Gethan urged.

Before he could refuse, he heard the carrion birds calling. They needed to move. He licked the proffered paw like a cat grooming before he thought about it anymore.

The surge was almost as good as the first time Gethan had shared his blood. Part of Arthan considered just how weak the dragon must have been earlier if a few drops were as potent as the mouthfuls he drank the first time. A few heartbeats later, he easily got to his feet.

"Thank you, Gethan." Turning to Shator and Melom, who were holding hands and giving looks that Arthan had last seen a bride and groom make at their wedding feast. Thinking that he and Shator needed to have a talk very soon, he said. "Let's go. The horses aren't far. We brought an extra mount for you, your highness."

Ummm, about that Gethan interjected…

"Well, it just sort of happened," Shator explained as she worked by a mixture of fire and moonlight that was nearly bright enough to read by to fashion a dragon harness from the bridle straps and other tack that their deceased mounts had no further use for. "We were together all the time, and she was, is, my closest friend. My soulmate."

The last caused Melom to coo and snuggle next to Shator. Arthan shook his head and smiled ruefully. He was using magic to meld their tent and blankets into a carrier the three could ride in back to the city. Arthan could have worked the leather as well, but Shator insisted that she needed to keep her hands busy. Princess Melom was cleaning up after creating a surprisingly good meal from the supplies in their saddlebags. Gethan had excused himself to bathe in a nearby lake.

The dragon must have been starving, Arthan mused as he worked. Other than some bloody patches on the ground, there was nothing left of the three horses. Not even bones, hooves, or hide.

"I take it that King Jaxom found out about your relationship," Melom sighed at Arthan's observation.

"Father is so old fashioned. The only requirement for an heir is it to be a child of my body. I know what I look like. I don't think that I will have any problem finding a sire when the time is right to produce a child and won't care that Shator will be my consort." The sharp look Shator gave the princess told Arthan that the pronouncement was news to Shator. "Although, I am pretty picky. I want a man who's strong, brave, and well-formed. Mage blood would be a plus." Melom gave Arthan an appraising look that wiped the concerned look off Shator's face in favor of a mischievous smile.

The fire flickering in the breeze heralded the return of a clean Gethan, whose arrival neatly steered the conversation to fitting the makeshift harness. Once adjusted to the dragon's satisfaction, he suggested that they start their journey to the city.

"I spent weeks imprisoned in that cave. Between that and absorbing the backlash of the late, unlamented Davan, I am too energized to rest. You three can sleep in the carrier while I fly back to Lapour."

"I think that is an excellent idea. Father must be frantic with worry. Flying a dragon back is so romantic," squeezing Shator's hand, who smiled in return.

Arthan realized for the first time that his partner had a soft side as he replied, "It's agreed. I'll snuff out the fire while you two load the carrier."

A few minutes later they were aloft. The moonlit view was spectacular. The stars in the heavens were radiant. And it was cold. So cold that the women insisted that he shut the flap. Arthan tried to get comfortable once it was tied off and found the arms of both Shator and Melom encircling him. Arthan dozed off to the rhythmic beat of Gethan's wings.

Arthan awoke with a powerful need to relieve himself. He reluctantly disentangled himself from the warmth of the still sleeping ladies and was untying the flap to ask Gethan to land when the dragon rumbled.

"This doesn't look good."

Bladder forgotten, Arthan released the flap and looked upon King Jaxom's castle. Purple streamers of mourning replaced the usual red, white, and blue striped banners that decorated the castle battlements that were clearly visible in the dawning sky.

"Perhaps the king thought his daughter dead?" Arthan replied.

"No, look at the flagstaff."

Peering at the flagpole located at the tallest tower of the palace complex, Arthan grimaced. The personal banner of the royal house, red, white, and blue stripes with a golden dragon emblem, flew at half-staff. That meant only one thing. The king was dead.

The king might have been dead, but his troops were not. Arthan could make out half-dressed soldiers struggling to don leathers and other items of protective clothing as they streamed out of buildings. Warriors on the walls pointed at the incoming dragon and notched arrows.

"Perhaps you should land out of arrow range. Not all of us have dragonhide."

"Good idea."

The bump of the landing woke Shator, who followed Arthan out of the carrier. "Good morning, all. Gethan you made good... Oh no." The last came out in a gasp.

"Oh no, what?" the princess interjected, rubbing sleep out of her eyes. Arthan saw Melom take in the castle, glance at the flagpole, and cry out, crumpling to the ground wailing. Shator rushed over to comfort her.

"Riders approaching, Arthan." The dragon had interposed himself between the grieving princess and the fast-approaching group.

"I see them. At least they have a parley flag." Despite the oncoming part's announced intent to talk rather than fight, Arthan readied his defensive shield and spells as they reined in their

mounts at the customary four lance lengths. An armored figure removed a helm to reveal a woman that Arthan surmised was what Shator would look like in thirty or so years. Her voice had the same lilt of Shator as well.

"What business do you have in Lapour? As you can see, we are mourning the loss of our ruler. Our markets are closed. It would be best if you departed and returned at a happier time."

"If only I could return to a happier time with my father still alive. What happened, Captain Marisa?"

"Your Highness!" The guard captain slid off her beast with the rest of her party following to join her on bended knee before the princess. Arthan noted that while her eyes were red and puffy, her voice was every bit the queen she now was.

"Rise, all of you. Tell me how my father died."

"Poison as far as we can determine, my queen. Or possibly heart failure. There were no marks on his person, nor sign of a struggle. The royal mage was also found dead, which hampers our investigation. Malock's cry brought the guards into the chamber where he and your father were conferring. I sent for the Healing temple archmage, but she's not yet arrived. In a lower voice she continued, "and I am so glad to see you alive, daughter of my heart."

Melom smiled and gave a slight nod of her head but said, "Fortunately, we have a skilled mage at hand. Be known to Arthan, slayer of my kidnapper, Davan. Be also known to Gethan, the dragon who saved all our lives. I think you know your daughter who protected me against four to one odds whilst Arthan dueled with Davan."

The older woman smiled. "You have done well, my child. Mage Arthan, I would be indebted if you would aid our quest to find out who struck down our king."

"Purple Lethe, it's broken down, but definitely present in the wine. Tasteless, odorless, and stops the heart after being ingested. The king died from heart failure," Arthan announced after turning from the table the late king was slumped over to start his examination of the dead mage on the floor.

"Isn't Purple Lethe a conjured poison?" Marisa asked.

"It is." Bending down he saw a familiar amulet around the dead mage's neck, partially obscured by the man's gray hair. Looking up at the guard captain he asked, "What time did the mage cry out?"

"Right before the rising of the third moon."

Arthan nodded grimly. "That was about the time Davan sucked the power from his minions. They cried out as they died."

"Malock was in league with Davan? I thought he was loyal. He had served my father and his father before that for decades." Melom paused, "Although, father had mentioned in private that it seemed to be more difficult for Malock to perform auguries."

"How old was Malock? I judged him to be about fifty or sixty years," Arthan interjected.

"Oh no. He was at least a hundred and ten. Very well preserved, from some of the tales of the maids." Marisa added.

"Magically augmented. Workings on our own bodies takes a lot of power. As mages age, we have to work harder to maintain our magic, the same as an older warrior keeping the fitness of their youth," Arthan explained.

Marissa snorted, speaking.

"And a losing battle. Old age bests us all sooner or later."

"Perhaps you and I should spar later, mother," Shator snarked.

"Silence, pup. You'll find that even an old dog can bite." Turning serious, Marissa mused, "Malock was chasing youth and vigor. And falling behind. Davan offered him vast power. He wouldn't be the first man to betray his oaths in order to extend his life and abilities."

"Nor the last," Gethan observed. They were meeting in a pavilion of the royal gardens to allow room for Gethan to attend. "Human life is so fleeting. I can understand why one would wish to hold on to it so desperately."

"Not just magical power. Princess, your cousin Perkins is next in the line of succession, correct?" Marissa asked.

"Yes, but he's an infant. And Uncle Arkin and Aunt Palese are the least political people I know. They aren't interested in anything but their bugs and butterflies."

"Precisely. Who would they reach out to if their child was elevated to the throne?"

Realization dawned in Melom's eyes at Marissa's observation. "Malock would be regent in all but name," she mused.

"And Davan pulling his strings," Arthan added, "But I wonder who was Davan's puppet master?" he continued.

"Exactly. Davan was a petty little man obsessed with adding to his magical power and little more. He did not strike me as a great thinker," Gethan agreed.

Shator and Melom looked doubtful. Marissa, on the other hand, looked thoughtful. Arthan continued.

"Take my duel with him. Had he ordered his minions to rush us rather than sacrifice them, they would have overwhelmed us, and he would have won. He didn't think strategically to use his assets to the greatest effect. Not the mind of a man who could envision subverting a kingdom."

"So, there's still a threat out there?" Shator growled, reaching out for Melom's hand. "Who?"

"The list is long. While the news of Prin... I mean Queen Melom's survival and ascension to the throne is spreading, it's trailing behind the news of the king's death and her kidnapping. There's unrest, and uncertainty in the kingdom that a twenty-two-year-old girl can hold the land together. Sorry your highness, but that's the truth." Marissa ended apologetically.

"And that's why I value your counsel. You always speak the truth. And who I want you to continue as the Captain of the Guard with the additional role as counselor." Melom looked about. "After learning that the royal mage that served our house for decades had turned traitor, I find myself in the company of the only individuals that I trust at present." She took a deep breath.

"Gethan, forgive my presumption, but a dragon has been part of our house standard since its inception. My father told me tales that our founder was aided by a dragon to first carve out the kingdom. Would you consider spending some time to help me keep it?"

"I know, And I would be honored to help ag... To help." Melom turned to Shator with a huge smile. "Shator you are to return to my side as my primary guardian."

"No, my queen," Marissa spoke up. Melom's face darkened.

"She's right, Mels. Your bodyguard has to be focused on external threats. They can't be distracted. I can't give your protection my complete focus when it's focused on you. I understand that now."

"Let's get back to that." Melom turned toward Arthan. I find myself in need of a royal mage who can wield a sword as well as a spell. I don't want you just at court. I need someone who I can trust to speak with my voice and be my hand of power to go forth and sort out the threats to the realm. Interested?"

"As long as I am not tied down to the castle, I would gladly enter your service." Arthan had anticipated the offer of royal mage and had dreaded turning her down. He was too young to be stuck inside a castle and its petty intrigues. Her vision of his job was perfect. "Your highness, I would wish for Shator to accompany me in my quests."

"I would be a fool to break up an effective team as you two are. The three of you, as Gethan is inclined. That's why I'm not naming her officially as my consort. Paints too much of a target. Queen's hand will have to do for now. I wish I could join you. But my place is on the throne."

"And you need to start thinking about an heir," Marissa added, looking pointedly at Arthan.

"Indeed," Gethan rumbled. Arthan thought that the dragon was smirking.

"The sooner the better," Shator chimed in, smirking.

Spending time at the castle might not be all bad, Arthan thought to himself.

Nothing Ever Emerges From the Sealed Chamber

By Frank Sawielijew

arcianus tossed another cup of wine down his throat. Rivulets of the honey-spiced drink ran down his chin, staining his greying beard redder than it had been in the prime of his youth. A few drops hit his cloak, expanding the mottled pattern of stains that had been growing steadily over the past year.

Panso burst through the door and interrupted his drinking session. He was the furthest thing from a man Marcianus had ever encountered: a lanky palace slave with droopy eyes and an upturned nose, not a muscle on his spindly limbs and no confidence in his timid voice. He smelled of rose and cinnamon, a scent more fitting to a dancing girl.

"Honored General, I come to remind you that the Empress requests your p-p-"

"My presence, I know." Marcianus pointed to a belt slung over a nearby chair, an ornate scabbard attached to it. "But I can't join the Guard without a sword, can I? And you know how hard it is to get dressed with one hand."

"Of c-c-course, Honored General."

The weight of the sword was enough to make Panso grunt with exertion. Marcianus rose from his chair and pulled his cloak out of the way so Panso could fasten the belt around his hips; it was the most strenuous physical task the soft palace slave had accomplished all week.

"Do you know how I lost my left arm, Panso? I was leading a cavalry regiment in a punitive expedition against the tribes of Gallthya. We crossed a dense forest when they jumped from the trees with scythe-like swords in their hands…"

The slave gulped. "P-p-please, Ho-honored General, d-d-don't t-t-tell m-me t-t-this gruesome st-sto-story again."

Marcianus laughed. He had related it many times before, yet it still revulsed the soft-hearted slave so thoroughly that it worsened his stutter a thousandfold.

He longed to be back at the frontier again, marching with men whose weathered faces bore the scars of battle, each telling its own story of struggle and triumph. Soft comforts bred soft men. The palace was no place for him.

But the Eternal Empress had promoted him into her personal guard after he lost his arm in her service, and who was he to refuse such an honor?

With a sigh, he placed the golden helmet with its ridiculous feathered crest upon his head and grabbed the spear with its colorfully painted shaft. Time to join the Royal Guard for yet another pointless ceremony. The tiled floor patterns swam under his gaze and his body swayed like a galley in a storm.

At least the wine was doing its job.

The Empress smiled at Marcianus when he took up his position among the Royal Guard. He returned a broad grin, revealing wine-stained teeth. His unwavering loyalty to Vitulia's Eternal Empress was the only reason he kept putting up with this charade.

Even drunk and one-armed, he was the most formidable soldier in her personal guard. The only soldier. The others were sons of patricians, soft young men who spent their lives sheltered within the palace district. Their white cloaks were supposed to symbolize the purity of their hearts and their devotion to the Empress; his was stained red and brown by wine and mud. Unlike these kids, he had gone through blood and dirt to serve Vitulia and wanted his garments to reflect it.

"I don't know what she sees in you, old drunkard," said Helvius with an arrogant smirk on his clean-shaven face. Marcianus resisted the urge to punch it.

"Unlike you, I'm a real man," he responded all too loudly. The other men shuffled uncomfortably. "You'd all run at the first sign of danger. She keeps me on the Guard to have at least one man come to her defense when the going gets tough."

Helvius chuckled. Of all the pampered patricians in the ranks of the Royal Guard, he was the most arrogant. Marcianus despised him with a passion. "Good for us then that nothing ever emerges from the Sealed Chamber, eh?"

Marcianus swallowed his retort. This was neither the time nor the place for a fight. The Ritual of Sealing was a tradition so ancient its origins were long forgotten, and even though he had no taste for pointless rites, he cared deeply for the Vitulean Empire and its Empress. He did not want to disrupt its traditions.

At the foot of Tellurnus, the hill the Imperial Palace throned upon, stood a tiny house with walls of thick grey granite. Its massive bronze door was engraved with magic symbols intended to keep whatever lurked within from breaking out. On the first day of each month, the Empress stood before the Sealed Chamber and sang an ancient song to refresh the magic of its forever-locked gate. The little building and its associated ritual was as old as the Empire itself, erected by the divinely touched sisters Vitalina and Vitella, Vitulia's founders.

In the seven-hundred years since the city's founding, nothing had ever emerged from the Sealed Chamber. Yet the ceremony persisted. The Royal Guard formed a defensive line behind the Empress, clad in ceremonial scale armor of gold and silver. Their cloaks were white as snow, their tunics the bright blue of a cloudless sky, their trousers yellow as a sun-kissed daffodil. Even the leather of their boots was embroidered with artful patterns.

Marcianus hated it, particularly the armor of soft precious metal. Were he to face the barbarians off the border in this garb, they would laugh him off. It was a mockery of all it meant to be a soldier.

But for the Empress's sake, he endured.

She struck an elegant figure, almost divine in her beauty. A long dress of purple silk so sheer it was almost translucent flowed around her body like a rippling stream. Her long dark hair was put into a braid so elaborate, it must have taken her slaves a whole day to weave. Thin red sandals and stockings of pale golden yellow adorned her slender feet. She stood before the Sealed Chamber's forever-locked gate, her arms spread outward, open palms facing the sky.

When the ancient song began to flow from her cherry-red lips, the onlooking crowd fell silent. The monthly spectacle attracted spectators from all across the city. Plebeians and patricians came together and mingled as equals on this sacred day.

The Empress's angelic voice, in combination with the copious amounts of wine he had imbibed, lulled Marcianus to sleep like a lullaby. He could barely keep his eyes open. When his head nodded down, he heard a snicker to his right – Helvius. Arrogant little bastard.

A sudden crash, loud as a catapult-stone thundering against a fortress wall, brought the dozing veteran back to attention. The Sealed Chamber's heavy bronze gate lay at the Empress's feet, torn from its hinges. Strange beings that moved like men but weren't emerged from the depths beyond. One wrapped its arms around the Empress and dragged her away, pulling her through the open passage.

His soldierly training took over and Marcianus shouted commands to the men of the Royal Guard. "Lock formation, men! Shields up, spears forward, protect the Empress!"

He marched ahead, spear held in an overhand grip. But instead of the familiar sound of hobnailed boots marching in lockstep, he heard the clatter of weapons against the cobblestone and the piercing screams of panicked men. The civilians behind him broke into a mass rout, throwing the entire district into chaos. He did not know how many of the Royal Guard remained to fight with him, nor did he care. Cowards like them were more burden than boon once the going got tough. He would have bet his right arm that arrogant Helvius was among the routers.

Marcianus drove his spear into one of the not-men's throats. A black liquid oozed from the wound, thick and viscous. When he pulled his spear out, the creature collapsed. The others formed a defensive line. They faced him head-on, wielding long blades fashioned from a brittle white material that reminded him of bone. Their bodies had a vaguely human shape, but their heads bore neither eyes nor mouths and their skin was as pale as the bone-like weapons they wielded.

Marcianus swung his spear to parry the not-men's strikes. Sharp edges bit into the painted shaft, shaving off flakes of colorful wood. Two of the pale white swords went past his spear and struck him in the chest. Their vicious blades scored deep gashes into his soft armor of gold and silver. Another blade went for his throat, and his left shoulder twitched as old muscle-memory kicked in, but no shield-arm came up to parry the strike.

From his right, a lavishly painted shield entered his vision and caught the blade before it met his throat. Marcianus glanced sideways – and hardly believed his eyes.

"Helvius?"

The young man's face was a grimace of fear, but his legs were steady, and his spear-arm drove the point into inhuman foes without hesitation. "For the Empress!"

A wide grin appeared on Marcianus's grey-bearded face. "For Vitulia Eternal!" With the youngster's help, he struck down the man-like beasts, leaving them bleeding on the ground. Their black blood was thick and sticky, pulling at his boots as he waded through it.

"Anyone else with us?" Marcianus asked.

Helvius shook his head. His eyes were wide open, staring into nothingness. His first real fight. His first kill, even though it wasn't human. Marcianus had seen that look on many a young soldier's face.

Marcianus stuck his spear into a corpse and unclasped his cloak, letting it fall to the ground. It would only be in the way. The young guard followed the old veteran's example. Marcianus smiled. Despite the boy's haughty arrogance, there was a soldier buried within.

Marcianus retrieved his spear and entered the Sealed Chamber. An opening in the far wall led deep underground. The sunlight did not reach far into its depths.

"Didn't think you had it in you," Marcianus said. "Think you can deal with whatever lurks down there?"

"I swore to protect the Empress with my life," Helvius replied, his voice measured and steady. With a sneer, he added, "Besides, how embarrassing would it be if a one-armed drunk turned out to be the only Royal Guard with guts? I can't let you get away with that."

Marcianus laughed. The arrogant youngster's attitude had returned. A good sign. Too many soldiers became withdrawn and distant after their first kill. Helvius remained himself, for better or worse.

They descended down a steep, slippery slope into the bowels of the earth. With each step the sun's light grew dimmer, but soon the passage widened, revealing a large underground cave. Luminous mushrooms illuminated the darkness with a bright blue. The cave's walls were stone, but much different from the white marble and grey granite Vitulia was built of – stripes of color went through the rock like veins: purples, blues, yellows, greens. Gemstones and ore veins glittered in the eerie blue light.

It was as if they had stepped into another world.

"Such wonders beneath our city's streets," said Helvius. "Vitulia is truly blessed."

"A blessed place it would be," Marcianus countered, "if not for the beasts that took our Empress. Keep your shield up and stay close. We will get her back, even if it claims our lives."

"The gods are with us, old man." Fear crept into Helvius's voice, betraying his doubt. "We won't die today."

Marcianus grunted. Excursions into enemy territory always claimed lives, but he was more than willing to give his for the Empress's return. She was yet without heir, and her death would end a bloodline that had reigned since the Empire's inception. Vitulia would be thrown into chaos. Its borders would crumble, and its legions would consume each other in civil war.

He kept marching ahead, only vaguely aware of his surroundings. The vibrant cave walls blurred before his eyes and his body swayed with every step. The wine that still coursed through his veins dulled his senses.

The attack took him entirely by surprise. Hordes of not-men emerged from behind the stalks of giant glowing mushrooms, their bone-like weapons biting into his armor from all directions. Scales of gold and silver tore from the leather backing and rolled across the ground like spilled coins. Marcianus drove his spear into a pale torso and drew his sword.

The steel of his blade sang with joy as it clashed with the creatures' weapons. Their movements were sluggish and awkward, as if they were children who hadn't yet learned how to use their limbs. The wine in his blood emboldened Marcianus, sending him into a frenzy of relentless blows. Black blood splattered everywhere as his sword performed its deadly dance.

When the not-men lay dead, he sheathed his sword and caught his breath. Apart from a few shallow cuts, he had sustained no injuries – only his armor, if it even deserved to be called that, had been massacred beyond repair.

Marcianus smiled. He hadn't experienced a fight like this since he lost his arm to the Gallthyan warrior who threw him off his horse and forced him to lead a panicked unit of cavalry on foot. It felt invigorating.

"What are these things?" Helvius asked behind him, his breath heavy.

"Foes of the Empire; what else, I do not care. We must ahead. The Empress awaits her rescue."

Marcianus picked up his spear and marched onward. Helvius followed at a limp, grunting as he walked. The old veteran threw a glance at his young companion and spotted a deep gash in his thigh. A growing red stain crawled down the leg of his trousers.

"Stay here. I'll go on alone."

"What? Why?"

"Your wound. You can't even walk without limping."

Helvius hissed through gritted teeth. "It's nothing. I can still fight."

Marcianus drove his elbow into the young man's thigh. He collapsed with a scream.

"A wounded soldier at the frontline only drags his comrades down. You stay behind and watch my back. With that leg, you'll be of more use as a rearguard."

Helvius got back to his feet, moaning with each movement of his injured leg. "It's only a cut. I'm still more use in a fight than a one-armed cripple like you." His eyes glowed with intensity as he tried to stare Marcianus down.

The old veteran shook his head. "Bandage that wound before you bleed out. I lost soldiers to lesser cuts before. And I saw wounded men endanger their comrades because they refused to pull back to the rear. This isn't a game, boy. Vitulia's future depends on our success."

"That's why you can't afford to go alone. Are not two swords better than one?"

"Stay here and watch my back," said Marcianus as he turned away from the wounded Helvius. A dimly lit pathway lay ahead. He could hear faint echoes of a woman's voice beyond. "The Empress is not far. I will return with her very soon."

He marched ahead, spear gripped tightly in his hand. Helvius screamed and fell again as he tried to follow. The boy had spirit, but he was more hindrance than help with that leg.

Marcianus had to save her on his own, and he prayed to the gods that they would grant him success.

Inhuman hands stripped the Empress of her garments. Their touch was rough and clumsy, as if they knew not how to use their fingers. Once stripped, they tied her to a thick mushroom stalk, hands behind her back. The not-men walked away, leaving her alone in the darkness.

Soon, a woman approached. Her bare footsteps echoed softly through the small subterranean chamber. She was clad in a dress whose color had long faded, and her skin was pale from lack of sun, almost like the man-like creatures she commanded. But her dark wavy hair, her piercing green eyes, and her delicate features were like a mirror to the Empress.

"I can see her in you," the woman said with a smile. "Your nose is a little narrower, your brows a little higher, but Vitalina's blood runs strong in your veins. She will live again."

The woman bent down to pick up the discarded clothes. A white-skinned figure approached behind her, this one much more intricately formed than the others.

"Who are you?" the Empress asked. She already knew the answer, knew it from the moment she had first met the woman's eyes, yet still she asked.

"You know it in your heart, daughter of Vitalina."

"But you must be seven-hundred years old by now. How can this be?"

"Seven-hundred? I lost count of the years down here. I still feel like it was yesterday when we last saw each other. Oh, dearest sister… why did you let fear take hold of your heart?"

The woman turned to face the creature behind her and dressed it in the Empress's clothes. Its face was an exact copy of the marble statues depicting Vitalina, the first Empress, founder of the eternal bloodline. Only the hair on its head was missing, and instead of rigid marble its limbs were flexible flesh. They moved in awkward, jerky motions, like a clumsy automaton.

"I recreated her face from memory," said the woman. "I still remember the look she gave me when we separated. So much fear and sadness in her eyes. Why would you be afraid of eternal life?"

The Empress rubbed her bound wrists against the mushroom stalk. It was no use. The stalk was too smooth to tear through the rope; it only chafed her skin. "But she has attained eternal life," she said. "What am I if not living proof of her immortality?"

The woman took a pair of scissors from her belt and turned to the Empress with a smile. The blades gleamed silver in the blue light of the luminous mushrooms. "The means of her resurrection."

The Empress drew a sharp breath when the silver blades approached her face, but they were not aimed at her flesh. Instead, the woman drove them into her hair. The Empress's heart pounded heavily, and beads of sweat formed on her skin.

She wondered whether she was going mad. According to legend, the founding sisters once faced a dark entity from beyond the mortal plane, whispering seductive promises into their ears. Vitalina resisted; Vitella did not.

Many scholars considered it a mere story; some even doubted the existence of Vitella, the imperial sister, altogether, believing her to be a purely mythological character.

Yet here she stood, a seven-hundred year old woman looking no older than thirty. Her hands sheared through the Empress's hair with skilled efficiency. When the long braid was fully severed, she carried it to the fleshen statue and placed it on its head. She worked her fingers across its scalp, as if pushing the hair inside.

Adorned with clothes and hair, the statue almost looked like it had come to life. Only its jerky movements and colorless skin gave away its inhumanity.

"My dearest sister… I will bring you back, and I will make you see that I was right. We will live forever, side by side." Vitella turned to the Empress, the scissors grasped like a dagger in her clenched fist. "I'm sorry, niece. But my sister needs her blood back."

A long spear came flying out of the darkness and grazed Vitella's shoulder. The scissors fell from her hand and black blood oozed out of the wound as she shrieked in surprise. It was thick and sluggish, like the tar used to seal roofs.

The Empress looked to the direction the spear had come from. A lone soldier stood at the mouth of the chamber, his single hand wrapped tightly around a gleaming sword.

"Marcianus!" she called. The hero of Tirrano, scourge of Gallthya, vanquisher of Kallixtos. He had come for her.

The warmth of joy spread through her veins and painted a smile on her frightened face. She knew she could rely on him, her greatest soldier. She had always known.

Marcianus muttered a curse. The wine in his blood messed with his aim, and the throw had gone wide. At least the Empress was unharmed. Anger coursed through his veins and made his muscles move by their own accord.

His legs drove him forward, closer to the vile sorceress. Whoever she was, she would taste the bite of his blade.

The woman stretched out her hand and shouted, "Stop in your tracks, warrior! I command thee!"

The words that left her mouth after were spoken in a tongue unfit for human lips. The unnatural sounds sent chills down Marcianus's spine but did little to stop him. He swung his sword in a wide arc, his trained muscles repeating motions that had been drilled into them a thousand times. It severed her hand at the wrist; the fingers still wiggled when it hit the floor, writhing like worms. Thick black blood spurted from the stump and coated the remains of Marcianus's tattered armor.

She recoiled, and the inhuman words upon her tongue were replaced by a wailing scream. With her oozing stump cradled to her chest, she ran for a narrow passage at the back of the cave. The white-skinned creature wearing the Empress's clothes followed on unsteady legs.

"Upon him, my children," she screamed. "Tear him apart for his violent deed!"

Hordes of not-men sprang from the shadows and assaulted Marcianus from all directions. More bone-like blades than he could parry descended upon him. One hit the ooze-covered front of his damaged armor and got stuck, but others cut through metal, leather and cloth to bite into the flesh beneath. He felt their impact, but not the pain. The wine was still strong in his veins, dulling his feeling and narrowing his focus. The multitude of swords swinging up and down before his eyes blurred like the horizon in the summer heat. To parry them all was a hopeless endeavor, so he stayed on the offensive, hoping to fell the beasts before they felled him.

"Marcianus! Watch out!"

He turned his head towards the Empress, her beautiful voice like a soothing balm upon his wounded flesh. Just a second before he met her eyes, he spotted a bone-white sword descending upon his head. He jerked up his left shoulder – only to realize too late that the arm was gone. The blade's impact knocked the helmet off his head. He crumpled to the ground like a sack of grain. A wave of nausea went through his body, and he vomited up a deep red liquid, which he hoped was wine.

"Marcianus! No! Don't die! Please, don't die!"

The Empress's voice implored him to get up and keep fighting. He climbed to his knees, but the ground was slippery and the swords pummeling his back kept pushing him down. He felt the soft scales of his armor dent under the assault, pushing into his flesh like a vice.

Suddenly, a not-man's head dropped to the floor and rolled away. Marcianus followed its path with curious eyes.

"For the Empress!" shouted a familiar voice above him. "For Vitulia Eternal!"

Helvius's sword slashed through the surprised not-men in a wild frenzy. The young man's bravery inspired Marcianus; he pulled himself to his feet and resumed the fight with a smile on his lips. The clumsy creatures fell under the renewed onslaught, and soon only a mass of crumpled bodies and black ooze remained.

"You old fool," Helvius said under heavy breaths, "you shouldn't have gone on your own. A second later and you'd be dead."

Marcianus shook his head. "I was just in time to save the Empress from harm. Had I waited for you to limp along, the sorceress would have drawn her blood." He walked to the back of the giant mushroom the Empress was tied to and severed her bonds with a quick slash of his sword. "Just like you arrived in time to save my life. Thank you, Helvius. There is more of a soldier in you than I thought."

The Empress rubbed her sore wrists and glanced towards the narrow opening through which the sorceress had vanished. "Thank you both, my loyal warriors. But I must ask you to stay here and let me deal with her on my own." She looked at Marcianus and showed him a warm smile. Her hand softly touched his cheek, making the blood rush to his face. "Don't worry about me. Tend to your wounds while you wait – I shall not be long."

"Empress," he replied, his breath heavy. There was something in her touch, something in the look of her gleaming emerald eyes. But no… no, the wine and loss of blood made him light-headed. There was nothing. "We must return to the surface immediately. There are only the two of us. I don't know if we can withstand another attack."

The Empress turned away and stared at the narrow opening at the far end of the chamber. "I cannot leave just yet, Marcianus. Not before I have talked to her again. Not before I have closure."

"But she is only a sorceress. Why would you risk your life, and with it your Empire's future, to confront her?"

"She is more than a sorceress," she said as she stepped over the fallen not-men, careful not to touch her bare soles against their sticky black blood. "She is a long-lost sister, and my heart could not bear to see her lost again."

She walked towards the opening naked as she was, leaving Marcianus to wonder. The Eternal Empress had no sister. Each Empress had one daughter, one heir, one unbroken bloodline without branches. Unless…

"Don't just stand there, old man," said Helvius. "Bandage those wounds before you bleed out, or do you want to leave her with a single guard?"

Marcianus sat down with a grunt and began to tear strips off his tunic. The youngster was right. He would be of no use to her dead.

The Empress ran a hand through her cropped hair and put the other to her quaking breast to steady her pounding heart. She wondered at the wisdom of her action, but there was no turning back. She had to do what her ancestor had failed to: lead her sister out of the darkness that had taken hold of her.

The blood that oozed from Vitella's wounds was black. She had spoken of eternal life, and how Vitalina had rejected it. Dark sorcery, no doubt. Its promises were seductive, but all who fell into its grasp paid the price with their humanity.

The Empress took a deep breath and squeezed through the narrow passage. After only a few steps, she emerged into a small chamber illumined by a scintillating pool of crystal-clear water. It sparkled with a lively effervescence and had a soft glow about it. Luminous water trickled out of a hole in the cave wall, chiming a beauteous melody as it fell into the pool.

Vitella knelt at the pool's edge, bathing her stump in its inviting waters.

"These are the waters of eternal life. My sister thought them dangerous and decided to seal them away. But she was wrong. See?" Vitella turned to look at the Empress and raised her right wrist. The wound had closed completely, leaving not a scar behind. The skin around her stump was smooth and without blemish.

The glittering water was alluring. Its melodious chimes turned into a whisper filled with wondrous promises. The Empress felt herself drawing nearer, her legs moving of their own accord. When her bare toe touched the pool's surface, she caught herself and wrestled back control over her body.

The water was cool to the touch, yet it spread a warmth through her body that went from her toes all the way up to her heart. The seductive whispers became louder, the promises greater. Eternal life, eternal youth, eternal beauty, things even an Empress couldn't attain were only a sip away. Yet there was something sinister about the pool's whisperings, something off about its sparkling glow.

The Empress stepped back and looked at the kneeling Vitella. She showed her an encouraging smile.

"All who drink of it are granted eternal life and good health. Look at me, dearest niece! I lived for centuries, yet haven't aged a day. Why would you shun such a gift?"

The Empress raised her eyes, looking over Vitella's shoulder at the facsimile of Vitalina behind her. The fleshen statue stood unmoving, its pale white skin glistening in the magical light.

"How did you make her?"

Vitella got to her feet and stroked the statue's arm with gentle fingers. "From the flesh He so graciously gave me, and from loving memories of a sister I always admired. I remade her exactly as I remember… only her soul is missing still, floating alone through the afterlife. But it will return once her blood flows through her veins again. Gods, how I miss talking to her! We used to discuss philosophy in the cool evening breeze, while the crickets chirped in the grass and the stars began to show in the sky. When we were together, all was right in the world."

A cold shiver crawled down the Empress's spine. A body crafted from inhuman flesh — it felt wrong, so very wrong. "Who is it who gave you this flesh?"

"He who speaks through the waters of life. He whose touch is wisdom and knowledge. All I know, all I am, all I achieved down here, I was given by Him." Vitella walked towards the far end of the chamber, where the pool's dim light barely reached. The Empress followed cautiously.

Deep in the shadows, she caught a glimpse of movement. Limbs of pale flesh pulsated like the fat white grubs often found in the soil of her palace gardens. What was an arm, what a leg she couldn't tell. All blended together in an amorphous mass of writhing appendages.

"The guards and servants I made for myself came from His flesh, as did my sister's new body. Without Him I would be all alone down here."

The Empress stepped back, away from the undulating abomination. Its very shape made her nauseous. Deep in her soul, she knew that it was not of this world. Its whispers kept creeping into her mind, but she recognized them for the lies they were.

"He taught me how to bring her back," Vitella went on. "He taught me how to return her soul to a new body. I want to be with my sister again. I want to tell her that I regret my mistakes and ask her forgiveness. But this… this wasn't a mistake. This one time, I was right. When she sees, she will finally say the words I longed to hear since the day I was born: Vitella, you did good. You did good."

The Empress closed her eyes and took a deep breath. She wanted to grasp Vitella in a tight embrace and give her the sisterly love she so longed for, but she couldn't. Not while this vile thing kept her mind in its fleshy grip. She, too, felt its corrupting touch on her soul, but like Vitalina before her, she resisted.

"Please, Vitella. Let us leave this chamber and talk outside. Only you and me, and no-one else to disturb our thoughts. There is much I wish to learn from you."

Vitella turned to face the Empress. Her eyes shone darkly with mistrust. "You want to take me away from Him, don't you? Just like you did all these years ago when we first came here. You were afraid of Him. You wanted to pull me from His embrace. You knocked the cup out of my hands so I couldn't drink. But I was right, and I will make you see, sister. You will see, and you will admit that I was right!"

Madness had taken full possession of her poor old soul. The Empress turned to walk away, but Vitella leapt at her with a roar. Their bodies collided and tumbled to the ground. The Empress felt something sharp dig into her arm, then warm blood coating her skin. She struggled against Vitella's grip to no avail. Her strength was inhuman, no doubt fueled by the black ooze that flowed through her veins.

Another weight bore down on the Empress's back, and something rough and wet scraped across her wounded arm. She turned her head and saw the fleshen statue of Vitalina lap up her blood like a starving hound. The red liquid filled its veins, making lines of red appear all across its pale white skin.

"Marcianus!" the Empress shouted at the top of her lungs. "Help! Marci—"

Vitella clamped her hand over the Empress's mouth. "Shh, don't worry. She only needs a little bit of blood. Only a little, and her soul will return. You have nothing to fear."

The Empress stared into the eyes of the fleshen construct. They turned red as its body filled with her blood. The soul that stared back at her was not human, if it was a soul at all.

Whatever it was, it was not of this world.

Marcianus rushed through the narrow passage. He was weak from loss of blood and his multitude of wounds throbbed with sharp spikes of pain, but his sense of duty propelled him. Helvius followed, dragging his injured leg behind him.

Two cripples against a sorceress. They shouldn't have let the Empress go alone. Her cries for help fell suddenly silent. Marcianus prayed she was still alive.

When he emerged into the chamber beyond the passage, he found a pale-skinned woman kneeling on the Empress's back, sucking up blood from a wound in her arm. Her flesh was the same as the not-men's, except for the dark red veins running through her skin in spiderweb patterns. She wore the Empress's clothes on her body and hair on her head.

Marcianus shoved his booted foot into the pale woman's ribs. She tumbled across the hard stone floor and landed in the pool of glowing water with a splash. An inhuman sound escaped her lips, like the buzzing of an insect swarm emerging from its disturbed nest.

The Empress seized her opportunity and jumped to her feet. She ran towards Marcianus and embraced him, but he brushed her off and pushed her behind. "Get behind me, Empress. The sorceress yet lusts for your blood."

Raising his sword to strike, Marcianus stepped forward and swung at the cowering Vitella, who raised her handless wrist protectively over her head.

"Not her," shouted the Empress, "it's not her fault! She was seduced by a dark, vile thing. Stay your hand."

Marcianus changed the direction of his swing and barely missed Vitella's shoulder. He looked across to the pale-skinned woman, who hissed and snarled like an animal as she climbed back to her feet.

"That beast? I thought it was a creation of the sorceress."

"Not that one. Another. Deeper in this chamber."

Marcianus looked where the Empress's finger pointed. He caught a glimpse of something moving, and it sent a shiver down his spine. He forced his eyes back onto the pale-skinned woman. Sharp claws had grown from her fingertips, the color of rusted iron. Her muscles were tense, her teeth bared.

"Helvius," he called to his companion, "shield!"

Helvius stepped forward and covered one-armed Marcianus with his shield. Together, they awaited the vile creature's attack, standing strong as a fortress before their Empress.

"Sister, what are you doing?" Vitella called to the pale-skinned creature. "Beloved sister, come to your senses! I have brought you back! Can you not see? I have taken you back from the realm of the dead!"

The pale woman laughed, her face a grotesque distortion of human expression. She spoke in the same inhuman tongue Vitella had used earlier, yet from her mouth it sounded much more grating. Her voice was like the creaking of a rusted hinge and the howling of the wind through a forlorn passage.

Marcianus grit his teeth. The sound made every fiber of his body shiver.

"No! I was wrong," Vitella whimpered. She looked across to the Empress, her eyes wet with tears. "Forgive me, sister. I was wrong. Please forgive me."

The pale woman leapt at the two guards, sharp claws bearing down on them. Helvius caught her with his shield and pushed her back. Marcianus brought down his sword in an overhead swing. The blade connected with her shoulder and bit deeply into her white flesh. Bright red blood was mixed in with the viscous black liquid that seeped from the wound.

He tried to pull out his sword, but it was stuck.

The woman jumped back, taking the sword with her. She grasped it by the hilt and ripped it out of her flesh. It clattered to the ground with a metallic clang.

"I forgive you, Vitella," said the Empress, meeting her ancient sister's eyes. "You are still my sister, even if you did wrong."

A warm smile spread across Vitella's face. It was as if a great burden had been lifted from her soul. "Yes. That is what you always said when I made a mistake. It doesn't matter if I mess up… we are still sisters, of the same flesh and blood."

Disarmed, Marcianus stepped behind Helvius, who now stood facing the savage creature alone. She charged at him and dug her claws into his shield, scraping them across the solid wood. Helvius drove his sword into her chest, right where the heart should be.

The pale woman jumped back again. Helvius lost the grip of his sword and stood unarmed like his comrade.

Vitella stared at the fighters, her body trembling with shock. "He is her heart," she whispered. "Beloved sister… He betrayed you." She crawled to where the fleshen construct had dropped Marcianus's sword and grasped it with her left hand. Her fingers were shaking. Everything she had believed for seven long centuries lay broken at her feet, shattered like glass. But she could still make things right. "I won't disappoint you again, sister. Not this time."

She got to her feet and rushed into the dark corner at the far end of the chamber. His amorphous limbs writhed and twitched in the shadows. She drove the sword into His flesh, slicing through a long thin appendage.

The pale woman went to her knees and screamed. Marcianus clasped his hand over his right ear and swore. Never had he missed his other arm as much as now. The sound drilled into his uncovered ear and went into the marrow of his bones. No thing that belonged to this world could produce such a hideous cacophony.

Both Helvius and the Empress went to their knees, their faces distorted by grimaces of pain. Marcianus grit his teeth and stepped forward. Even when a thousand Gallthyan war-horns sounded across the battlefield, he stood firm; what was one abomination compared to hordes of warlike foes?

He grasped the hilt of Helvius's sword still embedded in the creature's chest and pulled it out. With one mighty swing, he took off its head and the screaming stopped. The creature stumbled backwards and fell into the pool, where it sank into the glittering waters.

Marcianus shifted his attention to the writhing mass in the shadows and approached.

"Run, you idiot!" Vitella yelled at him. One of the creature's limbs was wrapped around her right arm; another coiled itself around her torso, squeezing tightly. She desperately chopped at it with her sword, but whenever she severed a limb, another appeared to take its place. "Bring my sister to safety!"

Marcianus turned around and ran. He nodded to Helvius, and the young man got to his feet. Together, they took the Empress by the shoulders and carried her out of the shadow-haunted chamber.

"You did good, Vitella," the Empress shouted after her sister as she was dragged through the narrow passage. "You did good, my dearest sister."

A starry sky greeted them when they emerged from the depths. A few guards stood behind haphazardly constructed palisades, and a handful of curious civilians out for a nightly stroll cautiously approached the scene.

The Empress dismissed them with a wave of her hand. When they hesitated, she said, "You did not hesitate like that when you saw me dragged away by creatures of the depths. Run like the cowards you are! Return to your homes. I have no need of men like you."

The guards exchanged quick glances, then left their stations without saying a word.

The Empress turned to Helvius. "What is your name, young guard? I have not asked it yet."

"Helvius, my Empress."

"Helvius, go find a blacksmith and a carpenter to fix that broken door. The chamber must be sealed again. Things remain below that should not emerge."

The young man nodded and went, limping as he walked. Despite his wound, he put the Empress's command before his own comfort.

"Hey," Marcianus called after him. Helvius turned around. "You're a good soldier, lad."

Helvius smiled at the old man and nodded. An unspoken understanding passed between them. No matter their previous differences, they were brothers in arms now. A bond forged in blood.

"As for you, Marcianus," said the Empress, "you are the greatest soldier the Empire has known under my reign. Your valor is without equal."

Marcianus felt blood rushing to his face. He hoped his greying beard was enough to cover the blush. "You flatter me, Empress. I only did my duty."

Her deep green eyes looked into his, gleaming with warmth. "Marcianus… you know the traditions of the Vitulean Empire. Once in her life, the Eternal Empress chooses a consort from the greatest men the Empire has to offer, so he can father her heir."

"Empress. You cannot mean—"

She softly laid a finger on his lips and smiled. "There is no better man in the Empire. I want you to father the next Empress."

He gritted his teeth and stared ahead, taking in the scene of ruin around him. Flowerbeds lay trampled and litter covered the streets. The barricades erected by the guards were a sorry excuse for fortifications. Even a barbarian would laugh at that mess. The Royal Guard had failed at its job so thoroughly, it was a miracle the city hadn't descended into chaos after the Empress's disappearance.

"Under one condition, Empress. You crown me Commander of the Royal Guard and allow me to recruit new men from veterans I served with. And they get to wear real armor, not these useless vests of gold and silver."

The Empress laughed. "Your wish shall be granted, my warrior." She wrapped her arms around him and pressed her lips against his. "But for now we shall retreat to the palace. The Empire needs an heir, and I have found her father."

Marcianus allowed her to pull him along. As much as he disdained the vain comforts of the palace, he was willing to bear any hardship his Empress wished him to endure. And soft pillows were not the worst thing he had to tackle today.

A rare smile appeared on his weathered face.

He wondered whether he'd be a good father.

The Burning Heart of Greed

By Moze Howard

Sitting in stillness, Adon communed with his Shaman, channeling the memory of his teachings, his prophecy. Eyes shut, that day in the Shaman's tent took form. Legs folded, the holy man hunched over the small brazier of burning incense held in his lap, breathing deeply, "To prevent destruction, you must take a journey, away from these simple lands, to behind the wall of fancy men, of silk and sugar. Find the fissure. Into the fissure a child of boiling stone, the son of a god and the Earth, will descend. If allowed to live, the fissure will grow, splitting Vaalbara, your home will slide into the ocean, and countless people will die."

"How can this be," he asked, "for one so new to wield such power? And how would I overcome such a foe?

The old man lifted his eyes from the incense, the source of his visions, "You know the way that we stack the stones? The way we chip away that which does not belong, that they may lay together as walls, and form arches?"

"Yes," the question made Adon uncomfortable, for there was clearly something he did not see, "We place heavy stones at the bottom, smaller ones at the top, fitting them together tightly. With these walls, we protect our women and young while the warriors deal with bears and other threats."

The Shaman hummed approval, "At the top of every doorway is a keystone. Remove the keystone, and the archway crumbles, taking with it much of the wall. This creature, a newborn god, has not nearly the power that he will one day yield, for now, he is but a keystone." Lowering a copper lid onto his brazier, the Shaman covered up the flame, "Remove him, and the apocalypse he would cause, crumbles to dust, never to be. Leave him to grow, and you place a heavy timber atop him, then a roof, and before anyone knows, all you've ever known will crumble instead." Whipping the lid off, he caused a plume of flame to erupt, incinerating the incense.

But a whelp at the time, Adon felt his heart pound, "What if I am not strong enough?"

"When the day comes, you will be the strongest that this tribe has ever borne up, son," said the Shaman, his eyes seemed to glow in the flames a bright amber.

Swallowing hard, cowering before this great figure, admired by all their people, he whispered, "When will he come?" "You will be a great man, hardened by the world, inured to suffering, and you will know. The tribe you walk with will pass by the wall in the mountain, and you will feel a pull." Using two fingers to scoop up soot from the brazier, the Shaman reached out, giving Adon a black streak across his eyes; the mark of a warrior.

With a flash, he was back, shaking away a mental haze. Adon had lived this day, the last with the Shaman, his father, many times. Now he watched the cart that brought him to the field overlooking the great wall roll through the gate in the wall in the mountain. Now, knowing what waits on the other side, he hesitated. Fate had brought him all this way, a nomad, flitting between caravans, learning the way of the world. His father knew the fate that loomed, knew that he was saying goodbye, that the neighboring tribe with their trained wolves would raze the tents and huts, killing all but a few warriors, and more than half the rest. He was but a boy, orphaned, searching the scorched battlefield that was his home, for bodies to bury, or in hope of survivors. There were few from both sides and he took comfort in making the injured invaders suffer. Then they wandered. What were once his people found other tribes on the road, but Adon kept going. If he was to fulfill his destiny, he could not stop. So many years, cuts turned to scars, fear turned to rage, boy turned to man until he became his destiny. Now, so close, he hesitated. Confronted with the enemy, he would draw his blade, but to walk among city dwellers was alien to him. He had no frame of reference.

"Pardon me, young man; are you lost?" asked a voice, and Adon tossed back his wolfskin cloak. Rising, reaching for his weapon, he glowered down at the newcomer. "Ah! I, well, you could just say no. The knife's unnecessary," an old man. Wizened, tiny, perhaps waist high to the tall plainsman. Slowly, Adon sheathed his blade, regarding the newcomer with curiosity. Somehow he'd managed to roll up on a small cart, piled high with wares, and drawn by a donkey, "It's just odd to see someone so young, so far outside the walls like this."

"I am a warrior, old one. What is your business with me?" He attempted to be as cocksure as the hero he was supposed to be.

"Ah, to the point, aren't you? Well, I've always been of the opinion that the old must guide the young so that they can build a better world. But it sounds as if you know your way around. Me, I'm off to the bazaar to peddle my wares, both magic and mundane." The old man started to walk back to his donkey.

Looking past him, at the tiny cart and its many wonders, he saw jewelry, tools, and weapons of strange, unfamiliar metals, gray and gleaming, like those of the city were supposed to possess, "Wait. Do you require escort?"

"Do I," asked the old man, without turning around, "Do you?"

Adon scoffed, "Warriors escort the weak and the small; They are not escorted by others."

Turning away, the old man took his donkey's reins, climbing up on the single seat of his tiny cart, "Ah, I see. Well, I don't really need protection, but I wouldn't mind company on the way. And I could explain what you see as we pass."

"I require no explanation," replied Adon, eyes locked on a short sword, lacking cross guards. It had an odd sheen, seeming to reflect more light than struck it.

"Hm?" The old fellow traced Adon's gaze, grabbing the blade in its engraved scabbard, "Are you interested in this gladius?"

Adon averted his eyes, "It is of an … interesting material. Something my people do not have."

"Steel, you mean. Well, steel and an infusion to make it more … effective." Exposing the blade, the old man struck its flat against the wood of his cart, causing it to wobble, "Incredibly flexible, but nearly unbreakable, and with an enchanted edge that never dulls. Well, I suppose you could dull it if you used it to break up stones, but it would take days."

Without meaning to, Adon reached out, "I would … would like to know more."

"Of course. What would you like to know?" Looking at Adon's hand, he understood, "Ah. Know the feeling, the weight. Know the blade itself. Well," and the old man sheathed it, then tossed it to Adon. "There. Pick anything, anything at all, and give it a whack. Over there, I mean. Don't go chopping up the merchandise."

Adon's eyes widened as he caught and clutched the precious blade, "You trust me with this? What if I were a killer?"

"You are a killer, son. I see that," smirked the old man, showing his teeth, both present and missing, "But you're also a plainsman. Nobody is more trustworthy."

Barely grown, Adon turned, spun, and swung the blade, dropping the scabbard. Thews tensed, veins swollen and pushing out. The blade was an extension of his being, like another finger; one that could take the head of an enemy, or his wretched, trained beast.

The old man laughed, "Are you just going to dance with it? Go ahead, pick something, give it a chop."

Adon's gasping breaths came in great gouts, "But … but you mean to sell it, yes?"

"I do! But before something can be sold for any great amount it must be tested, right?" With a grand gesture, the old man indicated the entirety of the landscape, "Go on, pick something. I guarantee you'll cleave it in two."

Excitable, Adon cast about, catching sight of a boulder, and charged in, thrusting the point towards the center, throwing sparks everywhere and turning a disc of the stuff into powder.

"No, boy, hack!" Adon looked back at the old man, shocked, "C'mon now. A strong boy like you could shove a tree branch through a man, but with that blade, you could chop him in two. Let's see it!"

Staring down at the edge of the gleaming shaft of magical metal, Adon roared, striking with all his might, and forming a crack on the surface. Flaming sparks sprayed across him and the field. He struck again, and again, perhaps a dozen times, with a sword no longer than his forearm, and, with a shudder, the great stone settled slightly, forming a narrow fissure. Wedging the blade into this, he twisted and pulled, and it, finally fell in twain. Sweating, thrilled, Adon issued forth a battle cry. Then, he stopped, "The fissure…" He stared at the blade.

"She's a true beauty, eh?" asked the old man, approaching, holding the scabbard, "Here." Taking the blade from Adon, he slid it into its home before turning away again. "At any rate, farewell. Perhaps we'll see one another if you come to the bazaar."

"Wait! Old one, are you sure you need no guard? No … help?" Adon felt desperate, and foolish, but suddenly believed that he had found the weapon that would help him to fulfill his destiny.

The old man laughed, "I've been buying and selling at this city for longer than you've lived, son. The city rents me a plot where no man may sell save me so that the people need not look for my wares. I need no help. But I could use a friend."

"Yes, of course," Adon agreed, far too eagerly, "Your wise ways impress me. Perhaps I could learn at your feet, old one. And you could benefit from   …   from   my…"

"Ah, your youthful vigor, perhaps?"

"Yes. Yes, that. The old lead the young towards greatness, do they not? This is their purpose. The young remind the old of themselves, in years gone by. My presence could re-invigorate you." Adon's grimly serious face was hilarious to behold, trying to justify remaining with the old man.

"Ah, but son, we can't be friends if we're strangers. But that's simple enough to fix. I am Woden, Old Woden to some. Wo to others." Extending his knobby old, wrinkled hand, Woden waited. "Wo. I … I am Adon." He almost felt ashamed as he gave a disingenuous smile and shook that hand.

Woden picked up on this immediately, "Ah, no need for that, boy," the old man had the grip of a blacksmith, popping Adon's knuckles as they shook, "I know your lot, remember? To be jovial isn't in your nature, so don't pretend for my benefit. Be grim. It's more honest."

Shakily, Adon's smile dissolved, and he nodded, "What would it take to get that blade from you?"

Woden chuckled, "Well, my boy, I doubt you could afford it. Do you even know the way of the coin?"

"My people mint no coin, but I have traveled with several caravans, watching the merchants work. I understand money."

Woden showed shock, "Ah! Well then, maybe we could figure something out after all."

Within the city, Adon felt no different. All around him were strangers, like the many villages visited by his caravan, but swarming in greater numbers than he'd ever seen. They were as a great herd, but lacking direction, and of such a variety that he could only marvel at the variety of cultures represented.

But as he struggled to comprehend his surroundings, there was a thrumming, waves of force that struck him continuously like a distant heartbeat drawing him onward. "What is that?"

"What is what?" shouted Wo, "We're in an absolute crush of humanity."

Almost on cue, Adon slammed into a giant, shaggy beast, causing it to stumble as he nearly lost his footing, "Beast," he shouted, cocking back a fist, stopping as the old man grabbed his wrist.

Beneath his bushy, white eyebrows, the little old man glowered, "Adon, please. It's just a camel. Come, closer to me, follow. Hold the back of my cart and nothing will run into you."

"It … it looks like a monster. A stinking, warped mockery of a horse," he panted. And the pounding!"

Cocking an eyebrow, the old man spoke sternly, "If you make a scene the constables will descend on you. No matter how strong you may be, a hundred men would be your end. Please remain calm."

"Yes. Of course…" Adon looked back at the camel, noticing its rider for the first time. It was heavy-laden with goods, no doubt bought in the bazaar that Wo was leading him to. He lowered his gaze, hiding beneath his long hair and wolf-skulled cowl, and did all he could to ignore the thrumming, distant heartbeat.

Still, smells and sounds assaulted him, triggering his instinct to fight back. Scat from the many beasts, swept to the side of the street, lay in great piles near stands serving exotic food with pungent, esoteric spices that burned the nose and throat. Hundreds of voices spoke in dozens of languages and all at once, keeping secret all meaning. All he could think was that any enemy that wanted to, could sneak up and he'd never know until it was too late.

"Well, this is it," shouted Wo. "As you can see, I have a permanent plot with a stand, locked shut. Help me get Hamid inside, would you?"

"Hamid?" called back Adon, finally opening his eyes. Wo stood, gripping the donkey's reins and reaching out to him.

"The donkey, Adon. Please. He gets spooked like you in the city and I need to unlock my stand," Wo shook the reins. Coming around to the side, Adon held tight to them, but Hamid tested his strength. He could certainly hold the beast but knew that if Hamid wanted to fight him, holding him still would be a mighty struggle.

Wo wrestled with the silvery, thick, disc of a lock, "There we are!" The thing hit the soil hard enough for Adon to feel the impact on the ground through his shoes. Picking it up, Wo overbalanced a little, then pulled it in close so as to keep his feet. "Magic, heh, and made of a fantastical material. So long as this lock is on the stand, no man can enter. Well, I suppose they could beat their way in, but the wood would be unnaturally tough, and picking it is impossible without circumventing the enchantment first. Certainly, the constables would find anyone attempting entry before they got in."

The old man entered first, then Adon, but the donkey brayed and pulled back, "What?" Adon glared at the beast, "I know you've been in here before. Why do you fight?" Rearing up, Hamid struck, catching Adon on the thigh, "Damn you!"

"Adon, no, soothing tones," said Woten, who then backpedaled as Adon nearly ran him over. Catching one of the striking hooves, Adon dragged both the shrieking donkey and heavy cart through the door. "Well, that was faster, I suppose."

The plainsman slammed the door behind them, "Your blasted beast of burden struck me, old man. I'll not take abuse from any living thing lightly." Adon glared at Hamid, who moved further into the stand.

"Young man, please don't hurt my pack donkey. Loyal ones that do well under the yoke are rare and expensive." Woden started spreading out his wares, taking boxes from the cart and tossing them on a nearby table, "He just has a problem with doors. Now help me unload."

Adon took the heaviest boxes and thumped them down on the table, making sure to place the special gladius not there, but bundled, still on the cart. "Is this how I will earn the weapon? Moving crates?"

"One way, yes. With you standing here I suppose it's far less likely that anyone will attempt theft or other bad business." Opening up containers, exposing different jewelry, uncut stones, nuggets, and so on, Woden chuckled, "And maybe an errand or two."

"This isn't an errand?" asked Adon, dropping a crate onto the table with a thump.

"No. No, that's a chore," said Woden, "Tell me, plainsman; now that you've walked the city a ways, do you still fear its streets?"

Adon tensed, "I fear no man!"

"Aha, that's good, but the streets are different. Loud, crowded, chaotic. Do you think I didn't notice that you were burning with fear?" Wo sneered, "By the gods, you nearly started a fight with a Camel!"

Looking away, Adon grit his teeth, "The great beast struck me. Any man would defend himself."

"But Adon, I need only one man accosted. A welcher. A man to whom I extended credit, and who has failed to pay several times. I come here every two weeks, two on, two off, and he has waived off three payments. He will not waive a fourth." Woden poked a finger into Adon's belly, "Do you understand?"

Adon scowled, "What would you have me do?"

Woden's directions had been precise, but still, it took longer to reach his destination than Adon would ever admit. The thrumming of the distant heart persisted but grew fainter as he entered the residential district, perhaps because of the many buildings now between him and it.

Grasping the hilt of his sword, a constabulary in padded silks and sewn metal plates approached, "You there, boy! What business have you—" The burly, fat guard stopped short, seeing the scroll given to Adon by Woden. He took it with a sneer, "What is this?" Reading, he chuckled, "A writ of credit, violated three times?"

"Yes. My … employer tells me that, per this document, the loan will be paid in full, with interest, or the man named here will die by the sword." Adon flicked the parchment, "I am glad that you've caught me here, for I am not of the city, and was not sure how to find you. The word is constabulary, yes?"

Nodding, the guard rolled the scroll back up, "You have that right, my boy. I feel that these execution clauses are barbaric, but I can see that the loan was for a hefty sum," he squinted, "Lino. Yes, I know the man. A potter. Come. His home is right over here."

Leading the way, the constable brought Adon to a well-appointed home of white stone with decorative columns. "This is the home of the welcher?"

"Welcher? Right, the merchant is the one who holds the debt. Yes, inside is your quarry, plainsman. He'll repay the debt or pay with his life. Be on your guard though; I'm here only to bear witness, so you're not called a murderer."

"Lino," called Adon. "You are called a welcher by one named Woden! Come, the time has come to pay your debt, in coin, or in blood."

Emerging from a doorway, wearing fine robes, came Lino. Curly-haired, well-muscled from working the clay day in and day out, he had an overly serious countenance about him, "What is this nonsense?" He noticed the constable, "Lukas? What is the meaning of this?"

Lukas the constable held up his hands, defensively, "It's out of my hands, Lino. Pay your debt or, by the contract you signed, this man may take your life."

Lino snarled, surprisingly aggressive, "I know the document. He can try, but I may defend myself! That old dwarf dares to send a boy for *my* head?"

Lukas sought still to call for reason, "That wouldn't absolve you of the debt. Think."

"Think? I did think, when I took the loan, I took the money of a senile old fool who was half my size. Now he sinks more of his money with this mercenary," Lino pointed a gnarled finger at Adon, "You. What's your name?"

"It will be executioner if you do not repay Woden," glowered Adon.

"I wanted to know the name of the man whose blood will be watering my garden, but fine," Lino flung aside his robes, leaving a loincloth. Adon began to draw his sword, and Lino scoffed, "Coward! You'd cut me down? I have no blade."

Lukas backed away, crossing his arms. Adon scowled, "What nonsense is this? Fill your hands with steel then."

"*That* would be unfair to you, savage," Lino laughed, "A copper blade? Come, let's just settle this with our hands. You do know how to fight without weapons, no?"

Adon pulled a strap and his scabbard and blade fell to the earth, then tossed his cloak on top of it, "Fine. You die slow then."

Adon dove in, only to have Lino swing about him, gripping him from behind and clasping his hands. He heaved, and Adon soared, crashing down with Lino on top of him, "It's been a while since I strangled a dirty savage," laughed Lino.

Looping an arm beneath Adon's chin, Lino squeezed, and Adon choked. At play with the village children, wrestling was not nearly so artful, so sudden. He'd been caught unawares by a superior combatant. Digging his fingertips in, his nails drawing blood, Adon struggled to loosen Lino's grip, getting just enough air to stay conscious.

"Why prolong the inevitable, boy? Do you think you're the first to try collecting that old fool's money? I was a champion in the stadium, holding dozens of lives in my grip, and, yes, killing several as the crowd demanded," he laughed, "My only regret is that our audience is only one man!"

Lino wrapped his legs around Adon's waist, locking his ankles together. Barely keeping enough control to keep breathing, Adon heard his blood pumping in his ear, keeping perfect rhythm with a second sound. The thrumming. His destiny. This man could end it, end him, never knowing that a newborn god would split Vaalbara, sending Adon's homeland and also this city into the ocean. Pulling up with his arms and down with his legs, Lino stretched Adon, whose neck popped painfully.

Adon released Lino's forearm, his arms falling to touch Lino's clasped feet, "I'll admit, you're probably the strongest who's come to collect, maybe stronger than the men I defeated in the arena. Still, I defeated them all, and—" Lino never finished his sentence, instead, he issued forth an inhuman scream. His bones ground and Adon had turned his foot backwards.

Gripping his horribly broken bone, Lino did nothing to defend himself, and so when Adon crossed Lino's arms across his chest and sat on them, he was rendered helpless. Without saying a single word, Adon rained blows that could shatter stones down on the face of the former champion grappler.

"Stop," groaned Lino, his head driven into the dirt, "I don't," more blows. Blood flowed freely, "I yield!" Adon paused in his assault.

"You yield? Does this mean you'll pay the debt?" asked Adon.

"I can't." Adon hooked his fingers in Lino's jaw, under his tongue, and began to pull as Lino screamed.

"Hold on," said Lukas, placing a hand on Adon's shoulder, "If he doesn't have the money, maybe he can pay in property."

Adon withdrew his hand, "Yes! Please, take anything," cried Lino. "This is the richest part of the city. My pots are widely sought, all over Vaalbara. Take them all!"

"Lino…" Lukas shook his head, "Your debt has grown since you took it on. The running total is over a thousand gold drachmae."

"No. No," said Lino, clearly panicking, "I'd be ruined!" Adon began to squeeze as Lino screamed, "Ah! Wait! I—take the house!" More screaming, Adon continued to squeeze when something in Lino's head popped, agonizingly, "Take everything in the house! Just spare me my life!"

Lukas pulled back on Adon's shoulder, and the tall plainsman looked back at the constable, "Enough, lad. If he signs over his home and all within, his debt will be expunged. Trust me, your employer would want to take the deal. Even at auction, if he takes half the value, the debt will be easily paid."

"I'll sign, just keep that animal away from me. No man wields power such as his," Lino whimpered, struggling to stand, but failing.

—

"You did well, Adon," said Woden, back at the stand. "Such a shocking success. Did he fight?"

Adon nodded, "He did. I found a constabulary as you said I should, or he found me. The man's knowledge of the law had me worried for a moment, but he chose a trial by fire."

Woden chuckled, "Which you used to strip him of all possessions. Well, certainly, he'll not to steal using the laws he helped write ever again. Did I tell you he was a former senator?"

"You did not…" muttered Adon, frowning.

Woden chuckled again, "Ah, don't be like that boy. It was nothing you couldn't handle. I knew he couldn't stand against you, though I thought you'd just run him through and be done with it. I'd get nothing, save satisfaction. This way I'm repaid much more than just the principle and interest, but more, and with greater satisfaction. A senator now lives that will caution against trying to cheat me. Invaluable."

"Yes, well, if my involvement has benefited you so greatly, then I expect my payment is now to be made," Adon stated simply.

With a clap the little old man bounded to his feet like an adolescent, "How could I forget! Of course. Let's retrieve it from your hidey-hole, shall we?" Woden unwrapped the sword and scabbard, "Here we are, a gladius of unparalleled beauty, edge, and strength. There isn't a beast alive that you couldn't end with a few strokes from this," and, with that, Woden handed the blade over to Adon.

Grimly grimacing, Adon pulled back the scabbard, staring at the gleaming weapon, eyes pulsing with the nearness of the thrum. It had grown stronger, closer. The grisly business was near upon him, and he would soon face his destiny.

Woden took notice, "I can't help but see, Adon, the way you twitch. It isn't consistent but it's always keeping with a rhythm that I can see. What's wrong, son?"

He hesitated but for a moment, sheathing the blade and staring at the floor, "A newborn god of rock and flame will soon bring about an apocalypse. This land and all to the west of the central Meridian will sink below the waves. The east … will suffer floods. It was foretold in my tribe for generations, but we never knew when it would come, or how to stop it. My father, our Shaman, though, he had a vision … I would slay the godling. The night I accepted my destiny, our village was struck. I went to sleep the youngest of my family, but woke the only one left…"

Standing on a stool, Woden gripped Adon's shoulder with the strength of an old smith, "I'm sorry that you've had to live with that, boy, and thank you for telling me. I've known for a while that something was coming, but something so devastating? I had no idea."

Adon flinched away, "You knew? What do you know?"

"Easy," Woden hopped down, "I am a creature of high magic, you know. I weave it into stone and metal, sometimes working in fantastic materials of great power. You think I can't hear the thrum? I hear it today louder, but I also heard it weeks ago on my last visit."

"Then you know I must go from here," Adon replied lowly.

"Is it that close?" replied the old man, "The thrum, it's been oddly … constant these past hours."

"The godling has stopped. For the first time since I entered the city, he rests, and so near," Adon affixed the scabbard to his belt, "The fissure; is it close to the city?"

"Very," said Woden, "Dynamis' Pass has only one wall because the fissure guards its back. The governor controls the only bridge. I can write you a voucher to cross–"

"No need," said Adon, turning to leave, "The godling is not on the other side of the fissure, he is within. I must go. None of Father's visions ever said how long it would take for him to bring about his destruction. Only that–" but Adon didn't finish, as the city began to shake. Woden grabbed onto his heavy table, the donkey, Hamid, brayed where he lay, and Adon gripped the stand's doorway. In a moment it was done, "No time. I must go!"

"Wait," shouted Woden, scribbling on a bit of parchment, then dashing up to Adon, "The constables may try to stop you. Take it! Use my name. Now go!"

The streets were a mass of chaos, all the people were stopped, wheeling about, shouting, questioning one another as to what had happened. No answers were to be had, and Adon had no time to explain. He slid by those he could, knocked aside those he could not, and avoided the crowds that barred passage through the city.

But one crowd was unavoidable; the one that choked the passage into and out of the city's rear. Constables had set up a barricade, only letting people out in a single-file line. The word "orderly" was heard over and over as Adon pushed his way through.

"I must pass! Woden the merchant has given me a voucher! Standing above most of the people, Adon managed to find the eyes of a constable; Lukas.

Recognizing him, the bulky guard pushed through from the other side, grabbing him by the hand and helping to pull him the rest of the way through, "What's that, lad? A note from your employer?"

"Employer, yes," said Adon, "I must go to the fissure. There is something down there, something magical. I must deal with it, or all is lost!"

Grimacing, doubtful, Lukas studied the document closely, "Woden?" he shouted, "The magic merchant? He's your employer?"

"Yes. He … he's the one who sent me. I have to deal with the threat," said Adon, telling his first lie, and also dishonoring his father by saying another sent him. A pang of guilt stabbed at him, but he felt it was for the greater good.

"That old goat holds immense sway in Dynamis' Pass. I suppose we have to let you go by," said Lukas, pressing him onward.

"Thank you, friend Lukas," beamed Adon, who, regaining his voucher, then sprinted onward towards the fissure.

After running over a mile from Dynamis' Pass, Adon showed his voucher a second time and was shown a path down the near side of the fissure. This was, for so long, the only way to cross over the wide canyon, a massive crack that spanned the length of Vaalbara. The path, a narrow, steep invitation to death, was better suited to goats than men, but Adon faced it unblinkingly.

All the while the thrum grew, "He's so near." Reaching the floor, Adon looked up at the sunlit sky but saw only a broad blue line that parted a rocky, gray sky. At the bottom, it was warmer, as stone baked hot by the summer sun. Feeling the rocky ground, Adon was surprised by the feverish feel of it, "So hot." The thrum struck his face, then hit on all sides, seeming to bounce back from the canyon walls.

Walking, stealthily at first, then with more confidence, hustling with great urgency, after what felt like forever, Adon beheld his target. Gray, blocky, with veins that glowed like the tears of a volcano, the godling was a horror to see. Softly, deeply, but with the cadence of a child, it spoke, "Cold. Too cold. Why so cold?"

"You," cried out Adon, pulling his sword, "Face me!"

The godling stood up straight, hunching toward Adon, "You! Why? You're cold. Why so cold?"

"Hot blood of the plains beats in my veins, creature," Adon's eyes narrow, "You are supposed to be a seed of divinity, birthed from the Earth itself. How is it you sound so simple?"

"Must find the warm. Cold. The world is so cold," as the creature neared Adon felt it, the heat of the forge. He realized that the thrum had subsided. It had done its job, and now he must finish it. Cocking its head to one side the godling reached out towards him, "You. You come to hurt. Why?"

This was unexpected. Adon assumed the creature was a force of pure evil, but it saw its fate, and questioned it, "You are destined to kill many," Adon looked about, spotting the apparent trail left by the creature. Its footprints were melted into the rocky floor and just its aura was enough to scorch the plants and debris on the canyon floor to ash, "You're too hot. I'm sorry, but if I allow you to do what you intend down here, everyone I've ever known will die. I've lost so many … I'll lose no more."

Sad, determined, Adon pointed his gladius at the beast and edged forward. It didn't seem to be a threat, not until its eyes, hollow pits in its lump of a head, before it roared, deafeningly. Snatching up a heavy stone in each hand, it hurled them both at Adon.

Dodging left, then right, Adon avoided what, certainly, would have meant his death. He paused briefly, in shock, for the stones struck and splattered on the floor, igniting whatever they struck. Then, ducking, he avoided the godling as it dove. As it passed over, Adon thrust his blade up, dragging the tip through the beast, then recoiling from the heat, "Blasted thing!"

Now, so close, he saw the creature in its full glory. A head taller than Adon, it was almost an animal, "Hurt!" Lunging forward, it flailed its great arms, and all Adon could do was dodge and swing his magical blade at any of the creatures that got too close.

Glossy black metal spurted out in rivulets each time the creature was cut, forming spikes that fell and stuck in the ground, "Gods, but you are a wonder." Backing away, Adon thought, for the first time, that victory might not be assured. "Listen to me. If you'll only leave this place now, there's no need for further hurt. I don't want to hurt you. Do you understand?"

The godling looked at its hands, "Hr. Words. How do I know … words?"

Adon could scarcely believe what he heard, "Words are learned, godling. Our families teach us."

"No. No family," said the creature, "Nothing!" It glared at Adon, "Only cold. Mother doesn't care. Must go down, find mother's warmth. So cold…" It attacked again.

Deflecting blow after clumsy blow, Adon rammed the tip of his blade into the godling, up to the hilt, and it fell to its knees, the great, ax-shaped scab of iron snapping off and falling, bent, to the earth, "I'm sorry, creature," said Adon, measuring a strike.

"Mother! Why? So cold. So—" and it fell silent, its head fell to the ground, and Adon watched the molten iron blood pool, then cool, as all fell still. He stared again at his blade; it remained pristine, as if untouched. The metal was cold as he ran his fingertips up and down the blade.

Abruptly, something knocked into Adon, who staggered, then fell. Somehow, it snapped his belt, as if bursting from inside his tunic, "What in all the hells?" He felt around, and found that his voucher had disappeared and, standing before him, was Woden.

"Excellent work, boy. Now, I'll just take my *cut*," said the old man, plunging his hand through the stone of the dead godling, and withdrawing a red crystal in the shape of a human heart. Adon saw that he wore some sort of mailed glove, which he then removed, and pocketed. "Thank you for taking care of the creature. It was so hot. Without you, well, I could never have gotten this."

Rising, angry, Adon shouted at the old man, "I don't understand. What are you doing here? How are you here?"

"I wrote your voucher on a magical scroll, my young friend. When the time came, I invoked its magic, and it and I changed places. Simple magic," said Woden, with a sweeping gesture, from the city to the canyon floor.

"You knew of the creature. You wanted its heart? You … used me to get its heart," gasped Adon.

"Of course. Your father was never the only one with a gift for prophecy. I often saw him, staring into the ether, and I stared back. I needed a weapon, the deadliest kind; a man of exceptional power and will. He gave me you," smirked Woden. "You plains folk are simple enough but, still, I thank you Adon. Couldn't have done it without you."

"You needed me?" Adon thought hard, "But I would not be as I was without the death of my father, mother, aunts, uncles. All my blood died that night, leaving me with disinterested neighbors and distant cousins," an epiphany, "It was you."

"Oh, Adon, don't take this personally, please. My ride will be here any moment," Woden feigned exasperation, "Don't you like the man you've become? You humans, you're so easily manipulated. By visions, like your father, by dreams, like the neighboring village. But, now, you're so strong," He smirked, he strutted, the little bastard, Adon could take no more, he struck!

Nothing. Blue sparks showered them both, and the magical blade given him by Woden flew across the canyon, "No!"

"Fool!" laughed the little old man, "Do you really think I'd give you something that could hurt me? All my magic, everything I sell, is incapable of doing me harm."

In a rage, Adon grabbed Woden by the throat, and the little man pretended to choke, rolling his eyes back, before focusing intently on Adon. Then, a third eye sprang open in his forehead, and he grew. Grabbing Adon back, Woden grew to look him in the eye, with giant hands, feet, and head, his body broad as an ox, "You're really just making it hard on yourself."

"No," Adon shouted, swatting Woden's giant hands aside before drawing his old copper blade and giving it a mighty swing, only to have it wrap around his back, "What are you?"

"Your kind would call me a pech, Adon, creatures of great might and mastery of magic," Woden batted Adon aside, "But I really don't want you dead, so stop this. I might have use of you again one day."

"Never!" Adon rolled, avoiding Woden's grasp, and snatched up the bent, cooled blood of the godling, "I'll repay you a thousandfold!"

"Foolish whelp! That's enough–," and Woden screamed, more sparks flying in every direction as the cooled iron pierced his side, "No! Blood of the godling!"

"You can be hurt! Die, old bastard," shouted Adon, clubbing away at Woden, mercilessly. Green blood splattered, but, though the broad end of his weapon looked like an ax blade, it was dull, and so Adon turned the broken-off point towards the pech again, "This is the end, betrayer!"

From behind, something slammed into Adon. No magic this time. As he found his feet, he saw it; a huge donkey, sized to carry Woden, "Ah, good, Hamid. In the nick of time."

Adon hobbled, finding his weapon, "You won't get away with this, monster!"

"Ah, Adon. Please don't change. We'll see each other again," said Woden, mounting Hamid, and dashing off, the godling's heart under his arm.

Leaning on the dull iron ax, the blood of a godling, Adon gave chase, but it was hopeless. For now, he would be satisfied, he told himself, that he averted disaster. But was any of the prophecy ever real or was he used from the very beginning? Pushing those thoughts away, he returned to the city, but only to pass through. He decided that he must become wiser in the ways of the world. Never again would someone take advantage of him. One day, however, he would have vengeance. On the memory of all that died to bring him here, he swore.

Red Seas

By Michael Morton

It happened on Gathering Day. Almost the entire village was at the reef, waiting in their boats for the schools of the black spotted fish to arrive. The island was home to their freshwater spawning grounds, and every year the villagers celebrated their arrival with something approaching a festival atmosphere. This year held great promise for the Gathering, as the seas were calm, and the sun was out. Children swam back and forth between the boats, chasing each other and playing games as the adults while they talked about this year's expected catch.

Keone and Rilea were in their own boat and made the most of the distractions offered to slip away to where they wouldn't be noticed. Although their Joining was only a few moons away, they still sought every moment they could to be alone. Their parents disapproved but also remembered what it was like to be young.

They were enjoying each other's company very much when they heard the screams. Peering over the edge of the boat, a chilling sight greeted them. They witnessed a massive shark, longer than a boat amongst the flotilla, jaws ripping and tearing. As they watched, it bit a swimmer in half and continued on to the next target without even stopping to feed. Other smaller sharks followed in its wake, snatching at the wounded and struggling swimmers.

One villager stood in his boat and jabbed his oar into the beast's flank as it passed by. The shark casually turned and slapped the boat with its tail as it went, overturning the boat and tipping the occupants into the water. Whirling with incredible speed, it shredded their bodies and turned the water red.

Rilea grabbed for a paddle, but Keone gripped her close. "Don't move," he whispered, hoping they wouldn't attract any attention. Boats were beginning to scatter in all directions, although none of their paths were coming near their hiding place. The massive creature seemed to pursue boats at random, ramming them or capsizing them so it could savage the helpless swimmers. His stomach lurched as he watched his parent's boat tipped upright, their bodies sliding into the water and lost to view. Almost, he grabbed for a paddle to go to their rescue, but he knew it was too late.

A conch horn sounded from the other side of the sandbar next to the reef. The hunters who had been further out to sea, waiting for their catch were coming back now. Mevosten, Rilea's father and chief of the village, led the pack. With their spears and tridents thrust out in front of them, they scattered the normal sharks, heading for their leader. But it ignored their approach, overtaking a struggling mother and babe and turning the water into a bloody froth as it shook its massive head.

Mevosten signaled the group to spread out as they attempted to herd the monster away from the rest of the people. Again, it ignored their prods and pokes as it sped towards one of the boats, ramming it broadside. The boat overturned, people flying as the flashing teeth tore into them. The rest of the boats closed in on it, weapons stabbing and opening numerous wounds. Mevosten himself drove his spear deep into its eye, seeking the brain. The shark rolled, flinging the chief into the water as the beast sped away, blood streaming from the wounds in its flanks.

Its escape path took it near the young lover's stationary boat. As it passed by, Rilea ducked down with a sob, but Keone continued to watch in a combination of terrified fright and horrified fascination. Despite the blood streaming from multiple wounds, it showed no signs of weakness. The undamaged eye tracked him as it went, and his stomach clenched as he realized it was not the dead black of a normal shark, but fiery red, as if molten lava flowed within their depths. He realized suddenly the tales the elders told of a Demon Shark that hunted men without remorse were true.

Its mouth opened as it passed him, closing with a massive thud on empty water, as if to say, *I could eat you in one bite.* Then the Demon Shark was gone, speeding into the deeper waters, leaving a blood trail behind that none were willing to follow.

"We have to hunt it down!"

Mevosten looked up from the seaweed bandage he was securing to a shredded arm. "It's miles away by now, Keone."

"It's leaving a blood trail! We can track it!" Keone gestured with his mother's necklace. It was the only intact thing he'd been able to recover from their savaged bodies. "We have to kill it before it kills again!"

"No. There are too many injured here. We'll have all we can do to help them survive. And we cannot lose any more hunters. Without the Gathering, food will be short." His voice was measured and steady as he spoke. "It will be dark soon. We need to get our people back to the village."

"But—"

The chief thrust his hand in the air. "I said no. I realize you're grieving, and I sympathize. But there are too many who need help and we have to see to them first. The Demon Shark is gone. The legends say it won't be back for years." He gave the bindings around the bandage one final knot, stood, and walked away without another word to more of his injured people.

Keone gritted his teeth as he watched the older man leave. *He isn't doing anything! It's going to get away with this!*

The mood in the village was somber that night. The injured with surviving relatives had someone to care for them, but too many families were left with only one survivor. The chief made sure everyone had someone to care for them, however.

Keone sat on the beach, staring out into the open water beyond the cove. He'd been there for hours, with only Rilea for company. She'd brought him some food but didn't try to talk with him, leaving only when her father called her away to help nurse the injured. That was fine with him. He had no one left to care for and Mevosten had made it clear that he wasn't to leave on his own to hunt down his parent's murderer.

He was still there when dawn arrived, and the surviving hunters headed out to the remaining boats. They needed to fish, even more so since the Gathering hadn't happened. Keone pushed himself off the ground, eyes sandy with sleep but filled with determination.

Over the next year, Keone worked harder than any other hunter. He learned to handle a boat by himself, judging current and wind to make it go where he wanted with ease. Long hours of practice with the spear gave him the ability to judge the depth at a glance and take his target with the first thrust, and soon his accuracy was unrivaled. Any type of sea creature was his prey, and he sought successively more dangerous predators as time went on. His body gained scar after scar, and his skill grew and grew with each one.

He spent more and more time with old Paiwa, a hunter long since gone blind from age but whose memory was undimmed. Many were the tales that began with, "Do you remember the time when Paiwa…"

From him Keone learned about the habits of sea creatures. He told Keone everything he remembered about life in the ocean. The two would sit for hours into the evening, Paiwa's dry rasp interspersed with the young hunter's eager questions.

All of this would have been acceptable, even praised if Keone hadn't tried to put to practice what he'd learned by hunting predators instead of food. Time after time he would seek out sharks to test what he'd learned, instead of gathering fish and other food from the sea. Again and again, Mevosten chastised the young man about forsaking his duties to the village.

Other days, Keone would take a boat out again after the hunt was done and search for the Demon Shark. He would patrol the reef, investigating every fin above the water, every carcass floating on the surface, until there wasn't light enough to see. On nights of the full moon, he would stay out even longer. Being that close to the reef took its toll on the boats, and even though Keone helped fix the damage, one day Mevosten finally had enough.

The whole village was there when Keone came in from another fruitless search. The chief stood in front of the crowd with Rilea a few steps behind him.

"Keone. This has to stop. Now."

The young man stuck his spear point first into the ground and waved his arm at the sea behind him. "It's out there, somewhere, and it'll be back. Do we just wait for it to come and kill more of us again?"

"No man can beat a shark that size with a boat and spear. Your hunt is pointless, boy! You waste time and damage boats. Food goes ungathered. I have told you time and time again, so this is the last time. End your obsession now or suffer the consequences."

He looked beyond the chief to the crowd behind him. Closed faces and hard expressions. His heart sank, but he tried one more time.

"Maybe one man can't beat it, but all of us, working together, can kill it! We have to be ready for its return!" He looked past the older man to Rilea, but her father put one hand on her shoulder and pushed her behind him. She didn't fight him as he did so.

The big chief sighed and turned to the crowd. "He will not listen, so this is my ruling. Keone is no longer a hunter. He is forbidden from using boats and other village resources to go to sea. Anyone helping him will share his fate."

Keone's heart sank at this pronouncement. He was no longer part of the community. Too old to begin learning a new vocation, coupled with the chief's ban meant no one wanted anything to do with him. The best he could hope for was charity from some of the more kind-hearted villagers.

That night Rilea came to see him. She found him sitting outside his parent's hut, the cooking fire only coals now. His spear lay across his lap, and he sat, hunched over and brooding.

As she sat next to him, she peered into the hut. The only thing she could see was his sleeping mat and the coral necklace, hanging over the door. Everything else was long since disposed of or traded away.

"Did you eat? I brought some taro and breadfruit…"

He took the offered food and began eating mechanically, not tasting it. She laid one hand on his arm. He didn't flinch away; in fact, he gave no response at all.

"If I talk to Father, tell him you're willing to renounce--" His harsh whisper cut her off.

"Until it's dead, we'll never be safe."

She glanced away, but not before he saw the pain in her eyes. "But Father says we can't kill it. That it will always win against a man in a boat."

Her lover sighed and poked at the coals. "Paiwa says the same thing too. "A man will never win against a shark while he's on a boat, and a shark will always win in the water." He jabbed the fire savagely now, causing sparks to fly. "There's got to be a way to beat it!"

Rilea began to speak but fell silent quickly. He looked at her. "What?"

"It's silly. Childish. You'll laugh."

"No, I won't. What are you thinking?"

"Mohi'ina. The old witch in the cave by the mountain. My mother always said that she knew everything about all creatures above and below the water."

He was silent for several long moments. She looked down. "I told you it was silly."

"No." He leaned over and kissed her cheek, softly. "It's the best idea I've heard in a long time. She will know how I can kill the Demon Shark."

Keone walked up to the old woman's cave carrying the fruit he'd gathered. As Rilea had instructed, he had collected only overripe fruit, very near to bursting its skin. The old witch had few teeth left and the sweet, soft fruit was easiest for her to eat. He set the collection on the rock outside the cave and waited.

Minutes passed but still he sat, unmoving. The patience learned from hunting served him well here, and eventually he was rewarded with the tapping of wood on the rocky floor. A figure came into view at the cave mouth, stooped with age and leaning heavily on a carved wooden stick. It paused at the cave mouth, inhaling the scent of the fruits.

A wheezy voice said, "Very well, boy. Your offering is acceptable. Bring it in." And she turned around slowly and began tapping its way back into the depths of the cave.

Keone rose, legs stiff, and picked up the fruit carefully. It wouldn't do to drop or split any and spoil his chances with the witch.

The cave mouth led to a tunnel that wound its way further into the mountainside. After several turns, he saw dim red firelight reflected off the walls, making it slightly easier to find his way. Mohi'ina sat herself carefully by the fire as he entered the cavern that she called home. In addition to the fire, there was a tangled mass of blankets that he assumed was her bed, several piles of bones, both fish and animal, and a small pool of seawater. All were in easy reach of where the old woman was seated. The cave smelled strongly of seawater, probably from the pool, but there was no smell of decay or waste. Overhead, a fissure in the mountain showed a small section of the night sky.

"Put that over by the wall, boy, and then come sit by the fire."

He did as he was instructed, waiting patiently again. Rilea was very clear about trying to rush her to action. She would do things in her own time or not at all. At this point, he was willing to do or try anything for a chance at the Demon Shark.

Several long moments passed as they sat there. He got the feeling she was studying him somehow, so he tried to learn what he could of her. The dim red light of the coals made it difficult to get a good look. Her body was thin and stringy, like dried out seaweed. Stringy hair fell about her face, unkempt but clean. As his eyes adjusted more to the dim light, he could see that she was bent over slightly. She appeared to be studying the fire.

Then she snored softly.

Stunned, Keone cleared his throat slightly. The old woman looked up at him. "Still here, heh? Well, good for you. I don't have time for those who can't wait for an old woman to have a nap."

"I will wait for your nap, for your sleep, and anything else you have to do if you can help me get the Demon Shark."

"Ohhh. Strong words for one so young. But then, you have lost much." She picked up a palm frond and gently waved it over the coals as she spoke, causing the coals to glow brighter. "Lost family. Lost friends. Lost a mate. Lost respect of your chief. All for revenge. Is it worth it?"

"If I kill that thing and rid the world of its evil, then yes."

She looked up from the fire into his eyes. "Is anything worth that?"

He kept her gaze. "Everything is worth that."

Nodding, she turned slightly to wave a hand at the pool nearby. "You can't kill it on the surface. You can't even really kill it, you know."

"What do you mean?"She continued to stare at the pool. "It's not really the shark's fault. The demon rides the creature until the body can't continue anymore. It lets that one die and picks a new host. That's why you can't find it. It's not the same shark that killed your family anymore."

"But… then how do I kill it?"

There was a long pause, long enough that Keone was afraid she'd fallen asleep again. Her next words were low enough he almost didn't hear them. "You have to kill the man who summoned the demon."

Turning to look at him, she rasped, "Only then will the demon be returned to where it came from."

"Who… who is it? Who summoned the demon? Why does he want to kill everything?"

She sighed, a wheezy sigh that was full of emotion. From the gear beside her, she gathered up a mortar and pestle and several small bags. Placing them on the ground in front of her, she began to drop a pinch from each bag into the mortar bowl. Indicating the pestle, she nodded at the bowl. "Mix."

He did as instructed as she added her powders and several small fish bones. Once it had achieved the consistency she desired, she took the bowl. Turning, she held it over the pool. "Watch. And be quiet." She started sprinkling the mixture over the pool, chanting under her breath as she did so.

The waters of the pool glowed slightly where the powder landed on it. It began to slowly swirl and soon, the whole surface was softly glowing. An image began to form on it, of an older man. With long black hair, a strong jaw, and muscular body, he was the very picture of strength. A carved wooden stick rested in his hands and an ornate chain hung from his neck, holding a polished disk of obsidian. The perspective changed as Mohi'ina spoke.

Many years before lived a strong shaman, stronger than any before him and any since. Many were his deeds, and much did he help his tribe with his powers. People celebrated him wherever he went, and he lacked for nothing. Not food, not valuables, not even women. But even he aged. As he did, his strength began to wane. Barrun was vain and wanted to remain the strongest of all. He began to study the old ones and their bodies after they died, seeking to know why they aged and how he could stop it.

The image shifted to show a much older Barrun, with gray hair and wrinkled skin. He was bent over the body of a young man that had been cut open. The shaman's hands were covered in blood and fluids as he removed organs for study.

Barrun's desire to know why the body aged reached the point where he was studying younger bodies, even killing them himself when no one of sufficient age was available. He was eventually found out but his chief, fearing Barrun's powers, banished him from the island instead of executing him for his crimes. In turn, Barrun forsook the dry land, taking the sea as his home and the creatures of the sea as his companions.

The image in the pool showed Barrun diving into the ocean from a cliff top as a crowd of angry people looked on. As he entered the water, his lower torso and legs merged into a shark's body and tail. Surfacing, the shaman tore away the obsidian disk and threw it at his pursuers in a final gesture. Sharks and other fish then came to him and formed an escort as he swam away from the island. The scene sped up until Barrun came to another island, this one with a smoking volcano towering over the landscape. He swam to a cave opening at the base of the volcano, disappearing into its depths.

Barrun called upon the spirits of the sky, of the land, of the sea, to answer his questions. But these spirits had no answers for him, since all they knew was the cycle of life and death that came to all creatures. So Barrun turned to the spirits of the netherworld, seeking forbidden knowledge of life and death.

The pool now showed Barrun underwater inside a massive cavern. It was a hellish scene, with channels of lava in the floor turning the water red, and massive columns of black smoke streamed upwards. Weak sunlight dappled the water at one end of the cavern, showing where it led to the sea. The old man, his body now covered in tough hide and scale, hovered across from a blood-red cloud that he had trapped inside a glowing circle on the rock floor. They apparently reached an agreement as Barrun gestured at the circle. There was a flash of reddish-orange light as the circle disappeared. The creature shot forward and exited the cavern while Barrun laughed.

Barrun formed a pact with the demon. In return for extending his lifespan, the demon would be free to kill in this world. Barrun placed a limit on the demon, however. It could only possess a shark and only one of sufficient size. Once the demon's current host dies, it must seek out a suitable host to take over. That is why the Demon Shark attacks are unpredictable. And also, why you cannot kill it. Barrun is its key to this world. The demon will be free to possess and kill until Barrun banishes it or until he is dead.

The pool stilled and the images on its surface vanished. In the darkness, Mohi'ina said, "You must kill Barrun to end this terror. Nothing else will suffice. And you must kill him while the demon is between bodies, or else it will not be banished."

Keone paced back and forth in the small cavern. "All the hunters tell me that the shark will sink any boat I use, and then I'm helpless against it in the water. If I can't go after it in a boat, how can I kill it?" The old woman smiled crookedly. "Do you remember when I asked you if revenge was worth the loss of respect from those around you?" "Yes, and I said it was. Somebody has to do something about this demon and Barrun."

"What else would you sacrifice to end this?"

Keone stopped pacing and held up empty hands. "I have nothing left. No possessions save my spear. What else can I sacrifice?"

"Would you say that you have nothing left above water that keeps you here?"

He remembered Mevosten banning him from the village, of the way he pulled his daughter behind him and the hurt in her eyes when he refused to renounce his revenge. "Yes. There's nothing left for me here."

She poked at the fire for several long moments. "You cannot defeat the shark from a boat. But you could do it in the water… if you could swim like it."

"How can I swim like a shark?"

"If you have nothing left for you above water, then you don't need your legs to walk the land. You need a tail to swim and hunt the demon."

Keone laughed. "And where would I get a tail?

She said nothing and continued poking at the coals. He remembered Barrun changing his legs into those of a shark and the realization hit him like a splash of cold water. "Can… can you do that?"

The witch nodded slowly. "It is very painful, and you would not be able to change back again. No more would you walk the land and breathe the air. The water would become your home and you would live there with the other creatures of the sea. But you would be able to meet the shark on equal footing and you would still have the mind of a man who has hunted creatures of the sea. The demon only knows violence and cares nothing for the host."

The young man stood still for several long moments; his eyes fixed on nothing in particular. "I'll do it. I've already cast away my old life. What else is left for me on land? But where can I find them?"

The waters of the pool bubbled suddenly, and a disk of obsidian attached to a leather cord surfaced. She gestured for Keone to take it. "As it was once his, it has an affinity to him. It will lead you to its maker."

He settled the necklace around his neck. "And Barrun can be killed?"

"He has extended his lifespan but is not invincible. A spear can kill him, if you can get close enough. But he can summon other creatures of the sea to do his bidding. And even when you get close, he is strong. Many hunters challenged him in feats of strength, and he never lost."

The young hunter took a deep breath and nodded. "When will you change me?"

She waved at the cave entrance. "Tomorrow night, meet me at the cove on the other side of this mountain. Say your goodbyes to the surface world, boy, for you will never walk it again."

The next morning as the hunters went to their boats to begin the day's fishing, they were surprised to see Keone waiting for them. Mevosten pushed his way to the front of the group.

"You were banned from hunting. Why are you here?"

"I'm leaving the island and will not return. I have come to say goodbye to Rilea. Will you permit this?"

The chief looked around at the gathered group. Most showed relief on their faces, glad that the young troublemaker would bother them no more. He looked back at the young man. "You will not try to talk her into coming with you?"

"I won't. Where I'm going, there is no place for her."

"Then yes, I will give you my permission."

Keone stood a few feet away from his former lover. He was afraid that if he touched her, his resolve would break. All he needed to do to be with her was forsake his vengeance and accept the life the rest of the village lived. That, and forever be in fear of the return of the Demon Shark.

Rilea stood with her arms crossed, face expressionless. "So, you're leaving me. For good."

He lifted his hands, palms up. "I didn't want to have to choose, but I can't just accept that we have to live with that thing out there. It has to be killed. What if it came after our children?"

"Children that we will never have."

Keone shook his head. "I'm not here to argue with you. I have to leave, and I won't be coming back to the village. I just wanted to tell you I'm leaving and to say… I love you. I will always love you, no matter where I go."

She blinked tears away. "But you don't love me enough to stay."

"Don't do that. Neither of us can change who we are. Just leave it at that. Leave it at what we had together." He turned to walk away.

"Wait! What if… what if I came with you?"

He paused, not turning around. "You can't. Where I'm going, you can't follow. And it's not your path to follow."

"Then I'll never see you again?"

"Maybe. Watch the ocean from time to time. Maybe we'll see each other."

When he arrived at the cove, Mohi'ina was already there, a fire underway and an earthenware pot set to boil over it. She nodded for him to come closer while stirring in various roots and herbs. There were two wooden stools next to the fire and a metal spear thrust into the sand.

She motioned to the spear. "Your wooden one will rot and be useless after too long in the water. Take this one and put it to good use. Now, sit on one and put your feet on the other. Do not flinch when I begin."

He did as he was told and watched with trepidation as she took up a wooden bowl and began to paint his legs with various colors of dye. Images formed on his skin as she painted; a person, a spear, the waves on the shore, a coral reef, various fish, and finally a dolphin jumping up out of the water.

Then the old woman, with the steadiness of hand of a much younger person, used an obsidian blade to trace the images she painted, carving shallow incisions as she went. He gritted his teeth at the bite of the knife and locked his knees, trying not to move. As his blood trickled down his legs, the images flowed with them. Red blood became blues, yellows, and pinks as the paint and blood flowed into the new bowl she held under his legs. Once all the images were in the bowl, she rose and tottered over to the fire. Carefully, drop by drop, she poured his blood into the pot.

As each drop hit the bubbling mixture, puffs of steam rose. The scent of salt water filled the air. His legs began to tingle at each incision site and the muscles began to twitch. Once the last drop was in the pot she gestured at the water. "Hurry, now. If you still wish to do this, you must get in the water! All the way in and lie on your back looking at the moon."

Wading through the surf, each step brought waves of stinging pain from the wounds. He soon reached waist deep water and sank onto his back, legs outstretched. They felt like they were on fire now, but soon that pain was overtaken by a body-wracking shudder. His leg muscles cramped up all at once, causing his head to briefly submerge as he doubled over. Spitting water and coughing as he emerged, he tried to lie on his back again, but the cramps were so severe now that he couldn't straighten out. He couldn't even move his legs! They were locked together at the knee and each convulsion doubled him over, submerging his face in the water.

The pain was immense now, a pulling and stretching of his leg muscles that felt like they were being twisted off his body. He screamed, not knowing or caring that his face was under water. Bubbles filled the water as the air was expelled from his lungs, and he didn't notice when water rushed in to replace it.

Suddenly, with a snap his body straightened and he found himself on his back, staring up at the night sky. It seemed blurry, as if the stars were smudged. He tried to take a breath and found himself gasping and helpless, as no air entered his lungs. The water in his lungs rushed out in a gush as his diaphragm instinctively compressed, and suddenly he could breathe again.

"Forgot to tell you that bit. You'll be able to breathe underwater too, but it'll take you a bit to change between the air and sea."

The witch was sitting on her stool, watching as he flailed about in the water. He gasped a few more times, getting the last bit of water out, and said hoarsely, "Did it work, then?"

She pointed with her bony fingers. "Look and see. See and swim."

He looked down. The faint moonlight reflected dimly off his legs. No, off the scales where his legs would have been. His skin glinted with the silvery dappling of overlapping scales, just like a fish. He tried to move his legs, but instead a tail swept up from the bottom to greet him. Instead of wiggling his toes, he saw the fins at the end shift slightly. With a growing smile, Keone turned and tried to swim the length of the cove.

He realized quickly that he didn't need his arms to swim. The tail propelled him through the water faster than he had been able to swim, faster than the most able swimmer in the village. He crossed the small inlet several times before returning to the old woman.

"It works! I can do it!"

She hmmphed. "Of course, it worked. I know what I'm doing!" She reached over, easily yanked the metal spear out of the ground, and tossed it to him. "Now go find Barrun and rid the world of his evil touch."

Keone caught the spear easily and watched as she trudged back up the beach. Very slightly, he could feel the obsidian disk tugging him to the east. *Well, that time will come. First, I have to find and kill the shark hosting the demon.*

A few days later, Keone admitted to himself that he needed more practice being half-man and half-fish before taking on the Demon Shark. Everything he'd learned about the sea was helpful, but he still had no experience living under the water. His hunting was awkward at first, limiting him to gathering mollusks and limpets. Eating them raw was revolting and he clumsily attempted to build a fire on rocks that jutted into the ocean. But the driftwood was wet, and the spray kept any sparks from growing beyond a smolder, so he gave it up. After a time, he was able to eat them without gagging.

He quickly realized he would need help. Since the land was closed to him, he turned to the sea. Dolphins had always been friendly to the villagers, rescuing struggling swimmers and chasing off the normal sharks. He decided to try and make friends, since the Demon Shark threatened them as well. Keeping in close proximity to their pod, he watched and waited for his turn. They watched him cautiously but a few of the younger ones made cautious overtures to him.

After a few weeks, the whole pod was used to his presence. He watched their hunting patterns and tried to help as best he could. He found that their body language was easier to interpret than trying to emulate the clicks they used. And one young dolphin in particular was watching him in turn. This one carried scars of what looked like bite marks near his tail.

Together, Keone and the dolphins roamed the oceans. He made himself as useful as he could and spent more time with the younger dolphin, who seemed to be fond of making a 'ka' noise when Keone was around. He took to calling the young mammal 'Ka' as they hunted and explored together.

It was Ka who came to get him one day while he was watching Barrun's island, trying to determine if the shaman was there. Ka's urgent clicks and whistles got his attention and he followed his finned friend to a scene of carnage. In the shallows above a kelp forest, nearly a dozen pilot whales were floating in the water, their corpses ravaged with bite marks. The Demon Shark was still feeding on one, tearing out huge chunks and gulping them down.

It was a different shark than the one that had killed his family, but the red fire in the eyes was unmistakable. *Well, you wanted to find him, and you have. What are you going to do? I can't fight it head on. I have to surprise it somehow.*

After an interminable wait in the kelp fronds, he heard Ka's high-pitched warning squeal from off to his left and high. Slowly he eeled his way through the fronds, trying to disturb them as little as possible. The demon would probably notice something like a frond moving against the currents, even though the shark would be focused on chasing the dolphin.

Ka sounded his cry again, this time a little to Keone's right and still high. The young dolphin must be leading the Demon Shark right towards his hiding spot, as they planned. Readying his metal spear with both hands, he watched the water above him. As Ka shot past his location, Keone launched himself upwards.

His timing was slightly off, as he appeared not directly beneath the Demon Shark but slightly below and in front of it. The beast veered down towards him immediately and Keone's heart jumped into his throat. With a desperate kick of his tail, the young merman shot up and over his enemy. He thrust the metal spear downwards towards one pectoral fin, sinking the barbed point deep into the flesh at the base of the fin. A gout of red blood filled the water and the huge body shuddered, but the shark's momentum and mass tore the weapon out his hands.

Keone dove again for the bottom, but not for the kelp fronds. Instead, he made for the reef where he had stashed his wooden spear. Zipping through a hole barely wide enough for himself, he felt the coral shudder a few seconds later as a massive weight hit it. Coming out the other side, he grabbed his spear and spun around.

The shark was swimming erratically above the reef, blood streaming from multiple gashes on its nose but more importantly, the metal spear was still embedded in its pectoral. That fin was barely moving, and the shark was having difficulty keeping level. It would dip up and down, overcorrecting for the damage and drag of the weapon. This was their chance!

The young merman rapped the butt of his spear on the reef three times and swam quickly towards the surface, away from the shark. It immediately followed him, focused on the prey that was proving far too troublesome.

Which is when Ka came speeding in from the deeper waters outside of the lagoon and rammed his nose into the shark's underbelly as it struggled up after the merman.

The great beast gave a convulsive lurch and tried to arc away from Ka. Blood seeped from the gills, and it convulsed, sinking slowly. The young dolphin turned and sped away, his tail seeming to mock the shark as he traveled out of sight. The beast recovered after a few seconds, but it was moving more sluggishly now and thin streamers of blood trailed from the gills.

Keone turned and began his own stalk, trailing the injured monster from several yards away. Each time it swerved towards him, Keone swam upwards, making the beast expose its belly from below. Ka would come speeding in and the shark would halt its pursuit, turning to swim back towards the bottom. This continued for several minutes as the shark tried to maneuver towards open water.

The demon must be planning something. Or it's losing control over the shark. But we can't let it get away, either. Let's see which it is.

He slid towards the bottom, moving slower to give the impression he was tiring. A few flutters in his strokes gave the impression of distress. Sure enough, the shark arced towards him, its path a spiral to encircle the prey and let it strike when it was ready. The actions of a normal shark, as the demon would have instead sent it straight at him.

Ka zipped past the shark, trying to attract its attention but the monster was solely focused on the seemingly weaker prey. Keone held his position near the bottom, spear held in one hand. *I have to time this just right. And hope that Ka sees his chance.*

Closer the shark swam in its spiral, massive jaws agape. The metal spear was still giving it problems and the shark kept its wounded side away from Keone. It was only a few lengths of his body away now. Soon…

Suddenly the eyes blazed red and the demon sent it rushing at him. This was no feint or nibbling bite either, as the jaws opened wide, and its eyes rolled back. Keone shot straight at it, so close to the bottom he could feel the sand scraping along his belly. He thrust his spear upwards as the massive creature came closer, piercing the underside of the jaw. The wooden haft snapped under the momentum, leaving the head and about a foot of spear trailing under the shark's jaw. It lurched aside, clearly not expecting the frontal assault.

He gave no thought to the loss of his spear; it wasn't sufficient for the job. Instead, as he came clear of the tail he rolled as quick as he could, then put all his effort into arcing over the gray torso. As it came past, he grabbed the embedded metal spear at the end of its haft. His shoulder screamed in pain as he put all his weight and effort he could muster and pushed to the bottom as hard as he could.

The shark, now off-balance and reacting to its injuries, rolled with Keone's motion. The vulnerable underside came up into view and Ka sped in. He rammed his target at full speed, snout crushing vital organs and rupturing blood vessels. The shark went limp, tail spasming as it sank. Keone swam away as quickly as he could, trying to avoid any injury from its death convulsions.

As the body hit the seafloor, a cloud of red shot out from the mouth. This wasn't blood, however, for it paused, hovering motionless in the water. Even though there were no distinguishable features, Keone could feel its attention on him.

<I WILL HAVE MY REVENGE!> The harsh voice sounded in his mind, sharp-edged with hate and sending shooting pains through his head as the words reverberated in his mind.

With that the cloud sped away into the depths of the ocean.

Keone and Ka sped through the waters, following the directions of the obsidian disk. They had scouted the island where Barrun made his lair previously, while searching for the Demon Shark. They knew that the old man left his lair occasionally, although for what purpose was unknown to them. If he wasn't there now, they would wait. For as long as it took.

The island was home to teeming sea life, drawn to the uprising the volcano created. As it created new land above water, the heat from the lava flows made the waters warmer than the surrounding ocean. Coral, algae, and seaweed grew in abundance, which attracted small fish and shellfish. These in turn attracted larger fish and the predators.

Strange, that the place a man who lives off death calls home is also home to so much life.

Ka was all for dashing in and taking care of their foe right away, but the young merman convinced the dolphin to take a more cautious approach. They followed the sea floor as it rose towards the underwater cave entrance, following the reef and using kelp forests as cover. And sure enough, they spotted the lair of a massive octopus in front of the cave entrance. The creature floated gently in the current, two limbs twined around the rocks to keep it steady. The other limbs were holding the body of a large fish as the beaked mouth tore chunks out.

We can't fight every creature here before we get to Barrun. Too much risk. He pointed at the octopus. "Think you can lure him away? Without getting hurt?"

Ka gave him a reproachful look and zipped off, running parallel to the shore and disappearing into the distance. Meanwhile, his human friend slipped into the rocks, keeping them between himself and the guardian.

Even he was surprised when Ka came in fast from *behind* the octopus, grabbed the fish carcass out of the tentacles' grasp, and sped away from the island. Staring in shock, it took a few seconds for the mollusk to release its grasp on the rocks and jet after the giggling dolphin, following him into the deeper ocean waters and away from the cavern entrance.

Shaking his head in disbelief, Keone made his best speed for the cavern in case the guardian came back. The opening was large, easily the height of two men and wider than three huts set side by side. The inside of the cavern was lit with a foreboding red light that emanated from the far wall. Streamers of lava boiled the water back there, warming the waters in the cavern to an uncomfortable level. Silhouetted against that light was a man-shaped figure in the center of the large room, although a shark's tail swept the water and kept him stationary against the current.

Keone entered cautiously, alert for any other creatures that might be on guard. The rock floor and walls were bare of plant growth and mostly smooth, leaving no obvious hiding spots for an ambush.

The shaman turned slowly, as the red light from the lava backlit him. His tail was dark gray and tough-looking, like the great sharks the demon chose as its host. The still human upper torso rippled with muscle and the body and tail were scarred. Long slashes stood out white against the gray and there were puckered marks in stripes that wrapped around his body.

He gazed at Keone with flat black eyes, just like a shark's. "You. A boy. They send a boy against me now."

"No one sent me. I've taken this task myself, to rid the world of you and your demon."

The older man cocked his head, examining the young man's tail. "Well, at least you have enough sense to meet me on even ground. More than those other fools. What did your chief promise you for killing me? His daughter? Leadership?"

"I tell you, I'm here of my own choice." The young man tightened his grip on the metal spear. "You killed my parents, you and your monster! I'm going to put this spear through your heart and I'm going to enjoy that!"

Burran chuckled and showed sharp, no-longer human teeth. "Well, young pup, let's see what you can do. It's been a long time since I had a real challenge. I'm thinking you have the makings of one." Before he had finished the last word he launched himself forward, shark's tail driving him forward in a burst of speed.

Keyed up on the adrenaline of the challenge, Keone dodged aside easily and thrust with the spear. His opponent rolled and dodged as he continued on to the other side of the chamber.

"You'll have to do better than that, boy. Do you have any idea of the number of challengers I've faced?"

They circled each other, Burran apparently content to draw the fight out. *Keep calm. Remember what you know about sharks. He's more shark than human now.* Certainly, he circled like his peers, waiting for the right moment to strike. *If I feign distress or distraction… Let's see what he does.*

In the next revolution, Keone pretended to be distracted by a gas bubble emerging from the lava flow. In an instant, the other man had reversed direction and charged in, tail sweeping furiously and hands outstretched. He was so fast the talons on his hand raked Keone's side before the young man could completely dodge aside.

Blood swirled in the water as Burran again let his momentum carry him to the far side of the chamber. He hovered there and brought his talons to his mouth. Sucking at the blood, the old man's eyes blazed with their own inner light. "Mmmm. Tasty. I'm really going to enjoy eating your flesh. Too bad your family is already gone. No more where this came from."

His side was on fire. Hugging one arm to the wound, Keone looked around quickly, daring to take his eyes off his opponent. The walls and floor were bare rock. It was the open sea at one end and the trench at the other, glowing red in the dim light. *This is it. I can't back down now. I finish him or he finishes me. No other choice.*

Letting go of his side, he beckoned to his nightmare. "You want more? Come and get it, then. Get your fill."

Burran smiled, sharp teeth flashing. "Oh, yes, I'm going to enjoy this very, very much." He swam forward with a leisurely flick of his tail, talons flexing, mouth slightly agape, beginning to circle his prey once again.

As Keone circled with him, his blood left streamers in the water. As the other came across them, he opened his mouth wider and gulped in the blood-scented water. His smile grew even broader, and his eyes came alight with predatory joy. He sped up, tail moving in great sweeps.

"More," he growled, and suddenly darted in.

Keone thrust awkwardly across his body as he tried to roll. The tip of the spear hit the other man's head at an oblique angle, merely opening a shallow wound as it glanced off. Burran didn't even seem to notice as he swam past, talon scoring his target's tail, about where the thigh would be.

They continued circling and darting, Keone's spear making touch after touch, but he could not land a serious blow. He was tiring and it was showing on his body. Scores of shallow cuts marked all sides of his torso and tail and even he could taste the blood in the water.

Burran was growing more erratic in his strategy. Each time he marked his opponent, and more blood filled the water, his rage grew. His tail lashed back and forth, no longer the controlled, mocking sweeps that drove his earlier attacks. Instead, he lunged in and out in a frantic motion, as if he wanted nothing more than to close with his prey and savage him with his own teeth.

It was a gamble. A desperate gamble. *But that's all I have left. The man inside of him is losing control to the shark. I have to time it just right.*

Testing his theory, he used the same tactic from his fight with the Demon Shark. His tail fluttered and he slowed and sank slightly.

Burran growled, "You've had it boy. You'll be mine and I will rip your flesh…" His words trailed off into unintelligible growls as he began snapping his jaws open and closed, biting off his words with growls and snarls.

Now. Keone faked a sob and dropped the point of the spear. The beast across from him lunged in an instant, arms outstretched, talons grasping and teeth gnashing the water. It was faster than he'd moved before, and Keone was caught in the act of drawing his spear back when the other man was upon him.

Desperately, he twisted his wrist, bringing the forward half of the spear between himself and the snapping jaws. Pain lanced through him as the talons speared his arms and shoulders. Barrun had grabbed him in a viselike grip. Sharp teeth closed around the metal spearhead mere inches away from his face and the momentum of the charge slammed their heads together anyway.

The crunch of his nose breaking was lost in the colors and bright light flashing in his vision. But no teeth slashed his flesh. Instead, as his vision cleared, he saw that Burran's jaws were wrapped around the metal spearhead. Several of his teeth were already broken, courtesy of the savagery of his attack, but he didn't seem to notice. In fact, his eyes were rolled back up into his head, just like a shark's. He continued to chew away at the metal and Keone became aware of a horrible screeching as the teeth slid across the metal.

They swirled around and around the cavern, locked in their horrific embrace. Keone's right arm was pinned between himself and Burran, holding the spear in place and preventing his throat from getting torn out. His left arm flailed about as they spun, every motion sending screaming pain up his shoulder as it moved against the talons impaled in his flesh.

Gritting his teeth against the pain, he began to slide the metal spear back in his grip. The reverse point, designed to hold it in place once a creature was impaled, moved closer and closer to the berserk monster just inches away. Slowly, it slid into the cheek of the other man, and his savage biting quickly widened the wound. He didn't seem to notice, lost in his frenzy.

I have to do this next part carefully, or he's going to get free. He stopped swimming against the swirl, letting Burran push him up against the cavern wall. The heat from the lava behind the wall was immediate on his back, already hot and getting hotter, but he needed his strength focused on the spear.

Working his left arm around his opponent's shoulder, he took a deep breath and grabbed the spear head in his hand. Then he began to leverage the haft backwards as he pushed the head. The edge sliced his hand open, but that pain was lost in the already-redundant signals from his other injuries. Slowly, he worked the tip of the spear into Burran's mouth, avoiding the gnashing teeth by the barest of margins.

In this, the forward motion of the biting jaws actually worked in his favor, as Burran began to pull the head of the spear into his mouth as chewed his way forward. Blood began staining the water around his mouth, but that only served to make him more savage. All Keone had to do was brace the butt of the spear against the rock as the spear point slowly entered Burran's brain, letting the other man's strength do the work for him.

So savage was his frenzy that the tip of the spear had exited the rear of the old shaman's skull before he began to slow down. The bites were less frantic and convulsive, as if he had forgotten what he was doing. His eyes briefly lost their wildness but were confused and stared at nothing in particular. With a final, convulsive bite, the eyes became fixed, losing their animation.

Keone gasped in relief as the talons released him. He slumped against the wall and let the spear handle slide through his hands as the lifeless body drifted away on the slight current. Burran's tail twitched twice as he floated away, rotating slowly with the spear sticking out of his mouth.

It hurt to move but he had to make sure. To come this far and leave it unfinished… Slowly, he straightened and with an effort swam towards the other man. Before he'd gotten a few feet a cloud of red streamed into the cavern from the outside. It went straight for the shaman and circled his body rapidly from head to tail. Keone backed away quickly, ignoring the pain of his wounds. Frantically, he looked around for something, anything he could use. Nothing came to his attention, although he noticed a dim light beginning to grow from the far end of the cavern.

The cloud paused in its circling, and he heard that buzzing voice again in his head. It was softer but it still caused him to wince.

<He was strong. But you are stronger. You can take his place. I will show you new power, new strength.>

Keone backed away, following the wall. His path was taking him towards the back of the cavern, but that was the only way he could go if he wanted to avoid the demon. It followed him, pulsing slightly.

<He hurt you. I can make you strong. Stronger than ever. Take the bargain, young one. Be young forever. Be strong and take what you want.>

With those words, the demon cast a vision into his head; Mevosten cowering on the ground, face bloody. The rest of the village on their knees, heads bowed. And Rilea clinging to him, the worry in her face replaced by shining adoration.

And it wasn't real to him because his parents weren't there.

"No. No! You killed my parents!" He could barely get the words out.

<They would only hold you back. I can make you strong. I will give you power beyond your wildest dreams.>

The light from the rear of the cavern was brighter now. He risked a glance over his shoulder and saw a glowing circle forming on the floor. It looked just like the one Barrun had used. Turning back, he saw the cloud was close now, only an arm's length away. But small pieces of it were breaking away and beginning to move towards the glowing circle.

<Take the power offered. Take the power and close the circle. It need not be sharks. That was HIS choice. Any creature will do for my host.>

"I won't. I won't let you be free to kill anyone else. This ends here!"

<You fool! If you won't take what is offered, then I will! You still wear HIS implement of power, which binds me. It will also bind me to you!>

The cloud surged forward and enveloped the obsidian disk around his neck. The feel of the cloud on his skin burned like fire. The matte black of the disk began to sparkle with dots of red and the cloud started to shrink into the disk.

Fumbling with the thong around his neck, Keone got the whole thing off his head. Holding it at arm's length, he looked around frantically. The cloud was more than half gone now and the disc was awash in red sparkles.

In desperation, he swam to the glowing circle. The glow was nearly as bright as daylight, and the floor inside the circle was a shimmering surface, like sunset on the ocean. Without hesitation, he thrust the disk at the surface.

His hand passed through without resistance. Instead of rock he found nothing beneath, but as he did the demon screamed in his head, a wordless, rage-filled shout. The thong was yanked from his grip and the scream faded away slowly, as if its owner was moving a great distance away.

Keone snatched his hand back and the circle collapsed upon itself, until a single glowing dot was left on the floor. Then it too was gone. He looked at his hand. Aside from the injuries done by Burran, he saw no new damage. *I did it. I killed the Demon Shark and Burran and banished the demon!*

Now what?

A solitary figure walked along the beach at sunset, as she often did. Her attention was on the sea, eyes searching the water beyond the reef as the onshore breeze streamed her hair behind her. Keone watched as she walked the entire length of the beach twice. He waited until she had left, following the trail back to the village. Then he swam ashore and left his mother's coral necklace on a rock above the waterline. Then he returned to the water to wait.

We hope that you enjoyed this title and look forward to many more to come. Please, leave us a review! Reviews matter to all of our authors.

Take a look at some of our other award-winning series at https://threeravenspublishing.com/series-universes/

Visit us at https://www.threeravenspublishing.com and sign up for our newsletter for the latest and greatest news on upcoming titles and events.

Other series and titles you might enjoy.

THE RAVEN
AND
THE CROW
MICHAEL K. FALCIANI
FIND ME
ON AMAZON

William Joseph Roberts Presents:
Misfits of Magic
Opening by
Piers Anthony
Edited by
William Joseph Roberts
& Kristina Barnes
Stories by:
Michael K. Falciani - N.V. Haskell - Michael Morton
Kristina Barnes - Jennifer Brinn - Megan Higgins
Jon Michael Kelley - Benjamin Tyler Smith - Wayland Smith
William Joseph Roberts

You can also keep up to date with our latest release announcements on Scifi.radio and get some of the best fandom programing on the planet.

Scifi for your Wifi

And don't forget to check out our other Sponsors and Affiliates

A southern Appalachian jewel for craft beer lovers, Buck Bald Brewing offers something for everyone.

To discover more visit us at buckbaldbrewing.com

Revolution X is a testament to the power of collaboration, blending four unique styles into a cohesive, revolutionary sound. When these four individuals unite, the result is nothing short of musical Revolution!

Would you like to learn how to write and market your own titles? The following affiliates links might be helpful.

Don't forget to check out the latest edition of Car Warriors: Autoduel Chronicle fiction series.

https://threeravenspublishing.com/car-warriors-autoduel-chronicles/

...or the latest in the *Car Wars* game series

http://www.sjgames.com/car-wars/

Or the other amazing titles from

Steve Jackson Games

http://www.sjgames.com

Comprised of active or retired servicemen and civilian volunteers,
Shepherd's Men enthusiastically raises awareness and funds for the
SHARE Military Initiative (SHARE) at Shepherd Center in Atlanta, GA.

This nationally renowned program focuses on assessment and treatment
for American military veterans who have sustained mild to moderate
Traumatic Brain Injury (TBI) and Post-Traumatic Stress Disorder (PTSD)
during post-9/11 service.

Find out more at: https://www.shepherdsmen.com/

www.ingramcontent.com/pod-product-compliance
Lightning Source LLC
Chambersburg PA
CBHW030136010826
48973CB00002B/582